SOLSTICE

LORENCE ALISON

SOLSTICE

{Imprint}
MAKE YOUR MARK

NEW YORK

An imprint of Macmillan Publishing Group, LLC
120 Broadway, New York, NY 10271
fiercereads.com

Our books may be purchased in bulk for promotional, educational, or business
use. Please contact your local bookseller or the Macmillan Corporate and
Premium Sales Department at (800) 221-7945 ext. 5442 or by email at
MacmillanSpecialMarkets@macmillan.com.

Library of Congress Cataloging-in-Publication Data is available.

ISBN 978-1-250-76282-5 (paperback)   ISBN 978-1-250-21990-9 (ebook)

[Imprint]
MAKE YOUR MARK

@ImprintReads
Originally published in the United States by Imprint
First Square Fish edition, 2021
Book designed by Elynn Cohen
Square Fish logo designed by Filomena Tuosto
Imprint logo designed by Amanda Spielman

10 9 8 7 6 5 4 3 2 1

To whoever defaces this book, or illegally downloads it, or makes up lies
about it, or uses its information to mislead a group of people to an
uninhabited part of an island with no resources: Beware the creature of
the deep, for it will spy you with its twelve eyes, devour you with its six
tongues and three rows of sharp teeth, and you'll never be seen again.

The Solstice Festival YouTube Ad, January 2020

A fast, rhythmic beat. Camera fades in on a lush, green ISLAND surrounded by turquoise water. Cut to an image of a PRIVATE JET on the tarmac. Cut to a beautiful GIRL in a bikini, glancing over her shoulder, beckoning . . .

Voiceover: (masculine, seductive, yet edgy) *The experience of a lifetime . . .*

Aerial pan over waves crashing onto a white shore. Cut to a DRUMMER onstage. Cut to another bikini-clad GIRL, winking, laughing, dancing . . .

Voiceover: *Just the sun, the music, the moment . . .*

Cut to a boat darting across the water. Cut to a HIP-HOP STAR standing onstage, arms outstretched, the crowd cheering. Cut to a girl's TORSO in water, fingers gliding across the ocean's surface . . .

Voiceover: *Three extraordinary days of music from the planet's hottest artists, all on remote and private MYLA ISLAND, once plundered by pirates for its riches, once a playground for kings and queens, sultans and monarchs . . . but now it's your turn.*

Cut to a bikini-clad GIRL lying on the sand, eyes closed. Cut to a bikini-clad GIRL doing a perfect jackknife from the bow of a yacht. Cut to a bikini-clad GIRL sipping a fruity cocktail and blowing a kiss. Cut to light playing off the strings of an ELECTRIC GUITAR. Cut to a bikini-clad GIRL at a farmers' market, holding a basket of ripe, luscious mangoes . . .

Voiceover: *Everyone will be there. Will YOU?*

Cut to a GIRL, hair blowing in the wind, looking straight at the camera. As we fade out, the superimposed graphic: *The Solstice Festival. June 19–21. Book through our website now. LIMITED AVAILABILITY.*

3,492 comments:

darkboy66: So pumped about this! Lineup says Lavender, Jay-Z, and Blankface, WAT! Already booked!

mfreek: PARTY OF THE YEAR!

lattelato: Booking three extra suites! Who's in?

bellyrubz10: Uh are there going to be dudes at this festival or just girls? #ReallyWannaSolsticeFestFling

fryeguy: Just FYI, tix cost $9,000 not including flight OR accommodations. But whatevs! Raiding dad's 401(k)!

@akellyz9: @fryeguy do you think that $9,000 includes food?

Replies (3)

> **fryeguy:** @akellyz9 Personally I think $9,000 is a total STEAL for the vacay we're never going to forget!
>
> **Arkolatto23:** @akellyz9 Doubtful food is included bc did you see the meals? Sushi, lobster tail, breakfasts in bed, organic only—we'll be eating like kings!
>
> **fryeguy:** @arkolatto23 uh duh it's organic only. I wouldn't eat regular produce if you paid me a million bucks.

BLankin: Is this the Myla in the Caribbean? Cuz I heard something kinda sketchy about that place . . . can't remember what.

Replies (3):

> **ChrisJacobs:** @BLankin Nah it looks sick!
>
> **JennyJenny:** @BLankin It's sketchy bc it's a pirate island, didn't u listen? There's treasure buried in the sand!
>
> **GucciwithaY:** @BLankin Yeah don't be a buzzkill! Zack Frazier is running it, so you know it's going to be incredible! Love me some Zack!

1

I WISH I COULD SAY that table nine was grateful when I set down the heavy tray of eggs, pancakes, Belgian waffles, and other random brunch items at their booth, but that would be a lie. Everyone at the table—they were college students, probably jonesing for sustenance to ease their hangovers—was staring intently at a video on a cell phone. They were so agape I thought something awful had happened—an assassination, a terrorist attack, the death of a major celebrity. But as I set down the scruffy-haired guy's western omelet and hot tea, I noticed it was a YouTube video shot on a pretty island beach. I figured it was a music video, but then I saw the logo: *The Solstice Festival*.

Oh, right. I'd heard about that.

Ms. One Egg White, No Toast, Black Coffee, and Large Fruit Platter—who was as skinny as you'd imagine—pressed her long, lithe fingers to the sides of her face. "Do you think this concert is for real? Lavender, Jay-Z, *and* Cardi B, all in one place?" She breathed in sharply. "I literally might die!"

"The weekend is after our exams," her seatmate, a tall, gangly guy with a buzz cut said as he dug ravenously into his steaming bowl of steel-cut oatmeal—without, I might add, thanking me for delivering it. "If I got to party with Ice Cube, my summer would be made."

"Do you really think the artists are going to have open-invite parties on their yachts?" Egg Whites cried, goggle-eyed.

"That's what this says." Scruffy Hair pushed his giant iPhone across the table. The title of the article read "The Music Festival for the 1%." It was from a clickbait site, I noticed, and not a reputable news organization, like the *New York Times* or the *Journal-Constitution*.

"I'm going to ask for this as an end-of-the-school-year present," said the fourth person at the table, an athletic girl with dangling gold hoop earrings. At least she'd cast me an appreciative smile when I set down her French toast. "But do you think there are still tickets available? And what about flights?"

"The flights will kick the cost well over ten thousand for sure." Ms. Egg Whites daintily bit off a tiny piece of melon. "And my parents are still pissed at me for crashing the Mini Cooper they got me for graduation—"

"Oh please, they can't say no," Scruffy Hair interrupted. "It's the concert of a lifetime. Surely *they* went to a concert of a lifetime when they were young? Like Woodstock or whatever?"

Egg Whites shot him a look. "My parents aren't *seventy*."

That was it. I could no longer resist. "I'm sorry," I blurted as I placed a pitcher of maple syrup next to the ketchup. "But did you just say tickets to that music festival cost *ten thousand dollars?*"

Everyone looked up at me as if I'd dropped a dead mouse beside the salt and pepper shakers. I didn't know what I'd done wrong—expressing astonishment over the steep price? From what I'd observed in people like this, wrinkling one's nose at all things expensive was a major faux pas. Or was it the fact that I, the waitress, a lesser person in their eyes, dared to speak . . . *period?*

I got attitude from these students sometimes. The private Atlanta liberal arts college closest to my parents' diner attracted wealthy and, let's face it, spoiled teens who'd usually never worked a day in their lives—unless it was a cushy internship at their dad's law firm or something, earning twenty dollars an hour for sitting around and every so often answering a phone. Maybe I should give them the benefit of the doubt; they had no perspective, insulated in their little bubbles as they were. But let's be honest—they were often rude to people who were only trying to make their lives seamless and easy. Don't get me wrong, they were good for our neighborhood's economy, buying up two-hundred-dollar T-shirts in the boutique my friend Andrea's mom owned up the

3

street, ordering Uber all hours of the night because they didn't want to walk home from the bars in their pinchy heels—and, more often than not, it was guys from the neighborhood who picked them up, Uber stickers on their dashboards.

But they also looked at everyone who wasn't like them with suspicion . . . and even disdain. I wished I could tell them that I could run rings around them academically. Then again, they'd probably just stare at me as blankly as they were staring now. Perhaps they thought I didn't know English. I didn't want to be obnoxious, and I didn't want to stereotype, but *you* try slogging through ungrateful shifts in this diner . . . and, well, maybe you'd be a little jaded, too.

I lifted my empty tray. "Anything else?" I muttered. My cheeks were burning. When no one said anything, I stormed to the kitchen, feeling humiliated, though I wasn't sure why. I'd asked them a totally legit question. Paying ten grand for a music festival made no sense to me, even if it was a whole bunch of cool artists on the roster and even if you did get the opportunity to party on a yacht with the bands.

"Adri!" my mother cried as I passed the hostess stand. "Come here for a sec, sweetie?"

My mom, Marguerite Sanchez, had an overexcited grin. Long ago, she'd declared she no longer wanted to work in the kitchen because bacon grease was giving her wrinkly skin, so she took over as hostess, which meant she got to gossip with all the customers. A tall, slender, freckled woman in dark-framed glasses stood with her. My mom pointed at the stranger eagerly, as though she was a celebrity. "Honey, you remember Mrs. O'Hara, don't you? She worked as an aide in your elementary school?"

I groaned internally. *Here it comes.* Every shift I worked, I prayed no one would come that we knew, but we'd lived on this block our whole lives, and our family diner had been here almost as long. And my mother was always looking for a way to humble-brag about my accomplishments.

My mom squeezed my wrist eagerly. "Tell her what you're up to, Adrianna! Tell her about college!"

Mrs. O'Hara turned to me, smiling patiently. I didn't recognize her, but then who recognized their aides from elementary school? "Oh, I don't want to jinx it," I said sheepishly. "It's not a sure thing yet."

"Oh please!" My mother turned to Mrs. O'Hara. "She's interning at Richards, Canopy, and Cairl this summer—you should have seen the essay she wrote to get the job! And one of the lawyer's wives is on the admissions board at Emory, which means Adri is a shoo-in!"

"My, my!" Mrs. O'Hara said. "Emory! How impressive!"

"Adri works so hard." My mother looped an arm around me, and I smelled her familiar scents—Dove soap, cinnamon gum, and, for some reason, oatmeal cookies, even though no one in our house eats them. "We're finally going to have a lawyer in our family. Of course, my husband wants her to go into medicine, but I just don't know. The malpractice insurance alone . . . and the *stress*!"

I hated when my mom got on this particular tear. It was 2020, music festivals were costing 10K a pop, women were CEOs and fed up and kicking ass, and yet I, Adrianna Sanchez, had no say in my future career. And my mom wanted the whole world to know it.

See, in my family, my destiny had always been mapped out like it was a square on the Game of Life board: Once I graduated from college, I would spin the rainbow wheel, and whatever number I landed on would determine whether I'd become a doctor or a lawyer. (Teacher and accountant were also job choices in the Life game, but those weren't options for me.) It didn't matter that I'd dropped lots of hints saying I didn't *want* to be a doctor or a lawyer. If I dared to bring up that I wanted to be a journalist—like when that guy in the CNN ID badge came into the diner for lunch and I screwed up my confidence to talk to him—my parents would just laugh it off. Or worse, they would look at me hard, their foreheads wrinkled, and say, indignantly, "Why have we been busting our butts for all these years if you're just going to be a *reporter*?"

"Anyway, nice to see you," I said to Mrs. O'Hara. I looked apologetically at my mom. "I gotta go. There's . . . toast burning." It was the first excuse I could think of.

As I hustled through the double doors to the kitchen, steam from the dishwasher hit me like a wall. Pots and pans clanged, and there were thick, pungent, comforting smells from the fryer and stovetop. Jamieson, our dishwasher, hummed as he sprayed syrup off plates. Patty, our prepper, diced tomatoes with knife skills as deft as a chef on the Food Network. My father, Roberto, stood at the stove, simultaneously flipping pancakes and cracking a jumbo brown egg onto the griddle. Dad reminded me of an octopus when he multitasked, a tornado of flipping and stirring and sautéing and browning. In the fifteen years since my parents bought this diner, he'd never allowed anyone else to cook. He claimed it was because he was a micromanager, but in truth, he loved every minute of it.

My father turned, catching my eye—and seemingly noticing my glum expression. His brow knitted in concern, but I hurried away before he could ask me what was wrong. He could always read me better than my mom. I knew Mom meant well, but sometimes the Emory/lawyer talk put me into a funk. I *did* want to go to Emory—that much was true. And I knew my parents wanted the best for me. They'd saved their whole lives, forgoing all sorts of luxuries first to purchase the diner, and then to send me to a decent private school in our neighborhood— not my older sister, mind you, just *me*. "Because you're smart," my mother told me in confidence once. "Because you're *different*."

We skipped vacations and spendy Christmases so I could go to Huntley Academy. I did without name-brand clothes, and my mom drove around in a zillion-year-old Hyundai. I loved my private school, and it had been worth it . . . but now it was like my parents were expecting something in exchange for all their sacrifices: a daughter who did exactly what they wanted. Which was fine when it was delivering trays of eggs over easy and blueberry pancakes to snotty, hungry people—I liked working at the diner, most of the time. But it was different when it came to the rest of my life.

"Adri?" My mother poked her head through the double doors.

I straightened up. "Yeah?"

"Can you watch the hostess stand? I gotta pee."

"Sure." I wiped my hands on my apron and headed back out to the front. The hostess stand was littered with evidence of my mother: her old iPhone, clad in its cherry-red case, a copy of *War and Peace*—she'd heard somewhere that reading big, important novels could stave off Alzheimer's—and, beneath that, a laminated menu, which had a picture of the diner on the cover. Our family's restaurant wasn't in an old classic Airstream trailer, but the outside was still pretty cool, with retro neon bars lining the roof and spelling out things like EAT and TAKEOUT and MAJESTIC, which was the name of the place when my parents bought it. My mother was an expert with Peruvian food, but my parents had decided the dishes we served at home might be a little too . . . *adventurous* for this neighborhood. So we stuck with what the diner was serving before: burgers, fries, breakfast all day. We kept the decor the same, too: The inside had checkerboard floors and bright-red tables. A jukebox stocked with Elvis and Patsy Cline and other oldies stood against the far wall. For a while, my parents even had the waitresses wear fifties-style poodle skirts, but when I came aboard, I put my foot down, saying that no woman had *ever* wanted to traipse around carrying heavy trays in thick wool midi skirts and three-inch heels. It wasn't like the lone man waiter, a guy we'd known for years named Hal, wore a poodle skirt when *he* took everyone's orders.

The bells on the front door jingled. When I saw who was walking in, I ducked. Why was *he* here?

"Hello?" his voice called. I could sense him standing above me, staring at the top of my head.

I rose slowly from behind the hostess stand, pretending I had a perfectly good reason for crouching on the ground. "Hey," I said, tucking my hair behind my ear, praying my smile wasn't too twitchy and weird. "I was just . . . there was something on the floor . . ."

"It's cool," he—Hayden Collins—said, with an irresistible grin.

Hayden Collins. Tall—as in taller than most heads walking down the hall in my school. Thick eyebrows. Green-gray eyes that seemed to change color depending on what he was wearing. A square jaw, broad shoulders, a quirky smile. I cursed not spending a little more time on my hair this morning. I also cursed the fact that I had a big chocolate smear on my Galaxy Diner T-shirt.

"I thought you worked here," Hayden said, smiling.

I wanted to gasp. Hayden was . . . *thinking* about me? "Yep, guilty as charged," I heard myself say. "So . . . what's up? You want some food?" *Duh, Adri!* my brain shouted. *Of course he wants food! He's at a diner!*

Hayden pointed to the kitchen doors. "I ordered takeout. Apparently you guys make a mean egg sandwich."

"You like egg sandwiches?" I blurted. "Me too." *Oh God. Stop talking. Just stop right now.*

But Hayden just nodded. "Oh yeah. I could eat eggs for every meal. In sandwiches, in salads . . . even in ice cream."

"Egg ice cream?" I asked, giggling.

Hayden winked. "And egg on a celery stick. Egg pretzel."

"Egg burgers," I suggested, getting into it. "Egg toothpaste."

"Egg toothpaste," Hayden repeated, stroking his chin like he was really thinking this through. "I like it. Don't think it would give you fresh breath, though."

We grinned at each other. Hayden had a goofy side. I liked that.

Then Hayden's eyes fell to the book on the hostess stand. "You like Tolstoy?"

"Oh." I touched the plastic cover of the library book, and it crinkled. "My mom's reading this. But I've read it, too."

His mouth twisted. "Of course you have. You've read everything."

I could feel the heat rising into my face. He *knew* this about me?

"No, it's cool," Hayden added, noting my red cheeks. "I work as a lifeguard at the rec center, and I *wish* I could read on the stands. But it's not allowed. They say it might distract me from noticing if people were drowning."

I giggled again. "Well, that *would* be kind of terrible."

I felt myself leaning a little closer. It seemed like he was leaning closer to me, too. My heart thumped wildly. I hadn't wanted to read too much into it at the time, but after our calculus final, when I came out the school's front doors, Hayden was . . . *there*. Waiting, it seemed . . . for *me*. He'd fallen into step beside me, chattering about the questions, asking how I thought I'd done, asking what classes I was taking next year.

I told myself it wasn't a big deal. Hayden was just being friendly. I didn't have a lot of experience with guys—it had always been drilled into my head that I could concentrate on guys *later* . . . that now was for school and working hard and *getting somewhere*. So I didn't know the cues.

"So," Hayden said now, propping his elbow on the stand. Behind him, I noticed that Ms. One Egg White had twisted around and was looking at Hayden with interest. I felt a little zing of satisfaction. "You going to Quinn's party tonight?"

"Uh . . ." I'd been invited to Quinn Carey's party—all of the Huntley juniors had. It was supposed to be epic: She had a huge swimming pool, a local band was coming to play, and I'm sure there'd be booze. It would be a mini Solstice Festival, actually—without the ten-thousand-dollar price tag.

I was about to tell him sure when I heard a voice behind me. "*What* party?"

My mother burst out of the kitchen, wiping her wet hands on her jeans. A brown takeout bag with a hand-written receipt stapled to the front dangled from her left hand. "A party?" she repeated, looking at me with narrowed eyes.

"Just this . . . end-of-school thing," I said meekly, wanting to melt into the checkerboard floor. "I won't be out late."

My mother set her mouth in a line. "You're meeting with Michael at the law firm in the morning, so that's probably not a good idea." Then she looked at Hayden, a businesslike smile on her face. "Are you picking up for Collins?"

Hayden nodded. She thrust the bag at him and punched the total into the register. A couple stepped through the front door just then, waiting to be served. My mother shot me a warning look, then scrambled off to seat them. This meant I'd have a few seconds with Hayden to myself, but I could tell that was exactly what my mom *didn't* want.

I could feel him looking at me curiously. "Michael at the law firm?" he asked. "You suing someone?"

"*No!*" I cried, aghast, though I knew he was kidding. "I have this summer internship," I muttered glumly. "Of all the annoying things, the guy I'm working with wants to train me on a *Sunday*."

"That sucks." Hayden sounded genuinely disappointed. "But that's impressive. An internship at a law firm will look way better on a college application than my boring lifeguarding."

"Yeah, well, I'd *rather* lifeguard," I said under my breath, nudging the register closed with my elbow. "Actually, what I'd really want to do is . . ." I trailed off, then shrugged.

"Is what?" Hayden goaded me.

His eyes were on me, which gave me a little jolt just below my belly button. "Forget it," I muttered. I felt silly telling him about the internship I'd seen posted on CNN.com. It was something I'd desperately wanted to apply for. My advisor at the student newspaper, Mr. Richards, said I should. The ad probably wasn't even up anymore, though. I'm sure they'd filled the position.

"Adrianna?"

My mother stood at the far end of the aisle, hands on her hips. The people who'd just arrived were ready to order, so I had to do my job. My mother's eyes flicked from Hayden to me, then back again.

I sighed, then gave Hayden a weary smile. "Back to work, I guess."

"Good luck," Hayden said, eyeing up my mother like perhaps he understood her type. "And I'm sorry you aren't coming tonight. Seriously."

"Me too." Abruptly, ridiculously, I felt like I might cry. *God, Adrianna, do* not *cry*.

Suddenly Hayden pulled out his cell phone and started tapping. My spirits sank—maybe I wasn't interesting anymore—but then I felt a buzz in my pocket, my own phone telling me I had an alert. Hayden gave me a cryptic wave before grabbing his takeout and turning for the door. I pulled my phone out and saw that someone named HHTK had followed my Instagram *and* sent me a DM. When I clicked on the profile picture, Hayden's own face stared back at me. I widened my eyes in surprise. Then I looked at the DM.

It was great to see you. Here's my cell.

My heart flipped. I wanted to text him with a dozen heart emojis right that second.

"Ahem."

When I looked up, I could feel my mother's steely, judging gaze. I tucked my phone back into my jeans pocket, trying to temper my glee. As she and I passed each other in the narrow aisle that separated the line of booths, I expected she'd be frosty, standoffish, maybe even angry, but instead she suddenly grabbed me in a strong, crushing hug.

I let out a bleat of surprise. My mother patted my back. She rested her head on my shoulder for a millisecond. Make no mistake—this wasn't a hug that said, *It's okay. You can have a boyfriend.* It was more like, *I know I'm hard on you, baby. I know I suck the fun out of things sometimes. But it's because we love you.*

And what can I say? I loved her, too.

From the Solstice website:

Welcome, friends, explorers, pirates, and party people! This is the official site of the SOLSTICE MUSIC FESTIVAL taking place on the beautiful Caribbean Myla Island on June 19–21! Yes, we know those dates have popped up quick and you might have to rear-range your schedule, but we have a good thing going down here, so let's make this HAPPEN!

If you are coming, please peruse the website for which items to bring and what you can leave to us. (Bring: bug spray, medications, chill vibes only. Leave to us: a decadent experience that challenges the borders of the impossible!) Please note: All travel arrangements must be made through private carriers. Also, you MUST fly to MYLA ISLAND AIRPORT. Those who fly to Myla will be brought to the Solstice Festival by private limousine. Your chariot awaits!

Check out our official Twitter account: @SolsticeFestZa

Comments:

@JaredJ1920: Wow. By limo? Nice! Takes some of the sting out of the ridic price tag!

@DiamondsZ20: I'd much prefer a Range Rover.

@MoniMone: Are those girls in the YouTube ad going to be there? PLEASE SAY YES!

@_jbird43: Heard a rumor that Blink-182 is going to play a pop-up concert? Need deets!

@redflagatnight: I heard tix are already sold out. Scalpers selling at double the price. Still interested!

@BLankin: Dude, that island is infested with sea monsters! Abort abort abort!

@ruskybex99: @BLankin stop being a troll! Sea monsters? What you smoking?

@UlrichGreen1: @BLankin Uh do you realize how amazing a sea monster selfie would be? Think positive!

2

"AND HERE'S THE COPY MACHINE," Michael Graham, the associate training me at Richards, Canopy, and Cairl said as he led me into a small room off the main office. The copy room was littered with papers and smelled pleasantly of warm ink. "To make a copy, you lift this lid, put the paper in here, and press this big red button."

No way! I almost wanted to gasp in mock surprise. *I had no idea a copy machine could do such a thing!* The knee-jerk part of me wondered if Michael was treating me like a kindergartner because he knew my parents owned a diner—and perhaps figured I'd never been in an office in my life. I guess he forgot the part of my résumé that said I was the school's office assistant for the last three years running. I could probably out–Microsoft Excel him any day of the week.

Michael showed me the desk that would be mine for the next three months. It was a plain cubicle, separated from the other desks by three low, beige walls that had a weird, fuzzy quality to them. The flat-screen monitor showed a screen saver bearing the company's logo. The keyboard was covered in one of those plastic protectors that always reminded me of the couch at my abuela's house. There was a tiny cactus plant in a ceramic pot next to the phone. I wondered who had put it there. The last intern, maybe? I wondered why they'd left. I wondered if they'd liked it here or felt as trapped as I already did.

"You're right next to my office," Michael went on. He was a slender guy about thirty-five with an eager face and thick, sandy hair that fell boyishly across his forehead. He wore clunky, square glasses and had a few tiny acne scars on his cheeks. "Which is great, because I'll need you to transcribe a lot of my depositions. It'll give you a good sense of how to interview people once you're a lawyer yourself."

He exchanged an excited glance with me that seemed to indicate we were part of the same club, like we'd just figured out we were both huge fans of the same super-hero franchise. Then again, in the letter I'd written when applying for this job, I'd gushed about how I'd known I wanted to be a lawyer since I was three years old. Which was absolute BS. What kid wanted to be a lawyer at *three*?

Ping. I glanced down at my phone. I'd set up a Google Alert about the breaking news that this housing developer, Morris-Evens Homes LLC, was going to raze an entire neighborhood of Atlanta—a cool, cultural, *historical* neighborhood—so they could build more McMansions. Today's scheduled protest got about 300 percent more people than they'd expected. Whoa. That was *huge*.

"You need to get that?" Michael asked, eyeing my screen, his tone suddenly testy.

"What? No." I dropped the phone into my bag. But immediately it started pinging again. More updates about the protest. God, I wished I was canvassing the crowd for quotes and reports. This was just the kind of story that interested me and that—I hoped, someday—I'd get to work on. But obviously there was no way I could be there.

"Probably best if you turned that off," Michael said, making a little face.

"Oh my gosh, of course." I held down the OFF switch, heat rising into my cheeks. It wasn't like me to be reprimanded. I needed to focus.

Michael went through the various computer programs I would be using—the Microsoft Outlook calendar, Word—and sometimes I'd have to transcribe depositions. He talked about the case he was working on—some boring thing about an insurance claims adjuster who'd run a scam on a bunch of buildings around Brookhaven. "Turns out, all of the buildings that had policies with him filed for insurance payouts at one point or another," Michael said. "We'd never seen so many pipes burst or houses randomly explode or sewer lines fail. It was like the buildings were doomed . . . until we realized the disasters were rigged—*by the insurance guy*." He eyed me, a way-too-excited smile on his face. "This guy got a big percentage for every claim paid out. The bigger the disaster, the bigger the payout for him." He leaned back on the edge of my desk, proud of his detective work. "He's going down."

I made careful notes to show that I was being the best intern I could, but the details were sifting through me like sand. This insurance guy was a criminal, but this case wasn't going to improve anyone's lives—it was just going to make the insurance company richer. How could Michael get jazzed about that?

My eyes drifted to the clock at the bottom right-hand side of the computer screen. I *had* to find a way to make this job more interesting. I had to find a way to shine for Michael, too—his wife was the one who worked in Emory admissions, and that was my whole point of being here.

A million years later, we finally wrapped up. When I turned my phone back on and checked the news, it seemed that the protest had ended. I packed up my purse, and Michael walked me outside. The air felt stale and heavy. Sweat immediately prickled on the small of my back, making my blouse stick to my skin.

"Thank you for coming in on a Sunday," Michael said. "I really appreciate it."

"No problem," I chirped.

The late-afternoon sun baked the top of my head as I walked to the parking garage. A whole day had passed, and I'd been stuck in a cubicle. We'd barely even stopped for lunch. My phone buzzed in my purse. I was elated to see Hayden's name at the top.

How's office life?

I leaned against the side of a bus stop kiosk. *Boring. Absolutely nothing to report. And that's saying a lot, considering I want to be a reporter.*

He texted back: *Nothing to report at the pool, either. Well, except someone puked in the shallow end, and we had to shut the facility down for 45 minutes.*

I snorted. *That's big news!*

Not if you were the one who had to clean it up, it isn't.

I couldn't believe I was texting with Hayden. I'd taken a risk yesterday—before the party that I wasn't going to, I'd texted him a jokey: *Hey, someone DM'd me using your Insta, tossing out your cell number—think your identity's been hacked!*

That's right, he'd written back, *this isn't even Hayden. It's a scammer overseas. And now I've got your personal information, too!*

If it were up to Elena Sykes, my very best friend in the world, she'd tell me that I had to wait at least three days after a boy gave me his number to call him . . . but Hayden had seemed overjoyed that I'd reached out so quickly. Suck it, dating rules.

After that, he and I had texted and Snapchatted for almost an hour—I'd even made him late to Quinn's party.

We talked about silly things, mostly—like how when I was really little, my older sister Maria and I used to dress up in wigs and sparkly dresses, pretending like we were the Latina Destiny's Child. Or stories about Maria's failed attempts to find a career, first going to school for dog grooming, then deciding she wanted to be a potter, then almost filling out a form to get a certificate in organic farming until my father found out and put a stop to it. *Maria still lives in her old bedroom in our house*, I'd written. *Which is probably why my parents put all their faith in me.*

Yeah, let's stop talking about Maria, Hayden had written back. *I'd rather hear about you.*

By the thrill I'd gotten, you'd have thought he'd said he loved me.

Hayden told me his single mom was a nurse and worked just as hard as my parents did to send him to Huntley. His older brother had enlisted in the navy after high school, which would give him a free ride to college. Hayden had thought about following that path, too— especially since he wanted to go into engineering, for which there were a lot of opportunities in the military— but he wasn't sure he could endure boot camp.

I'd never really bonded with a boy before. I'd had a few brief boyfriends—hidden, of course, from my parents—but those had mostly been surface flings. Talking to Hayden didn't feel any different from talking to Elena. I liked that our trajectories were the same. I liked that we were square pegs in a round hole in the privileged, easy-life sea that made up most of our high school class. For example, Hayden was lifeguarding not so he could work on his tan, but because he legitimately needed the money. We understood where each other was coming from in a way a lot of people around me didn't, and that felt like an instant bond. I just wish I'd gotten to know him sooner.

An added bonus: He was so *cute*. Whenever I saw those little bubbles appear on his end, indicating he was typing, I pictured his handsome face bent toward the screen, his lips pursed just so, his long, slender fingers tapping . . . and I got tingles all over.

Now, I was about to write back to Hayden when another alert came in. It was Elena, sending me a Snap. I opened the message and saw a picture of Elena with the koala filter—she had a cute round nose where her sloped one should have been and a pair of fuzzy gray ears on top of her head.

How's the internship? read big, round letters beneath her chin.

Meh, I answered back. *But it's over for today.*

A new Snap came in. *Maybe I should get a job there, too*, she wrote. *Then we could spend the whole summer together.*

I wrinkled my nose, trying not to feel exasperated. But I loved how Elena, who'd never had to work for anything in her life, simply thought she could just call up the law firm and score an internship—and that it'd be *fun*.

The office definitely isn't for you, I wrote back. *Do*

something cool this summer like working at your cousin's boutique on Peachtree.

A half minute went by with no new Snaps, but then Elena sent one that read: *Can you come over right now? I have something to tell you.*

Everything okay? I asked. *It's not about Steve again, is it?* Steve was Elena's on-again, off-again boyfriend. He was a college student and rubbed me the wrong way. Long, long story. Elena swore that the last breakup with him was for good, though. I hoped she'd finally learned her lesson.

Nope, Elena wrote back. *I have a surprise!*

I was at my car by then. I checked my watch. I probably had time to pop over to Elena's before my mother sent out a search party. It wasn't like we had a big Sunday dinner at the Sanchez house—usually, my parents were too busy finishing up at the diner to throw together much more than leftovers. A surprise seemed perfect right about now.

I always felt a little breathless and out of place when I pulled up to Elena's dad's house in Buckhead. The place looked like a fancy wedding cake: white facade, white columns, a fountain in the center of the circular drive. I didn't know what a weed would do if it found itself in her front yard—probably slink away in shame. There were Juliet balconies on the second floor and a long series of double doors along the side that opened into a massive outdoor kitchen, seating area, and pool. And though Elena's father lived only a block from a major road, the property had a hushed feeling, as if it had an invisible barrier around it, stopping the noise.

I pressed the buzzer at the gate, feeling the usual mild embarrassment about coming here in my rattling old Toyota, which had primer spots all over it and sometimes sputtered to an agonizing slow speed on the highway. Elena's picture popped up on the video screen, and she squealed when she saw me. She buzzed the gate open, and by the time I pulled up to the house, she was bouncing out the door. "You are not going to believe it you are not going to believe it you are not going to *believe* it!" she shrieked as I stepped out of the car.

"Whoa, whoa, *whoa*," I said, pushing her back so I could breathe. "Slow down! What's happening?"

There were spots of pink on Elena's cheeks. She pushed a piece of butterscotch-blond hair over her shoulder and blinked her wide, lash-extensioned, sapphire-blue eyes. Elena was pretty. Like almost *I hate you* pretty . . . though I never got girls who hated other girls because they were good-looking. It struck me as a waste of energy—and besides, Elena's sweetness and humor and loyalty mattered more than her appearance. Okay, there were moments when I questioned why she was friends with *me*—I was pretty enough, but I wasn't *Elena* caliber, and I certainly didn't come from the same universe she did.

But I liked to think Elena appreciated the same qualities in me as I appreciated in her.

"Okay. Okay. Something really big just happened. Something that's going to change *both* our lives." Elena jiggled up and down.

I frowned. What could *that* be? Was Elena moving? No way. Maybe her parents were getting back together? But that wouldn't affect my life. Besides, Elena's parents famously hated each other. Their divorce was like a battle scene in the latest *Avengers* movie—mind-blowingly anni-hilating.

Elena dragged me through the door and sat me down in the living room, an enormous space off the kitchen. After Elena's mom left, her dad had let Elena redecorate the place any way she wanted, sort of as a bargaining chip to get her to spend more time there. There were a lot of chunky knit blankets, glowing Moravian stars, a giant faux-tiger-skin rug, and some huge art prints that Elena had bought on eBay because they'd allegedly once belonged to Zendaya. I'd tried to argue her out of it—she could have bought a grand piano for what they cost, or donated the money to an animal shelter, and did anyone really *need* stuff that used to belong to Zendaya, anyway?

She plopped us down on one of the gray leather couches and held both my hands. She was literally vibrat-ing with excitement, which reminded me of the day we'd met at casting for *My Fair Lady* in ninth grade. We'd both gotten parts in the chorus. I was kind of bummed—I'd wanted a speaking part—but Elena was thrilled, because she'd thought she wouldn't get cast at all. That day, she'd turned to me and crowed, way overenthusiastically, "We're chorus buddies! Want to come to my house after this and run through our songs?" Which was so sweet because, well, no one actually *hears* the chorus. But it led to an instant friendship.

"My dad gave me a graduation present," Elena began.

I pulled my hands away, confused. "But you're only a junior."

"I know. I guess he lost track of the years. Which means I guess I'll get *two* graduation presents out of this—his loss, my gain. Yay, divorce!" She put her hands in the air in a raise-the-roof style, but I could sense the pain in her voice. The divorce hadn't been easy on Elena. She was often trapped in the middle of vicious arguments and never knew where she was spending Christmases, and then there was the awkwardness of meeting her parents' new significant others—neither of which she really liked. "Anyway, he gave it to me last night—and you're not going to believe what it is. *Guess.*"

I shrugged. "A car?"

"Nope!" She threw her hands up again, gleeful. "Guess again!"

"Just tell me, El," I said, growing impatient. In Elena's world, the possibilities were endless. I wouldn't be surprised if she said a pet Bengal tiger.

She leaned forward a little. The way her eyes bugged

28

out, it looked like she was about to explode. "My father. Got us tickets. To the *Solstice Festival*."

My jaw dropped. "That thing on the island?"

"Yes!" Elena was bouncing excitedly. "He got us tickets! And flights! And . . . *everything*! We're going!"

I stared at her wide pink mouth. "What do you mean . . . *we're*?"

"Me and you!" Elena gave me a look that telegraphed, *Duh, obviously!* "He said I could take a friend, and who *else* would I choose? Adri! You're going to finally meet Lavender! Isn't this amazing?"

"Yeah, but . . ." I ran my hands through my hair. Lavender, the singer who was better than Lady Gaga, Beyoncé, and Ariana Grande combined, had been my favorite for years—and she *never* toured. She was the biggest reason I was paying attention to Solstice in the first place. "The concert is ludicrously expensive. There's no way I could pay for a ticket."

Elena waved her hand. "We've got it covered. He doesn't want me to go alone, and he *flipped* when I told him I was choosing you. You know how responsible my dad thinks you are."

I frowned. "So I'm only coming because I'm responsible?"

Elena play-hit me, rolling her eyes like she wouldn't even dignify that with a response. Then she flopped back onto the couch dramatically. "*Please* say you can come, Adri. Please?"

I stared at the large, blown-glass bowl that sat in the middle of the coffee table, remembering that this, too, cost as much as a small appliance. Should Elena have really poured *Doritos* into it? I did sometimes worry that Elena saw me as the "responsible friend"—book smart, reliable, boring. It was kind of true: I wasn't a risk taker. I did my weekend homework as soon as I got home on Friday afternoon. The few times I'd drank I didn't like it, and I stayed far, far away from drugs, terrified that my mother would surprise me with a drug test—they'd been through so much heartache with Maria, after all. I was always the designated driver. I'd never gotten a traffic ticket, not even for blowing a stop sign. I had a savings account with the money I'd earned from the diner, though it didn't have nearly enough in it to pay for Solstice.

"Aren't you afraid Solstice . . . isn't me?" I then asked.

Elena cocked her head. "What do you mean?"

"Just . . ." I took a breath. "Everyone going can afford the huge price tag. What if I don't fit in?"

Elena guffawed. "Of course you'll fit in! You'll *be* there, won't you? No one's gonna judge you or anything!"

But I wasn't sure. My whole life, I'd felt judged for one thing or another. As a different ethnicity. As the daughter of a blue-collar family at a preppy private school. And now, as an outsider at a concert for the 1 percent. Or maybe that was irrational. Would I be able to get out of my own head and even enjoy myself? On the other hand, it did sound amazing. The adventure of a lifetime. And it *would* be fun to bond with Elena.

But then I remembered my internship. And everything else. My shoulders slumped. "My parents will never go for it."

Elena's face fell. "But if you can't go, then I can't go!"

"I know, and I'm sorry. I guess you should take someone else." It pained me to say it. Now that the festival was a possibility, I desperately wanted to go.

"We just have to convince them," Elena decided. She sat up straighter, suddenly in debate mode. "What can our arguments be? That it's a once-in-a-lifetime trip you'll probably never get to do again?"

I thought for a moment. "Maybe we could give it some kind of this-will-be-good-for-a-college-essay angle." I grabbed a Dorito from the bowl and crunched down loudly. "Who's running it again?"

Elena narrowed her eyes. "Zack Frazier. The YouTube star."

I wrinkled my nose. My parents wouldn't be impressed by a YouTuber. "I could just say that I'm pretty certain Post Malone's going to invite me on his Jet Ski, and I could write a college essay about *that*." It was a joke, though. My parents wouldn't buy that, either.

Elena snapped her fingers. "Or about how, on this trip, you're going to become best friends with Lavender!"

"And a bunch of supermodels and influencers," I snickered. "Or maybe I'll become a supermodel myself." I did a few hip pops, though there was really no chance that was going to happen—I didn't know if I had a supermodel vibe or not, but the idea of living my life with a camera stuck in my face 24-7 made me twitchy with anxiety.

We collapsed into giggles, but then a weighty silence fell over us. I stared at the shimmering pink curtains I'd helped Elena choose. On top of the TV was the silver metal sculpture we'd found at a cool design store—Elena liked it because she said it looked like a metal cloud, though I'd said it looked like a boil on someone's butt. In less than a year, Elena and I would be off to college, starting new lives. Even next school year, we'd be in fewer classes together—I was in honors and AP everything, and Elena was more on an arts track.

I worried about us growing apart. This trip felt crucial, suddenly. If we went, we'd make more memories to carry our friendship through.

"I really want you to come," Elena said as though reading my mind. "Please say you'll talk to your parents."

I looked over at her, grateful she wanted to go with me as badly as I wanted to go with her. "Okay," I said, leaning my head on her shoulder. "I'll try."

@SolsticeFestZa: Greetings, fellow explorers, music lovers, and marauders! First things first, our lineup for next weekend is INCREDIBLE. Aside from the teasers we've already given, we're keeping the rest of the roster SUPER TOP SECRET—but know that your mind will be BLOWN. (1/4)

@SolsticeFestZa: Second, festival tickets are sold out—we repeat, SOLD THE F OUT. But! Tag two friends below and send us a pic of your $250+ purchase at the SOLSTICE FESTIVAL ONLINE STORE, and we'll give two lucky winners tix for FREE! (2/4)

@SolsticeFestZa: We particularly like the Solstice cashmere sweatshirt ($180), the Solstice Festival poster, signed by the artist ($230, unframed), or the Solstice chemical-free bug spray in a limited-edition graffiti-inspired designer can ($39 for 6 oz.). Shop on, my friends! (3/4)

@SolsticeFestZa: (Disclaimer: Prize tickets do not include transportation fees, food, lodging, drinks, medical services, merchandise, or other basic needs. But again, mind-blowing adventure comes free!) (4/4)

Replies:

@SeedSpore16: I'm in! Outfit ideas? How hot is it down there? Are we really going to need bug spray? The scent's going to clash with the perfume I had custom-mixed in Paris.

@Mahalo_Star: @SeedSpore16 I'm just bringing a big beach hat and TONS of bikinis! #BikiniInfluencer

@jhhj99: @Mahalo_Star Ooh, then I'm bringing my camera!

@FinniganDefine: Is it me or does Myla look pretty uninhabited? I kind of can't believe they even have an airport. I have diabetes and I worry about medical attention/getting quickly off the island in case of emergency. Or am I freaking for nothing?

@bb8-kool: @FinniganDefine I'm sure Solstice has this all figured out! Or just raid Zack Frazier's boat! (Someone told me he travels with a 24-7, 365 on-call doctor and an MRI machine!)

@FinniganDefine: @bb8-kool Good thinking! By the way, is anyone else having trouble finding Myla on a map?

@MunchausenFantasee: @FinniganDefine Yep, I Google Earthed it a few days ago. Half the island looks like a big field of nothing.

@bb8-kool: @MunchausenFantasee A big field of AWESOMENESS!

3

IT WAS THE FOLLOWING NIGHT after dinner. Dishes were washed. The kitchen was clean. My older sister had already gone out for the evening, which was her routine because she didn't want to sit around with my parents watching *Masterpiece*. The house was quiet. Peaceful. The sun was setting, but it wasn't too-too late, and my parents had drunk their single glasses of wine at dinner, which meant they were as relaxed as they'd ever be.

Go time, then.

Butterflies did gymnastics in my stomach as I padded into the den and stood in front of the TV screen, blocking the image of a Victorian-era British woman in a bustle scuttling down a flight of gloomy stone stairs. My parents were in their normal places: my mother on the ancient velour couch, the diner's accounting books in her lap, my father in the La-Z-Boy, half watching *Masterpiece* and half skimming an article in *Gourmet* magazine. He read *Gourmet* to get inspired at the diner, though I found that laughable—the menu hadn't changed since I was three, and gravy fries and western omelets were hardly gourmet food.

"Mom?" My voice croaked. "Dad? Can I talk to you?"

My mother hit PAUSE and lowered her hands to her lap. My father marked his place in the magazine. I fixed my gaze on the big bookcase in the corner that held our antiquated encyclopedias and about three hundred photo albums from when I was a baby because I was too afraid to look my parents in the eye. My heart was a jackhammer.

"So listen," I said, starting the speech I'd spent the last hour constructing and memorizing. "I've worked really hard this school year. My grades are great. My SAT scores are great. I've never missed a day of work. And I'm looking forward to this internship at the law firm. But I'm wondering . . ." I took a breath. *Here goes.* "I'm wondering if I could take a little trip with Elena next weekend. To, um, this island called Myla in the Caribbean. To a music festival. To see my favorite singer."

Their brows knit in confusion. My mother started twisting her plain gold wedding band around her finger, something she did when she was displeased.

"Her father is paying all the expenses," I said quickly. "No questions asked. And I've looked into it—the facilities where we'll be staying are safe, and there are security and medical teams on staff, and I promise I won't drink. Like I said, my favorite singer, Lavender, is performing, and she *never* tours. And also, I've never been anywhere—

maybe this would be good for a college application. And as far as the internship goes, I'll only miss two days. I can work extra hours with Michael when I'm back, and obviously I won't take any time off for the rest of the summer. And Elena and I will keep each other safe. So . . . can I?"

It came out of me in a rush . . . but a persuasive rush, I hoped. A safe, secure, all-expenses-paid music festival that could also double as college-essay potential? A mercy gift for the girl who never did anything wrong? If Adrianna Sanchez were *my* daughter, I'd totally let her go.

My mother finally let out an incredulous snort. "You're joking, right?"

"It sounds like a disaster," my father added.

It felt like they'd sucker punched me. "Wait, what? Why?"

My mother's pencil tapped her accounting pad. "Myla Island? I've never heard of it, and I won the geography bee my senior year."

I gritted my teeth. My mother never let me forget she'd won that damn geography bee, probably because geography was the only subject I didn't score 100 percent in.

"And furthermore," my mother went on, "I've already read about this festival. It looks slapdash. Poorly planned. How do you know security is tight? From their *website*? What if they're lying? What will you do if you're in trouble? From what I've read, there's only one way off the island—*by boat*. What if there's an emergency?"

"They have medical facilities," I said weakly, though I wasn't entirely sure if this was true.

She looked at me hard. "What, a first-aid tent? And what about the threat of Zika? Is that present in that country? You want to have babies someday, don't you?"

I threw my hands up. "Are you kidding me? Zika? Babies?" I looked at my father. He often let my mother take the first round of offense. "What's your case against it?"

My father stroked his chin. "Adrianna, there are far better experiences you could be having this summer than going to some dirty music festival on a desert island."

"It won't be dirty! And Myla looks beautiful! There's . . . sea life! Endangered species! The people who live there look friendly and cool!"

"And more than that," he went on, seemingly not hearing me, "I take offense at you saying you've never *been* anywhere. We all went to Peru last year to visit your grandparents. That's a whole different continent."

"I wasn't talking about Peru," I grumbled. Not that I *saw* much in Peru except the inside of Abuela's house.

"And you went to New York City on a class trip," he added.

I shut my eyes. "With the debate team. And it was *outside* New York City. In a hotel in Newark, New Jersey."

"You don't have to go on a harebrained luxury trip to write a good college essay," my father added, crossing his arms over his chest.

I gritted my teeth. "Forget the essay part. It's just . . .

this means a lot to me. It will be great for Elena and me, and it will also be great to refresh my brain. I need a little break, okay?" My parents looked at me skeptically, but I rushed on. "And also, I sort of already promised her I'd go. If you guys say no, that means she doesn't get to go, either—and her dad's out all that money."

The corners of my father's mouth arched down. "You shouldn't have given Elena the impression that you were allowed before asking us."

"Nor should her father have bought a ticket for you," my mother added. "That's very wasteful. And I raised you better, Adrianna, than to accept someone else's charity."

"Charity?" I squeaked. "I'm going as Elena's guest. And her dad won't even *miss* the money." But I knew that wasn't the point—like me, my parents took offense at the cavalier way some people spent money. "If none of the ticket costs go to charity, I'll find a charitable organization *I* can donate to—I'll use some of my internship funds." Maybe that would make this karmically square with the universe.

"But also," my father piped up, barely hearing what I'd said, "we haven't taken you anywhere, as you say, because we're saving every penny for you to go to college. We always thought there was more to life than frivolous excess. We wanted to give you the best future we could."

I opened my mouth, about to protest that I *was* grateful, and *blah blah blah*. But there was no point. I'd wounded my parents' pride. To them, I sounded like a bratty kid complaining that her family didn't go on all the fun trips her friends' families did. Which, yes, was the truth—how many times in elementary school did I quietly vibrate with jealousy when my classmates took weekend jaunts to Disney World while we slogged away at the diner? How many international class trips had I skipped because it wasn't in the budget? It was amazing that my parents sprang for that New York debate trip, actually. But it wasn't what I'd meant. I knew trips or material things weren't the meaning of life, nor did they necessarily make a person well-rounded. I'd hoped my parents knew that about me, too—but maybe they didn't.

I realized I had one last play and straightened up. "The thing is, I'm old enough to go without your permission. Having turned eighteen and all."

My parents stared at me hard. But it was true: I had just turned eighteen last week. It was a long story why I was eighteen going into my senior year—I was a summer baby, on the cusp of the school cutoff anyway, and I'd been anxious and shy in preschool, so much so that my teacher at the time had suggested that I hold off on going to kindergarten until I was six. All these years, my being a little older hadn't meant much . . . but today, it meant everything.

My mother's lips were set in a tight line. "You're going to have to tell Elena that you need to refuse her very generous offer. End of story."

"But . . ." My thoughts scattered. I didn't know what

else to say. I wanted to bring up that I'd never asked for anything before—and also, this was costing them *nothing*. Remind them of how good I was, how easy I'd been, how I wasn't prone to mood swings or wild behavior like my older brother and sister. It was why my parents were so strict with me—because they felt they'd failed with Anthony and Maria. But it didn't mean it was fair to *me*.

But I could tell nothing would convince them. My mother had already gone back to studying her accounting books, a clear indication the conversation was over. My father stared at the magazine.

I felt my whole body wilt. "Thanks for nothing," I mumbled, and then went upstairs. I wasn't even enough of a moody adolescent to stomp. I just walked.

I didn't have the guts to tell Elena the news over the phone. Even writing a text seemed impossible. I erased three different versions before settling on *I'm so sorry, I tried, it's a no-go* and adding a string of sobbing-face emojis.

After I hit SEND, I flopped on my bed and stared at the ceiling. Above me, in the attic space we'd converted to a bedroom, I heard telltale creaks and thumps. Maria was home. Should I talk to *her* about this? Maria used to wheedle all kinds of unthinkable things out of my parents—like living at her best friend Lulu's house for the summer of her sophomore year, or auditioning for a job as a character at Disney World (she didn't get it), or forming a band with her friends and practicing in our garage on weeknights. My parents didn't lord it over her schedule or decisions; she went to parties, dances, out on dates, lied about sleeping over at such-and-such's house when she was actually out with a guy, and one time, turned up on the eleven o'clock news for a crowd interview outside Eminem's tour bus after his concert in Atlanta—when she'd told my parents she was at the mall.

There were nights when my parents couldn't find her, when she didn't answer her phone. They stayed up all night, waiting for the police to knock on the door or someone from a hospital to call. The summer after her junior year, she ran away. For three whole days, Maria didn't come home. Didn't call. Went totally off the map.

I swear my father's hair turned completely gray just in that single weekend. They were grateful when she finally turned back up—she'd gone to Memphis for a few days with some friends but, oops, forgot to mention it to anyone—but also shattered and wounded. After that, they were just relieved she graduated high school without getting pregnant or arrested or kidnapped. Their standards were so low for her—they were never pushing her to actually do something with her life, certainly not to be a *lawyer*—but she also had freedom to do what she wanted as long as she paid for it with her own income.

Which way was better? Which life was more grat-
ifying? What would Maria do if she were in this same
situation as I was right now?

I couldn't talk to Maria. She was almost ten years
older than I was; besides a brief stint of being friends
when I was teeny-tiny, we'd always sort of been ships
passing in the night. It would be strange to try to strike
up a heart-to-heart after years of either being intimidated
by her or ignoring her. As I lay in my bed, I wished we
were closer. I needed a big sister to tell me what to do.

My phone rang. I felt a clench in my chest—it had to
be Elena. She would be heartbroken, I figured, but not
devastated. She'd probably just take someone else. While
I was sitting in that windowless, airless cubicle at the law
firm, transcribing depositions, my Instagram would be
pinging with pictures of Elena and her guest on the beach,
at the concert, on Lavender's yacht.

But it was Hayden's name on the caller ID. I answered
it with a gloomy hello.

"You okay?" Hayden asked, sounding worried.

I sighed and explained as best I could about Elena's
invitation and my parents' swift and decisive dashing of
my dreams. "Wait a minute," Hayden interrupted. "You
were offered a free ticket to the Solstice Festival?"

"I *was*," I muttered. "But I just gave it up."

"Adri, you have to go." Hayden's tone was urgent. "It's
supposed to be the party of the century. Like, *history* will
be made. You explained that to your parents, right?"

"Yeah, but they don't really care. They think Myla sounds dangerous. My mother can't find it on a map."

"That's because it's a tiny island. But the guy who set it up, Zack Frazier? You know who he is, right?"

"Sort of . . ."

"He, like, *invented* the concept of the YouTube influencer. His channel has one hundred million followers."

"Really?" I asked incredulously. I'd *sort* of heard of Zack Frazier, but YouTube wasn't really my thing. Still, 100 million followers was unthinkable.

"The guy's a marketing genius, and whatever he touches is really well done. The Solstice Festival is going to be safe; it's going to be well run; it's going to be an *experience*. This guy knows how to put things together. He threw a festival last year in New Orleans that was amazing."

"You sound like the president of his fan club."

"I admire what that guy's doing. So seriously, you need to find a way to go. With that guy running it, it's got to be legit."

"How can I go?" I slumped on my pillows. "They already said no."

"Couldn't you just . . . go anyway? You're eighteen, right?"

I'd told him about my birthday a few weeks ago. The bed creaked as I turned onto my side. Out the window, the streetlights turned on, casting long, golden shadows into my room. "I don't know. I'm not even sure the concert is me, anyway. It's going to be a bunch of rich kids."

"I'm not going to tell you to do something you're not comfortable with," Hayden said. "But it really will be the experience of your life. And if you already have a ticket, you have nothing to lose. Call your parents once you're in Myla. It's not like they're going to fly down there and haul you back."

"Clearly you don't know them," I muttered. But maybe Hayden had a point. *Could* I sneak out? It was certainly what Maria would have done. I remembered, when Maria returned from her three-day stint in Memphis, how my mother had been so angry until the moment she saw her daughter's face, and then she'd burst into tears and thrown her arms around Maria tightly, sobbing into her shoulder, just grateful she was okay.

"Look," Hayden said. "I'm going to tell you a story. A few years ago, before our freshman year, my family went on this trip to Arizona. And we got in a car crash. A . . . a terrible one."

I drew in a breath. "*What?*"

"We were driving on this winding road, and my dad lost control of the car, and . . . I don't know what happened, really. I just remember rolling, and glass breaking, and then nothing. We were stuck, Adri. In the middle of nowhere, in the desert. No one could see us from the road, with no cell service, no way to yell. Nobody helped us for *hours*. I really thought it was the end."

"Oh my God." My skin suddenly felt cold. How did I not know about this? But I'd come into Huntley as a sophomore; if people knew about this, the stories had blown over the following year. "I'm so sorry," I whispered.

"Don't be," he said. "I mean, we were eventually rescued. It all turned out okay. No one was badly hurt. And in a weird way, it was a great thing. It gave me clarity. I don't worry about the little things anymore. I mean, obviously I don't make choices that are going to screw up my life, but instead of being afraid to go for something I want, I just remember those hours in that canyon, thinking I wasn't going to live. If I were you, this concert would be a no-brainer. I'd absolutely go."

"Huh," I said thoughtfully. I was still rattled by the idea of a younger Hayden lying in a ditch in Arizona with no food or water or chance of help. Something like that *must* change a person. I wondered how that sort of trial would change my parents. I wondered how it would change *me*.

I told Hayden I'd text him tomorrow, then hung up. I felt unsettled but also honored he'd trusted me with his story. It felt so intimate. Were we becoming . . . *something*?

If I didn't go to Solstice, I'd regret it. If I *did* go—sneak out, in other words—would I even enjoy the festival, or would I be riddled with guilt and worry? But then, what was I worrying about, exactly? What could my parents really *do*? They wouldn't take my college fund away—

that would be like cutting off their noses to spite their faces. They certainly wouldn't kick me out of the house, either, when they were still letting Maria live here. Was it possible that if I went and sent them an "everything's okay" message once I landed, over the course of the three days, they'd realize they'd come down too hard? That I was busting my butt and doing everything they wanted, and I needed to have a little fun, too?

I *could* just go. I was eighteen. No one was going to arrest me. I wasn't doing anything illegal. And, like Elena said, I was the responsible one—I wasn't going to binge-drink or take weird drugs or even crowd-surf. I would work eighteen hours a day when I got back to make up for my missed internship time. I would work double shifts at the diner on weekends to say I was sorry. But, hopefully, I'd have an amazing experience that I'd always remember. And, like Hayden had said, that mattered.

I picked up my phone from the bedside table. Elena hadn't replied to my text yet—chances were she was sleeping and hadn't seen it. I pulled up my last message and started to type. *Forget that! Please don't take someone else! I'M COMING. Pick me up for the airport early Thursday morning!*

The text made a *whoosh* as I sent it off. This message Elena saw right away, and she quickly replied. *Yes! YES! Can't wait!*

I sat back, my heart hammering, my brain humming.

I had to keep quiet about this for two days, but I knew I could do it. This was the best decision. This would be the most amazing thing I'd ever done. Next weekend, I was going to have the time of my life.

Or so I thought.

@SolsticeFestZa: Aloha, Solstice Travelers! We know many of you are boarding flights to make your way south very shortly. Here are the details on how you can find the limousine that will ferry you toward the bucket-list experience of a lifetime ... aka Solstice. (1/7)

@SolsticeFestZa: If you are coming to Myla by private jet, a concierge will be waiting for you as you deplane; vans will take you to the waiting limos. (2/7)

@SolsticeFestZa: If you are flying commercial, it's an easy walk outside the airport and past Long-Term Parking to reach the port. (3/7)

@SolsticeFestZa: Smart Cartes for your luggage can be rented for a nominal fee, or you can reach out to our Solstice Concierge (email below) and he will book you with a SOLSTICE SHERPA, who will schlep your stuff for the low, low price of $500. (4/7)

@SolsticeFestZa: If you by chance live on the island (lucky you!), the limos will be one street past the airport. We'd suggest hiring a private driver because there's no public parking. (5/7)

@SolsticeFestZa: And this is totally one for my gratitude journal: Reports say that the weather is going to be BEAUTIFUL for our three days of decadent splendor. MAYBE a pop-up t-storm here and there—but hey, it's the tropics! (6/7)

@SolsticeFestZa: So bring extra sunscreen, your skimpiest bikini, maybe an umbrella if you so choose, and your sense of adventure—we will see you SOON! (7/7)

Replies:

@ukulele7: On my plane now, first class, bitches!

@free_da990x: already into the Veuve!

@SOLSTICE4-EVA: I am freaking! Literally cannot breathe! Lavender, mofos!

@JAZrreK: Commercial fliers: def wear sneakers once you get off the plane because that walk to Long-Term Parking is NO JOKE. At least 3 miles! But still super pumped!

@AnonymousA: You spoiled millennials disgust me. I hope a shark eats you all.

4

"*HOT TOWEL?*" A flight attendant in a crisp blue uniform leaned over me, her green eyes wide and her mauve-painted lips stretched into a sincere smile.

I looked down at my hands. They were still red from the last hot towel I'd been wrenching for a good hour. "I'm fine," I tell her sweetly. "But thank you."

"You're *welcome*!" She looked thrilled that I'd been cordial. I wondered if flight attendants, even first-class ones, got pushed around as much as diner waitresses did. Probably. I wanted to tell this woman—*Traci*, read her name tag, though she looked too serious to be a Traci—that I didn't belong in this oversize leather seat at the front of the plane, gorging on chocolate-covered strawberries and practically being forced into underage drinking. (Everyone in first class was a teenager, though the airline didn't seem to blink an eye at serving us alcohol. My flute of champagne had gone mostly untouched, but Elena was already on her third and tipsily giggling at everything.)

Speaking of Elena, she peered at something out the

window. "I think we're getting close. What are we going to do first when we land? We have a whole day to just *chill*. I hear they're running free hot yoga classes in the main tent. Or maybe there will be helicopter rides, like on the video? Or maybe everyone will get their *own* helicopter? Do you think there will be shopping? What sort of food do you think they'll have? Everything, I bet. Probably really good sushi—I read that Zack Frazier is a sushi *fiend*."

"I read that, too." I'd looked Zack up—research was my thing. His résumé was impressive. At only twenty-three years old, he'd launched a YouTube channel that was essentially a mix of comedy, pranks, and skateboarding, and gained enough sponsors to make millions of dollars. Zack had a zillion investments in other companies; a TV option on a short story he'd written at eighteen; he was sponsoring an X-Games-esque sporting event for extreme sports in Oregon next summer; and he was even thinking of getting into the space-tourism game. He'd also started several charities in LA; one was to bring music education to underprivileged children, and one was something about improving California public gardens without the use of harmful chemicals. I liked that he'd used some of his money for the greater good.

I'd also tried to do research on Myla Island. The Wikipedia page showed a lively tropical paradise with several towns, a capital, and some commerce. It didn't seem as built up as some of the other islands nearby, but serenity and wide-open space was kind of the idea, right? Also, the page talked mostly about Myla *West*, where all the tourism was, and very little about Myla *East*, on the other side. As far as I could glean, Myla East was much less populated and not very easy to get to from the west side of the island.

I trolled for Solstice subreddits, too, but all I found were eager Solstice Festival attendees also gossiping about where we were going. According to some, Myla was like an island of paradise with a secret resort only accessible to the rich and famous—except for this weekend, when the great and powerful Zack Frazier would open it up to all of us. There were shadowy pictures of the Myla resort where we'd be staying—sleek terraces, negative-edge pools, nearly empty beaches, stunning sunsets. Some said the resort had been closed a few years ago, and we'd all be camping instead. I was okay with either. My family often did camping vacations because it was cheaper than hotels, resorts, or theme parks. I didn't mind sleeping in a tent, as long as there was bug spray.

"Or, oh!" Elena squeezed my upper arm a little hard. "I think I read there are Jet Skis to rent, too! That would be fun to cruise around the Caribbean Sea, huh?"

"Is that what it's called?" I asked. "The Caribbean Sea?" I felt like Elena might be wrong—wasn't it just the Atlantic? But then geography wasn't my thing, so I wasn't sure.

At the thought of geography, I felt a pang of guilt.

I'd texted my parents after boarding the plane but then promptly turned my phone off because I wasn't quite ready for the hysterical responses I knew I'd receive. I hadn't paid for Wi-Fi access during the flight, either, still too afraid of their reaction. They couldn't be *too* angry, could they? They wouldn't do something rash like call the Mylan police to arrest me once I deplaned, right?

On the other hand, *I'd* never done something this rash before. I couldn't quite believe I'd gone through with it. When I hopped into Elena's car early this morning, it still felt like a hazy dream—like it was an alternate Adri going, not the real, levelheaded one.

The tone of the plane's engine shifted, and the captain made an announcement that we were dropping in altitude. As I leaned across Elena to look out the window, I noticed we'd burst through the clouds. Below me, stretching as far as I could see, was glistening turquoise-blue water. I gasped. "Is that the *ocean*?"

"Yep." Elena beamed. "Gorgeous, right?"

"It's so *clear*." My heart started to thump with excitement.

"The water's super warm, too," a girl across the aisle in gigantic Gucci sunglasses piped up. "It's going to be perfect for swimming." She reached under her collar and showed us the strap of a pink bikini. "I'm going straight in. Someone told me that there's a guy there who'll get you selfies with the dolphins that swim around the shore. He just holds them tightly so you can pet them and everything."

I felt my smile waver. What did the beluga whales think about that? But whatever—it wasn't like *I* had to support beluga-selfie guy.

A flight attendant named Andrea, on her way back toward the front of the plane with her cart of beverages, stopped and looked at us. She had flawless brown skin, coiled braids on the top of her head, and the straightest teeth I'd ever seen. "Oh no, you don't want to swim in the ocean." Andrea pointed a long fingernail out the window. "We've had a lot of jellyfish lately. Really painful."

"Wait, you're *from* Myla?" I asked excitedly.

Andrea blinked at me, as though this was the first time someone had asked her this all day. "Yes. I grew up there."

"Oh wow!" I exclaimed. "What's it like? Is there a traditional greeting I should know about? Are there any customs we should be aware of?" I wanted to be respectful of the people living on the island.

Andrea raised an eyebrow, and I realized a moment too late that I must sound like an airheaded tourist. But before she could answer me, a voice rang out from the front of the first-class cabin. "Stewardess? Um, stewardess?" A girl waved a champagne flute in the air. "Can you possibly get me some champagne that's a little *less* bubbly?"

Andrea pushed back the curtain to head into coach. I

felt a pang of disappointment, hoping to catch her again before the plane landed.

"Ooh, you know what else?" Elena grabbed my arm excitedly. "Someone told me some of the acts are going to do pop-up concerts on the beach this afternoon." She widened her eyes. "Would you just *die*?"

I imagined Lavender doing an impromptu concert on the beach. I had never been one of those screaming über-fangirls, practically fainting whenever Lavender released a new video or I came upon her picture in a magazine, but I had a feeling being up close and personal with her would be very, very different.

The plane droned on. Andrea the flight attendant scuttled all over the plane, satisfying requests. Soon, the tip of land emerged. It was all golden beach and thick, beautiful treetops. A sense of wonderment swelled over me.

"Is that Myla?" I said, pointing down.

Elena's eyes boggled. "Maybe? It's gorgeous."

She called Andrea, who happened to be passing by again. "Ah, yes," she answered, with a little bit of a sarcastic laugh. "Well, that's the *west* side."

I squinted out the window, and sure enough, I could see an airport ahead.

"Solstice is on the eastern part of the island," Andrea added. She thumbed the top of the window, out on the horizon. "I don't know it well at all." I squinted. Beyond the trees seemed, well, *deserted*—just like the Wikipedia page said. I couldn't even make out any roads. I felt a tug in my gut. Still, I had to believe everything would be fine.

Right?

The same brief worry flickered across Elena's face, too, but then it quickly disappeared. She looped her elbow through mine and swigged down the rest of her champagne. "We are going to have such an amazing time together."

"Totally," I said. But as I glanced down the aisle again, I saw Andrea watching me . . . almost like she wanted to say something. But when I turned to ask her what it was, she was gone.

Text message log:

To: Marissa

From: Bethany

Hey! Just landed! Where are U? Where's this airport's Starbucks? I can't find it anywhere.

(Message unable to send)

To: Marissa

From: Bethany

OMG. Just found out there IS no Starbucks here. WTF?

(Message unable to send)

To: Marissa

From: Bethany

Bitch! I know your flight got in. See it on the Arrivals board. Did you walk to the ferry without me? WTF? Why aren't you texting me back?

(Message unable to send)

To: Marissa

From: Bethany

Holy shit! All my texts to U just bounced back. Is there cell service here? Please tell me this part of the world knows about cell phones. The airport is in the dark ages. I'm afraid to use the bathrooms. How can we know this place is clean if they don't even have a Starbucks?

(Message unable to send)

5

AFTER A BUMPY LANDING at Myla Airport, we grabbed our carry-ons and deplaned. My stomach trembled nervously as I walked off the Jetway, but when I looked around the terminal, I noticed that though there were a few police officers scattered around the terminal, none of them were glancing my way. I guess my parents hadn't gone totally DEFCON 5 and sent the law down here to retrieve me.

I pulled out my phone, turned it on, and looked at the screen. No signal. I nudged Elena. "Your phone working?"

She hiked her tote higher onto her shoulder and frowned at her iPhone. "No bars."

I looked around. The Myla airport was nothing like the massive monstrosity I was used to in Atlanta, which housed every shop and eatery one could think of. But it was clean, and it was nice to see unique-to-the-Caribbean gift shops. I noticed that everyone else who'd descended from planes—most of them as young as Elena and me— were also looking at their phones in despair. "Excuse me," one girl said, tugging on the sleeve of a woman pushing a cleaning cart into a restroom. She waved her phone in the woman's face. "Do. These. Work. On. Your. Island?" she said in slow, exaggerated English.

The woman's nostrils flared. "Yeah, honey, we have cell phones. But sometimes the service is spotty."

Then she pushed into the bathroom. The tourist girl grumbled and stared at her phone. "How could people *live* like this?"

"I guess a tower is down or something," I said breezily to Elena. But I could still use my phone to record a video to eventually send to Hayden. He'd made me promise to send vlogs of everything I experienced.

I turned the camera on myself, not wanting to miss these very first moments of setting foot on Mylan soil. "Um, hey, Hayden!" I said, hoping my face didn't look too puffy and tired and overwhelmed. "Just got here. It's sunny, and I have a feeling it's hot outside. And here's Elena!" I swept the camera over to her, and she waved. "I'll film more once I get to ground transport—I mean *our limo.* Hope you're not fishing puke out of the pool as we speak!" I considered making kissy-lips at the camera before signing off, but since we hadn't kissed yet, that seemed a little forward. "Check in with you later!"

I pressed the STOP button and dropped the phone into my hoodie pocket. Elena eyed me as we stepped through a small doorway marked CUSTOMS. "So what's up with you and Hayden?"

"We're . . . friends," I said, not meeting her gaze.

Usually, it was Elena talking about boys, not me. It felt weird to admit a crush. "We've been talking a lot, though. He's super nice." To my surprise, Elena frowned. "What?" I asked.

"Just . . ." She shrugged. "Didn't Hayden move here from . . . ?"

I shot her an incredulous look, silently daring her to say the name of the small, lower-class town across the state.

"Oh, never mind." Then she smiled. "Maybe you guys could double date with me and Steve when we get back."

I stopped short in front of a duty-free shop. "I thought you and Steve were over."

She shrugged, then pointedly looked away.

"Oh, Elena . . ." I gritted my teeth. "Are you sure that's a good idea?"

Elena sidestepped a family dragging what looked like ten overstuffed suitcases toward a gate. "He made a mistake, Adri. That's all."

I made a *harrumph*. So here was the thing with Steve. When Elena and I met him, we were both charmed. Steve was nice, polite, funny, and smart, and seemed genuinely interested in Elena. At first, I'd even felt a little jealous when I saw them go off together and make out! They became a couple fast. Elena dropped me for a little, choosing to hang out only with Steve. I tried to be okay with it, figuring she needed time with her new boyfriend, but once, when I was working at the diner, I saw Steve come in with a group of people—but *not* Elena. I guess he didn't realize my family owned the place—and certainly didn't notice me among the waitstaff. A redheaded girl sat next to Steve, and they flirted all night. Nothing actually *happened* between them, but I could tell that it was going to. Later, I'd texted Elena, casually poking around, asking what she'd been up to that day. *Well, I was supposed to go out with Steve, but he had to go to his grandma's. It's so sweet that he visits her at the nursing home every week.*

That was when my opinion started to change.

After that, every time we'd get together as a group, I'd be skeptical of Steve's sweetness. I'd wonder what he was doing behind Elena's back. He seemed to make more and more excuses to not be with her, too—though they were always noble reasons, like volunteering or tutoring sessions or helping out his mom. I wondered what he was *really* doing. But when I tried to tell Elena about my concerns, she looked at me like I wasn't making any sense. "Steve's been nothing but wonderful!" she cried.

Things came to a head, though, when Elena actually caught him cheating about a month ago. It was at a party; Elena and I hadn't planned on going, but we decided to after all at the last minute. Elena had texted Steve she was coming, but I guess he was too busy to get the message. We came upon him in a back bedroom, making out with a redhead—a *different* redhead, I might add—on a daybed. Elena broke up with him immediately, and I felt grateful. Finally, she'd seen what a jerk he was.

"He came to me last week," Elena admitted. "*Sobbing*. He was so upset at what he'd done. He was so heartbroken that he'd hurt me. He *begged* for me back."

"Why didn't you tell me?" I asked.

Elena shrugged. "Because I wasn't sure you'd understand. But I really believe he just made a mistake. He's not going to do it again. He *loves* me, Adri. I believe that."

I felt Elena watching me, maybe gauging what I was going to say. I wanted to tell her Steve wasn't worth her time . . . but I yoga breathed through my annoyance. I had to let Steve go. We were on vacay. This was all about fun.

And so I grabbed her hand and pointed excitedly at a neon sign ahead that read AUTHENTIC TROPICAL DRINKS. "Coconut-banana smoothie to get you in the mood? It's on me!"

Customs took a while. Then the baggage-claim belt spun around and around before spitting out anybody's bags. Other concertgoers waiting grumbled that this airport was amateur hour; nobody around here even seemed to be working. "Maybe it's a cultural thing," some jackass guy in a Phish T-shirt said. I wanted to remind him that the bags often took forever to hit the claim belt in Atlanta, too.

When we stepped outside for ground transport, the heat clung to me like a thick sheet of saran wrap. Even my *eyeballs* were sweating, and my hair, which was normally curly, turned into a frizzy puffball in the humidity. Elena and I consulted our instructions from the Solstice website—I'd printed them out ahead of time—and headed out the door to the ferry. So many young, hopped-up people were walking toward the parking lot with determination, so Elena and I fell in step with them, figuring that the lead person knew where she was going. I tried to soak up the atmosphere of this beautiful, new place, though everything looked airport generic: concrete parking structures, whizzing taxis, tired-looking people dragging big suitcases. As we passed a sea of cars in a parking lot, the sun beat down on the part in my hair, and sweat rolled slowly down my back.

"There'd better be a big glass of ice water waiting," I mumbled.

"There'd better be a big glass of *vodka*," Elena corrected.

Parking Lot A led to Parking Lot B led to Parking Lot C. Finally, after passing Parking Lot D, I saw what looked like a wide, empty lot . . . and then ocean. This had to be where the limos were . . . except I didn't see a single vehicle. People were squashed under a tiny shelter on a small strip of sidewalk, trying to escape the sun. Elena and I strolled up next to them and managed to co-opt a few inches of shade.

"Here for Solstice?" Elena said to two tall, pretty blond girls in tie-dyed crop tops.

"Yes!" the girls squealed. "You too?"

We nodded. A bunch of other newcomers burbled about the Solstice Festival, their flights, the acts that would go on tonight, and why no one seemed to be getting a phone signal. "I heard a tower near the airport is down," a white guy with bleached hair in a dirty attempt at dreadlocks said sagely, shrugging. But then his friend shook his head. "I heard that tower is fine. It's something with the satellites." One girl bemoaned, "I promised my followers I'd post *every hour*. I don't want them to be disappointed!" Another guy was angry because his Fitbit steps weren't uploading to Facebook, and if his friends saw him slacking, he'd never hear the end of it. One girl was panicking because she really wanted to skype with her cat nanny to see if everything was okay. *Cat nanny?*

"I can't wait to get in a limo," one of the blonds in tie-dye said.

White-Guy Dreads cocked his head at her. "Wait, you didn't hear? The yacht is having engine issues. They're sending shuttle buses instead."

The girl looked horrified. "A *what?*"

"Like . . . *Greyhound?*" her friend spluttered.

As if on cue, a line of blocky, utilitarian buses chugged into the lot, straight for us. They certainly would fit more people. And as long as they had air-conditioning, I didn't really care they weren't limos.

But the girls in tie-dye backed away as though the buses were leaking toxic waste. "Oh *no*," one said. "I will *not* get on those. I'll wait for the limos."

"Really?" I piped up. "You're going to stand out here, baking in the sun?"

The buses heaved to a stop. The door to the first one opened, and the driver, a skinny white guy with a goatee, peered out. "Solstice?" he asked us. "Climb aboard!"

Most of us lined up, tickets in hand, eager to get out of the punishing sun. Even the tie-dyed girl surrendered, though she didn't dare touch the stair rail or the seats. Another girl back in the pack grabbed the driver. "Um, does this bus have Wi-Fi?" she simpered. "I *have* to reach my cat nanny."

"Indeed we do," the driver said cheerfully.

The bus also had A/C, and it felt blissful. I put my face up to the vents until I began to shiver. Elena and I took a seat at the back and tried to relax. I glanced at my phone and was pleased to see an available Wi-Fi server pop up on my screen. I clicked it, typing in the password the bus driver had provided. The upside-down triangle in the upper-corner of my screen blinked, trying to connect. A message came up that a connection couldn't be made.

"Okay, I'm going to have a panic attack." When I glanced over my shoulder, it was a guy in a Nike tee holding his cell phone aloft, presumably also trying to connect to the Wi-Fi. "I *need* to reach her."

The driver glanced at him in the rear-view mirror. "Is

it urgent?" he asked. "Because I might be able to arrange for you to use the bus's satellite phone . . ."

Nike Tee set his jaw. "Can the satellite phone open TikTok? Because that's the only way my girlfriend and I communicate."

His buddy, who had close-cropped hair and looked a lot like my brother, nudged him. "Dude, watch how loud you're talking. Your *real* girlfriend? She's heading back from the bathroom."

Ripped guys in Solstice board shorts and perfect-bodied girls in Solstice bikinis pranced around passing out water, Terra chips, and coupons for a free drink at the Conch Bar on the Solstice site—"as an apology for missing out on the limo experience." Elena, along with most everyone else, brightened at the idea of free drinks. "This is going to be amazing, Adri," she said, snuggling close to me. "Just you wait."

When we were filled to capacity, the bus pulled away. We turned onto a lively thoroughfare; people in resort gear strolled into restaurants and shops or rode on Vespa scooters and bicycles. Everyone knocked on the windows and waved excitedly. POINTS EAST, read a sign on the side of the road; the bus took the roundabout exit. So we *were* going east, then? To Myla East? I watched the grocery stores, hotels, and quaint shops recede into the distance. I liked it over here.

The roads became pitted, twisty, and narrow, and I started to get carsick and shut my eyes. When I opened them again, we were driving along the coast, but there were no signs of life around us. Waves kissed the smooth shores. We passed a copse of pint forests with tall, thin trees with most of the growth concentrated on the top . . . and barely any signs of human habitation.

Eventually, the road dead-ended into sand. Another bus had already stopped and turned off its engine, and I could see people climbing down the steps and looking around, confused. Elena frowned. "Is there a rest stop around here I just don't see?"

A boy behind me who wore a shirt with a colorful cartoon character smoking a joint looked my way. "No, the concert's through those trees," he answered, pointing. "But the path is undeveloped—buses can't get through."

"Oh," I said. My heart skipped a beat. At long last, we were here.

6

OUR BUS SHUDDERED TO A STOP. Elena and I grabbed our luggage and filed off, the heat even stickier than before. The moment the last person was off, the bus departed, presumably heading back to the airport in Myla West to pick up more guests.

I looked around. To the left of us was the beach, the sand smooth, the water clear. It reminded me a little of the beach in the Solstice video, but no one was in the water. That surprised me, considering how sweltering it was outside. But then I thought of the jellyfish the flight attendant had mentioned on the plane. Maybe it was true.

I glanced around for a path where the other people had gone, seemingly over some dunes and into some trees. Everyone milled around aimlessly.

"So . . . where are we, exactly?" Elena murmured as I fanned my T-shirt away from my stomach.

Finally, a guy in red board shorts with SOLSTICE printed down the leg appeared over the dunes. "Ahoy, marauders!" he exclaimed. "My name's Indigo! Come with me! Excitement awaits!"

"*Indigo?*" Elena said out of the corner of her mouth. "Like the color?" I giggled, just grateful someone had come to fetch us.

Indigo started over a small dune and around a few overgrown bushes. A girl behind me made a scoffing noise. "I'm not dragging my luggage in the sand. This is Louis Vuitton!"

"It's not a very long walk," Indigo said cheerfully. "It's fine!"

The girl grumbled as she hefted her monogrammed suitcase into her arms. She looked like a waddling designer penguin as she forged ahead. Away from the ocean, there was no breeze, and the air felt even hotter. Swarms of gnats buzzed. A mosquito landed on my arm. It probably wasn't the best idea for me to have worn thin-soled Toms sneakers—the sand was in my shoes in a matter of seconds. On the other hand, I was in a better position than most of the girls, who were wearing towering wedges, block heels in soft suede, and, in one girl's case, stiletto booties that wobbled so badly that a few steps in, she kicked them off.

"How's everyone doing?" Indigo called cheerfully. "It's not much further, friends. We're supposed to have four-wheelers to transport you guys over the unbeaten path, but they haven't arrived yet."

"What's with nothing arriving on time?" Elena muttered. "Is this what they mean by *island time*—nothing is punctual, and no one cares?"

I shot Elena a look, startled by how easily that casual, rude generalization fell from her lips. Okay, so the Solstice Festival had a few hiccups, but she didn't have to insult the island itself. But maybe she was just tired.

We finally came to a flat field of cleared land, hemmed in on all sides by pines. Young, attractive people packed every square inch. A lot of them were lugging their bags, and quite a few were drinking out of red Solo cups. I could smell the booze.

"Ooh." Elena's eyes lit up as she spied a pretty girl wearing a yellow Solstice bikini carrying a tray of Solos. She snatched drinks for herself and me, but I declined—the last thing I wanted was to get dehydrated so quickly in this heat and sun. I needed to get rid of my stuff first. Charging my phone would be great, too. Or, at the very least, another bottle of water. Was this deserted field really the concert area? Then again, the concert didn't technically start until tomorrow. Maybe they were still working on getting everything ready.

"Excuse me." Elena elbowed a girl in a beautiful peasant dress who was standing beside us, squinting around as confusedly as we were. "Do you know how far the venue is from here?"

The girl's big blue eyes blinked. "Someone told me *this* is the venue."

"Wait, *what*?" Elena spluttered.

"I think she's right," I said. When I stood on my tiptoes, I noticed a stage surrounded by speakers and lights.

Beyond that was a huge semitruck with its back hatch wide open. Next to that was a food cart—smoke billowed out its top, and there was the smell of something being fried wafting through the air.

Okay, not quite what I was expecting. Though I still got a little thrill—soon enough, I'd be seeing Lavender, *right here*.

But Elena looked horrified. "Where is the VIP area? Where are the cabanas? Why are we standing in the middle of a Best Buy loading zone?"

"Shh," I whispered. "I'm sure we'll get this figured out."

"Y'all got your tickets?" a voice called. A perky blond girl, also in a Solstice bikini, had approached. She held a big electronic scanner that looked like a cross between a price gun and an iPad. Elena and I rummaged for our Solstice passes, and the girl scanned them with the machine.

She was about to move on to the next group when I tapped her arm. "Is this where the concert's going to be?"

"Yep!" she cried brightly. Though her eyelid twitched. And she kind of cringed, like she worried we were going to hit her.

"And where are our accommodations?" Elena demanded—a little bossily, I thought.

The girl cocked her head. "You didn't bring camping gear?"

Elena snorted. "No! Do I *look* like a camper? I reserved a suite. The highest-priced package available."

The girl chewed on her lip. "Um, you'll have to speak to someone else. Look for someone in green Solstice board shorts, okay? They're on lodging detail." Then she walked away, waving her scanner in the air like a beacon.

"Green Solstice board shorts," I repeated, then glanced at Elena. "Listen, camping isn't *that* bad."

Elena stared at me, wide-eyed. "Maybe for *you* it isn't."

I bristled. "What's *that* mean?"

She seemed to realize her gaffe and sighed. "Sorry. It's just so hot. I just meant—I hate camping. I can't sleep on the ground. I need my down pillow, my Sleep Number mattress—you know, the *basics*."

"Okay, Your Highness." I was joking—sort of.

I grabbed my duffel and marched through the throng of people, trying to tamp down the feelings of uneasiness that were beginning to rise. I'd never traveled with Elena before, but I hadn't figured we'd clash. I didn't want to bicker with her. And she was right—the Solstice website *did* make it out like this festival was a little better put together than what was here. Still, I found it ironic that I, Adri, the boring one, the responsible one, the predictable one, was rolling with the punches, while Elena was panicking at every unexpected turn.

I spied plenty of girls in Solstice bikinis, but I didn't see anyone in green board shorts. We did, however, come upon an angry mob gathered around a sign on an easel near the stage. I moved closer; on the easel was a schedule of festival acts. Over the logo for Blankface, tomorrow's headliner, there was a big stamp that read CANCELED.

"This is bullshit," a beefy guy with dark skin grumbled. "Blankface was the reason I maxed out six credit cards to come here!"

"This was my quinceañera gift," added the girl next to him, who had long dark hair and fingernails painted with sparkly polish. "I should have gone on that African safari after all." She whipped out her phone but then scowled. "And I can't even bitch about it because there's no freaking cell service here. Are we in hell?"

"That isn't even the worst," a sardonic-sounding girl piped up. "I heard a rumor that Blankface isn't the only band that's canceling. Other people are planning to drop out, too, now that they've seen the conditions."

"Like Lavender?" I felt a streak of panic.

The girl gestured around, seemingly not hearing me. "Have you noticed it smells like garbage around here? Someone told me the flies cause mega-huge hives that leave *scars*. My friend's already planning to see a plastic surgeon when she gets home. Imagine, a fly bite eating away at your face!"

I opened my mouth, about to say that perhaps she was overreacting. Then someone else piped up, "And what's with there being only *one* food truck? I looked at the menu—it's hot dogs and hamburgers. Nothing keto. Nothing paleo. How am I going to get my macros right?"

"I *need* chia," someone else said. "I *need* soy protein."

"Hey!" another voice rose from the din. "I heard someone's trying to build a wireless router behind the food truck! We should check it out!"

A stampede headed in that direction. I turned to Elena. She looked like a traveler in the desert who'd just found out the beautiful oasis she'd come upon was all a mirage.

"Where are the spas?" Elena said in a small voice. "Where are the pop-up boutiques? Where are the beaches and Jet Skis?"

"Come on," I said, grabbing her arm. "Let's at least find a campsite."

After much shoving and elbowing, we finally neared the stage and the big semitruck I'd noticed earlier. A line of people stood by it, passing their suitcases to a guy inside the trailer. A guy wearing *green board shorts*. Aha!

I rushed up to someone waiting in line, a girl dragging two enormous Tumi wheelie bags. "Why's everyone throwing their bags in there?"

"Because this, apparently, is *bag* check." The girl lowered her big, glamorous sunglasses to take a closer look at my Marshall's bargain-rack valise. "I guess *you* don't have to worry about a luggage tag. Nobody will want to steal that thing. But what am *I* going to do?" She gestured to suitcases, which were made out of alligator skin. "These are a limited edition. I can't just *leave it*."

"Oh God, oh God," Elena murmured, rocking back and forth. I patted her shoulder. The sun beat down on the tops of our heads, singeing our necks—I could already see that Elena's skin was getting bright red. Then she whipped around to me, her eyes wide. "Adri," she said with horror. "Have we been scammed?"

"Scammed?" I repeated.

"We've *totally* been scammed," Glamour Girl echoed. "I am so suing this place when I leave."

Elena looked like she was going to have a panic attack. But suddenly she spied someone across the field, and her eyes lit up. "*Hey!*"

I followed her gaze. A broad-shouldered, floppy-haired guy in a sun's-out-guns-out muscle tee stood about twenty feet away, talking to a group of tipsy-looking girls. He blended in with everyone else here—young, attractive, privileged, drunk. But when he turned and spied Elena, I realized . . . I *knew* him. Knew him well, actually.

"Is that . . . ?" I started to say, but it was too late. Elena was sprinting toward him. He turned and held out his arms for a hug. Elena squeezed him tightly, rising on her tiptoes. I blinked hard, aghast. It was Steve. Elena's on-again, off-again, total-jerk boyfriend was . . . *here*?

"Hey!" Steve said, smiling brightly at me. "Adri! Amazing to see you here!"

I just stared. This had to be some kind of joke.

"How was your flight?" Steve asked. "Is this your first time in the Caribbean? Do you need some water?"

You aren't going to win me over with your sweet-guy act,

I thought acidly. I glanced at Elena, who suddenly looked a little guilty. "This is quite a coincidence," I said slowly.

"Um, well . . ." Elena's smile wavered. "Look, it all came together *super* last minute. But it's going to be so fun!"

"Fun?" I repeated. I still didn't understand what was happening.

Steve slung his arm around Elena. "I'm Zack's cousin— as in the guy who founded this thing. So we have a total in. You too, Adri!"

I blinked hard. "*You're* related to Zack Frazier? Funny, Elena never mentioned that." I looked at her hard, but Elena wouldn't meet my gaze. Terrible conclusions were forming in my mind. Did Elena's father really surprise her with tickets . . . or did she nudge him to buy them for her when she found out Steve was going?

"Adri." Elena's voice came out like a squeak. "Don't be . . ."

"Be *what*?" I knew my voice was sharp, but I was so caught off guard—and hurt—I couldn't see straight. Why wouldn't Elena have told me? Then again, I knew full well why.

Steve just smiled. "Me and Zack went through many torturous family Christmases together. In fact—" He waved at someone in the crowd, and in a blink, a handsome, hip, familiar guy was before us. "Zack!" Steve said. "Say hello to my girlfriend, Elena, and her friend Adri."

"Hey there." Zack had a moon face. Dorky dark-framed glasses. He was too skinny, too short, but he had an expensive haircut and probably an expensive watch, because didn't all zillionaires have expensive watches?

The mood in the crowd shifted with Zack's presence. Everyone whispered like he was royalty. Even I felt a little flutter—I knew I should turn on the video app on my phone and record him while giving Hayden a shout-out. Except I was still so, *so* angry. I didn't want to give Elena any indication this was okay.

But then I realized that we had an audience with the leader of this festival—and maybe we could get answers. I turned to Zack. "So what's with the false advertising? Elena's been a little upset that we can't find the luxury accommodations you guys promised."

Elena's smile wavered. "Uh, I'm not upset!"

"It's all good," Steve said quickly. "Zack's got it covered."

Zack smiled at me reassuringly. "You just wait until tomorrow when the music starts. We'll work out all the kinks. I've got an incredible team on it, and they've promised me that everything will be up and ready by the time we get going."

"But, um, what about tonight?" I asked. "Are those luxury suites . . . somewhere? If we have to camp, I wouldn't mind setting up a tent and getting out of the sun for a while."

Steve looked horrified. "You don't *actually* want to camp, do you?"

"I don't see any other options," I argued. "I didn't realize camping was so *beneath* everyone."

"Adri," Elena warned. "There's no need to be nasty."

Um, have you forgotten what Steve did to you? I wanted to shout. That *was nasty.*

"We'll have it all worked out," Zack said again, grinning. "I was just talking to my guy right now. The facilities are on the next ferry from the other side of the island."

"Wait, *how* were you talking to your guy?" I asked. "Do you have cell service?"

Steve laughed politely. "You have a lot of questions, Adri. Why don't you just relax, enjoy yourself? It's all going to work out."

Elena giggled. I tried to catch her eye, but she wouldn't look at me. "And what about the food truck?" I gestured to the growing line at the only food establishment on the field. "Some people are vegans. Some people have food allergies. Are you addressing any of that?"

Zack smiled at me wanly. I wondered if he was stoned.

"And what about the porta-potties?" I remembered a girl complaining about that earlier. "Are you bringing in more of those? And where's the first-aid tent?" Okay, now I sounded like my mother, but it was a good question. When I glanced around, I didn't see any area that would address medical needs. In fact, all I could see was a tent for something called CBD Beauty, its logo a big pot leaf. "What if someone gets hurt?"

"You've really thought all this through," Zack said, grinning. "I hope you're not a reporter!" He clapped his hands together and laughed loudly as though he'd said something truly hilarious. Elena laughed, too—though nervously. I didn't crack a smile. "But you guys have seen nothing yet," Zack went on. "Through those trees is the beach—and a ton of yachts are already docked. Jay-Z's, Lavender's, a bunch of Silicon Valley bigwigs' . . . and more are en route."

"Through *those* trees?" I asked, pointing to the pines to our right.

"Yep. There's a yacht full of hot models, too." He nudged Steve, and Steve, like a jerk, grinned lasciviously. I glanced at Elena to gauge her reaction, but she wasn't watching. Of course. "It's going to be a real party. The trip of a lifetime."

Maybe it was the relentless sunshine, maybe it was my exhaustion, or maybe it was my annoyance at Elena, but I suddenly felt a strong sense of injustice. "So . . . you're going to invite *everyone* on that yacht?" I gestured around to the crowd. Even though I found most of them spoiled and ridiculous, I didn't want them to bake out here in the sun.

"Adri." Elena's eyes were wide and pleading. She was looking at me like she couldn't believe I'd just crossed the famous, do-no-wrong Zack Frazier. Even Zack backed up, a little shocked. But all of a sudden I didn't feel like waiting for answers. I was so angry at Elena for keeping this from me, I broke from the group. I just needed to be alone for a while. I needed to clear my head.

"Adri, wait!" Elena cried. "Where are you going?"

"To find some water," I shouted behind me. "To get the lay of the land." And maybe to find a tent, because I would rather stick needles in my eyes than get on a yacht with *that* guy.

I felt Elena watching me as I stepped away. It suddenly felt symbolic, my leaving the group. If Elena followed me, I would let her lies about Steve slide. But if she stayed where she was . . . well, I didn't know.

I took another few steps, then peeked over my shoulder again. Elena hadn't moved. And there was my answer.

@SolsticeFestZa: IMPORTANT UPDATE FOR ALL FESTIVAL TRAVELERS! Due to unforeseen circumstances, our limos are having engine issues, so we'll be sending shuttle buses instead. But because space is extremely limited, IF YOU CAN FIND YOUR OWN TRANSPORTATION TO THE FESTIVAL SITE, PLEASE DO SO. (1/2)

@SolsticeFestZa: Some options: Jimmy's Limo Service, Whirlwind Private Aircraft LLC, or the Highwinds Helicopter Charter, which is located only two miles from the Myla airport! See y'all soon! (2/2)

Replies:

@B. YOLO: Dude. Have you looked up the prices of those plane and heli charters? I don't exactly have three grand to spare just to get me to Myla. (PS: I'm posting this from an internet café in Myla—there's no service anywhere else! Have we landed on another planet?)

@VendoCh88: DON'T GO WITH HIGHWINDS CHARTER. Yes, they have wifi on board, but we ran out of gas halfway to the festival site and THERE'S NO SIGN OF RESCUE. #LostonaDesertIsland

@CiCiCutie: Guys! My uncle's chartering a seaplane for a bunch of us—there's still space! And don't worry about paying—his hedge fund's footing the bill. They're able to write it off as a charitable donation/state of emergency rescue! Isn't that rad? #NotLostonaDesertIsland

@HaydenATL: Has anyone seen a girl named Adrianna anywhere? Dark hair, big smile, probably wearing a Lavender t-shirt? I can't get in touch with her and want to know if she's okay.

@B. YOLO: @HaydenATL, uh, didn't you read my tweet? NO CELL SERVICE. No one can reach anyone. But also, haven't seen your friend.

7

BEYOND THE SEMITRUCK/BAG CHECK was a road. Down it, only an eighth of a mile or so, were a few more roads, homes, a small white church, and—miracle of miracles—a little market with a Coca-Cola sign in the window.

I stamped through the parking lot. Several bicycles were tipped up against the building's facade, and I could hear voices inside.

"Rich kids dropping garbage everywhere," one of them said. "It's a disaster."

"They can't contain them all on that field," another voice grumbled. "And do they even know about—"

They all fell silent as I stepped across the threshold. One was a youngish, darker-skinned man, another a youngish woman with a cool, natural Afro, and a third an older woman with lighter skin, colorful beads in her braids, and wearing an oversize T-shirt I swore I'd seen on sale at the Gap. They sat on folding chairs around a small register. A radio tinkled between them, playing, of all things, Britney Spears. I'd been expecting Bob Marley, but now I realized (wincing internally) that of course Mylans would listen to any music genre, just like Americans did.

The man half rose from his chair, looking me over. "You need some water?"

I offered a wobbly smile. "H-how'd you guess?"

That got some chuckles. Then the woman said, "Fridge in the back. It's not ice cold, but—"

"I don't mind," I interrupted. "Water is water."

The man grinned. "I like your attitude."

The door chimes rang behind me, and a few more people walked in. They were most definitely from the Solstice Festival, too. A few wore Birkenstocks and Lululemon gear. Others had quilted Chanel purses looped over their shoulders and eyelash extensions. A tanned, muscled guy didn't bother wearing a shirt. The locals gave them friendly-enough smiles, but I noticed they didn't continue with their conversation.

A girl in a bikini wrinkled her nose at a bunch of bananas on the shelf where I was standing. "Why are they so *weird looking*?" she whispered to her friends.

"Um?" I said carefully. "They're actually not bananas. They're plantains. They're really good fried." My mother always bought a bunch when we managed to make it over to the grocery a few miles from our house. (And I absolutely loved the bags of plantain chips you could sometimes find at a bodega, if you searched hard enough.)

The girl blinked hard as though I'd spoken in Swedish.

Then she turned away, giggling, and wafted to another part of the store.

I could feel the Mylans at the register watching me as I shuffled toward the fridge cases and extracted several bottles of Poland Spring, downing nearly a whole one right there on the spot. I reached back in to grab a few for Elena, then put it back. Let her get her own.

I couldn't believe she'd tricked me. It was clear she'd known about Steve for a while . . . but hadn't mentioned it to me because she knew I wouldn't have come if I'd known he was going, too. But what about all that stuff she'd told me about badly wanting me to come? Was that true, or did she want me along because I was her responsible friend . . . and that was the only way her dad would buy the tickets?

Did she even realize how much I'd put at risk to come? Maybe not. Maybe she wasn't thinking about me at all.

Melancholy overwhelmed me, coupled with an intense jolt of homesickness. I plopped my bottle of water on the checkout counter, but then Plantain Girl cut in front of me, piling water, sodas, candy, and other random snacks next to the register. "Do you have Wi-Fi service?" she demanded of the shopkeepers.

The woman with the Afro shook her head as she started punching in the prices for the girl's stuff. "Sorry, no."

"But you know what Wi-Fi *is*, right?" the girl pressed.

"Internet service? Cell phones? Do you have that, in this country?"

Her buddy nudged her and said, sotto voce, "Piper, they probably don't. They probably, like, ride goats to work."

My mouth dropped open. *Goats to work?*

The woman at the register scanned the girl's items as if she hadn't heard a word they'd said. "Twenty-two fifty," she said. The girl passed her American dollars; the woman gave her change in what I presumed was Mylan currency. Plantain Girl looked at it like it was Monopoly money. "What the hell is *this*?"

When they left, I shot the woman a mortified smile. "I-I'm so sorry about them."

"They friends of yours?" the woman asked.

"No! Of course not! They were so rude, and . . ."

"Barrier Reef one oh one," the man murmured, cutting me off.

"What?" I asked.

"Of course we have Wi-Fi." The man rolled his eyes. "The password is starfish five five one four. Please don't pass it around, okay?"

"I . . . *thank* you," I said, flattered that he had deemed me trustworthy—and nothing like Plantain Girl.

The older lady in the oversize T-shirt eyed me pityingly. "Poor dear, coming all the way here for this sham of a *music festival*. I hope you didn't spend your life's savings."

I looked up in surprise. "What do you mean 'sham'?"

She smiled cryptically. The younger woman eyed her with warning, as if to say, *Let it go*. She waved her hand. "I'll just say this. They made it out like you were coming to the Four Seasons. When in fact, what they've built for you is more like . . ." She glanced at the others, looking for a comparison.

"A roach motel?"

She smiled. "Something like that."

Then, after a beat, she dropped a can of bug spray into my plastic bag. "You're going to need this in your tent tonight. They're not kidding about the biting flies."

"Thanks," I said. Then I held up my phone, which I'd unearthed from my pocket. "And thanks for the Wi-Fi password, too."

In the doorway, I uncapped the second water bottle and drained its contents practically in one swallow. Then I tapped the Wi-Fi icon on my phone. Sure enough, the Barrier Reef router appeared as the only available connection. Making sure no one was looking over my shoulder, I typed in the password. I was astounded when the little triangle in the corner lit up with a signal. I had a feeling it would take my phone a while to download all my messages—I dreaded what I'd be getting from my parents—but I didn't want to wait. I dashed off a quick text to them saying I was in Myla and perfectly fine. Then I wrote to Hayden. *Got here. A little different than I expected, but I'll deal. Elena screwed me, though. And met Zack Frazier . . . but not quite impressed. Miss you!*

I sent it off before I could second-guess the *miss you*. Too much too soon? Suddenly I felt someone looming over me. It was Plantain Girl. "Are you using your phone?" she brayed. "Do you have Wi-Fi? Is there a signal?"

A few more heads popped up. All at once, I felt like a crust of bread on the beach, at the mercy of a flock of hungry seagulls above. I didn't want to betray the store-owner's trust, so I dropped my phone back in my pocket. "Nah, just looking at photos. No signal anywhere."

The girl scowled, then slumped away. I was dying to pull out my phone again and read the texts that had come in . . . but there was just no way. Besides, I felt a little guilty not sharing. What if someone here had an emergency and needed to reach the outside world?

At the edge of the festival site, a few guys in Solstice board shorts were hauling something out of a truck that must have appeared while I was in the shop. I squinted hard. They were unloading what looked like tents.

"They're military huts, in case you're wondering."

I turned and saw a fit, ruddy-cheeked guy with dark, shiny hair, and keen, intelligent eyes wearing a red shirt that read EVEREST on the front. Like me, he held a bottle of water and bug spray from the shop. "So not tents, exactly," he went on, "but not four-star hotel rooms, either." He twisted his mouth. "And believe it or not, those are the suites that cost more."

"Hmm," I said. "A lot of people are going to be disap-pointed."

"Not me." He shrugged. "I'm used to camping out."

"Me too," I admitted. "I think it's kind of peaceful to sleep outdoors, actually."

"Same." He extended his hand. "Eric Jedry."

"Adri Sanchez," I said, smiling.

"I'm from Maryland. You?"

"Atlanta." My eyes flicked to the tents again. Was it me, or did they look sort of flimsy? And how could there possibly be enough of them to accommodate everyone?

"Hey, it's going to be okay," Eric said, as though reading my mind. "A lot of festivals like this come together at the last minute. And hey, even if it's not what it was advertised as, this island still rocks."

I looked around. "It *is* beautiful here."

"Right? There are some pretty cool places to rock-climb around here—I'm into that sort of thing. I've heard the beaches are awesome, too—though a lot of them tough to get to. That one nearest us? It's got a killer rip tide."

I nodded. That explained why no one was swimming, anyway.

"Or maybe you're here for the music?" He eyed the Lavender T-shirt I was wearing. "Not *every* band is going to cancel." He arched his back and looked at the sky, which was a brilliant, cloudless blue. "Now that we're here, we just have to make the best of it, you know?"

I downed the rest of my water and wiped my mouth. I liked Eric's attitude. We were on a tropical island full of mystery and wonder. We could make this a miserable three days, or we could make it an adventure. And suddenly I realized how to tailor it to be *my* kind of adventure.

Eric tossed his bottle into a large trash barrel. "You want to do some rock climbing this afternoon? Nobody from my group is interested, but you'd be in good hands. And I'm not drunk—I promise."

I laughed. "I can tell you're not." He wasn't slurring his words. Then I gazed back at some of the people wandering out of the shop; one girl was walking in big, crooked steps. Someone else was throwing up into a bush, her friend holding back her hair. A couple of brilliant-colored birds skittered away to avoid her projectile puke. "Thanks anyway," I added. "It sounds fun, but I have something else I want to do."

Eric nodded, looking a little disappointed. "I'm going to head out, then." He peeled off his red T-shirt and tucked it into the waistband of his shorts. On his muscled back was a small tattoo of a mountain peak. "See ya around, Adri. Maybe on Lavender's boat, huh?"

"I hope so," I said . . . though not *quite* as certain as I'd been before. In fact, I wasn't even sure Lavender's boat was here.

But I wanted to find out. That was what *I* was going to do with my time on this island: not get drunk, not watch Elena and Steve grope each other, and not panic like everyone else because Solstice was a hot mess and no one was getting the five-star treatment they'd expected. I was going to do some reporting. I was going to figure out what was real about this festival—and what wasn't—and turn it into a story.

I don't know if it was because there was no cell service (that they knew of) and people weren't afraid of me leaking anything, or if they were as bewildered as I was and just wanted to share their concerns, but it wasn't hard to round up people in Solstice gear to get their take on the situation. I didn't tell anyone I was low-key reporting on this; I was afraid they'd run for the hills. Just that I was a curious, sober, non-whiny member of the crowd.

Adam, a short, muscular guy, explained that the festival was stashing everyone's bags in the trailers because they wanted to keep them dry in case a storm came. "Oh, that's cool," I said brightly. "What do you have planned for the people if it storms?"

Adam just shrugged. "Everyone should have brought ponchos, boots. It's hurricane season."

I thought of the list of items the Solstice website had told us to bring. There was a vague mention of *perhaps considering* an umbrella, but certainly not head-to-toe rain gear. Then again, maybe we all should have read up on the island's climate. Adam added, "It rained at your Woodstock concert in 1969, and you people can't stop talking about how great *that* was."

I stared at him evenly. "So true! But also? Woodstock was *free*."

Faith, a small, muscular girl with a Simone Biles vibe about her, had a walkie-talkie on her belt that wouldn't stop blaring. I tried to ask her some general questions—was she from this island? Had she lived here all her life? She was terse with me, but I persisted and finally wore her down. "We will be getting more porta-potties in by six p.m. tonight," she reported about the bathroom situation.

"Oh, great!" I cried. "And . . . how about *better* bathrooms? Like, ones with real plumbing and soap?" I prayed my phone, which was lodged in my pocket, was picking up my voice.

"And what about the ecological footprint this concert is making on the grounds?" I asked next, after Faith had mumbled a nonanswer about the bathrooms. "How are you planning to deal with the mess everyone leaves behind once they leave? All the extra boat fuel in the water? Any plant or habitat damage from hikers and campers?"

Faith frowned. "I don't handle that stuff. Also, *who* are you again?"

And then there was Stuart, a bulky guy with a shaved head who looked like he'd just gotten out of the military. I found him by the food trunk, unpacking boxes marked with a popular food-distribution logo. "What's in those boxes?" I asked.

"Food." He opened the box and showed me bags of

Doritos, packages of Oreos, and plastic-wrapped cheese sandwiches.

I took a picture of the contents. "This is all awesome, but the website said there was going to be sushi—which, *totally* fine if there isn't. But my friend can't eat dairy. You'll have something for her, right?"

"Talk to the boss," Stuart said cheerfully. "I just unload it."

Just then someone pushed through the crowd and put his hand on Stuart's arm. "What's going on, Stuart?" The guy was tall, had a square jaw, expressive eyebrows, warm brown skin, and sharp, dark eyes. I guessed he was probably in his early twenties. He'd be cute, I thought, if he weren't so damn angry. Something about him screamed that he was in charge.

"Oh, hey, Paul." Stuart suddenly looked nervous. "Just . . . you know . . ."

But Paul was glaring—at me. "I've seen you around, asking a lot of questions, keeping the staff from doing their jobs. Can you tone it down?"

"Are you the boss?" I asked brightly, avoiding his question.

"I'm the local team leader." Paul's frown deepened. "Trying to keep all of you guys safe and happy. But if you keep interrupting my staff, they can't get work done."

"I'm just curious," I said. I gestured around the site. "Is there security here? Clean drinking water? Do you have medical facilities?"

"*That's* what you've been asking my people?" Paul looked offended. "If their island is civilized? Most of the people on my team are from Myla, you know. They're island people, born and bred—and proud of this place." He gritted his teeth like he wanted to say more, but then just mumbled under his breath, "*Rich* kids."

I blinked. "I-I'm not a rich kid!" I *empathized* with this guy. I'd been in shoes like his before. At the diner, I grumbled under my breath about the spoiled private school and college students who expected things to be handed to them, who never said thank you, who complained because their pancakes had a little bit too much powdered sugar and they were going to exceed their calorie count for the day.

At the same time, I wasn't going to let him dodge my questions. I placed my hands on my hips and eyed Paul. "I never meant to insult your island. I'm sorry. It's beautiful here. The Mylans I've met are lovely. What I'm asking about, instead, is this *festival*. The ads for this state that this is supposed to be a resortlike experience. Just because most people here had enough money to make this trip doesn't mean Zack Frazier has free rein to trick them."

At Zack Frazier's name, Paul's eyebrows shot up. But then his expression snapped back to annoyance. "I don't have time for this." He turned and stomped away.

A whistle blew, and I stared into the crowd. Someone let out a drunken cheer. The line for the food truck was so long that Solstice workers were handing out wrapped sandwiches to the people at the end. People wrinkled their noses, but they had to be hungry, because they pawed at the Reynolds Wrap and ate the things in only a few bites.

When I searched the sky, I was surprised to see that the sun was low in the trees. When had *that* happened? Soon enough, we'd all need a place to sleep. Where were the tents? Where was the organization? I was certain it wasn't this island's fault. It was the person running this circus. Zack Frazier.

"Adri? *Adri!*"

Elena emerged from a crowd playing beer pong. She'd taken off her jacket and tied it around her waist, and I noticed she was no longer dragging her suitcase. "Thank God!" she squealed, wrapping her arms around me. "I was so worried! And with no cell service, I couldn't call, and . . ." She looked at me, her eyes big and wide. "Where *were* you all this time?"

"I . . ." I felt my anger dissipate. Elena really did look worried. And I certainly had a lot to tell her.

I breathed in, about to get into my hours of reporting, when suddenly Steve appeared behind her and wrapped his arms around Elena in a bear hug. "Gotcha!" he squealed.

"Oh, you!" Elena squirmed and twisted around for a kiss.

I turned away, an oily feeling spreading through me.

Elena grabbed my hand. "C'mon, Adri. We need to find shelter—it's supposed to storm."

"Where?" I grumbled, shooting daggers at Steve.

Elena grinned excitedly. "Steve pulled some strings for us . . . and we're invited onto the yacht where Zack Frazier is staying! Can you *believe*?"

I rolled my jaw. *No.* There was no possible way I was getting on a boat with that guy.

Elena seemed to sense my disgust. She grabbed my hand. "Adri, *please*," she begged. "I don't want to go alone."

I studied her face. She was right. Just because I was pissed at Elena didn't mean I could send her onto a yacht with a bunch of grown men by herself. Who was to say Steve would watch out for her? Still, I glanced around at the festival site. This was great news for us, but what about everyone else? I felt like a hypocrite. A fraud.

But Steve was already pulling my friend away. Elena glanced back at me, her eyes pleading. Slowly, reluctantly, I followed her.

BREAKING NEWS: Blankface, one of the headliners of the Solstice Festival, pulls out of performing due to "poor performance site conditions." Is Zack Frazier in too deep?

MYLA ISLAND: Blankface, one of the most anticipated bands to play the Solstice Festival, the $10,000-a-ticket music festival where elite Gen-Z-ers could hobnob with celebs, influencers, and models, has canceled their performance. Timothy Cornish, Blankface lead singer and front man, could not be reached for comment, but he tweeted the following statement: "It's to my great disappointment that Blankface will not be able to perform in Myla this weekend. We were really looking forward to it, but we've assessed that the infrastructure isn't up to par, and we want everyone to have the best experience possible. Stay safe, everyone."

Reports say that over 6,000 concertgoers have descended on Myla Island this weekend for the concert despite news of rough seas and storms in the area. Internet access and cell phone connectivity is limited to none—though it's unclear *why*, exactly—so reports on the conditions are scarce, but aerial footage shows what seems to be "a football-field-size gravel pit" of a concert area, "Gen Z swampland," and then "about sixty yachts" on the water. News of strange circling shapes in the water is concerning as well—a jellyfish bloom has affected the Myla shores in the last month, but these shapes seem a little ... *different* from jellyfish. We're thinking a really big shark. With ... a lot of eyes?

(This is a developing story.)

Comments:

@H1990K

The entire festival was a scam. Of course Blankface pulled out.

@BMittenBoy

Smart move, Blankface! You wouldn't get ANY infrastructure . . . not even toilets!

@SSSKJ12

Shame, Zack Frazier. SHAME!

@HaydenATL

Anyone there at the festival? Trying to find out if anyone's seen a friend of mine. Adrianna. Is there seriously NO cell service?

8

STEVE'S FLASHLIGHT MADE A WAVY BEAM down a sandy path toward the water. As I slapped at the bugs—they thought my skin was made of ice cream, even *with* loads of bug spray—Elena sidled up next to me. "I was really worried," she scolded. "Running off with no cell service? Not cool."

I felt a flare of anger. Was she really trying to make *me* feel guilty when she drove me away? "I just wanted to check things out. And I figured you were busy with Steve."

I tried not to make Steve's name sound like a synonym for *toxic waste*, but Elena caught my disdain anyway. "I'm sorry about that, Adri. Really and truly. I meant to tell you before we came, but . . ." Elena pushed a low-hanging branch out of our way. In the distance, I could see a break in the forest and what looked like the edge of a cliff. "Like I said, he came to me sobbing. I've never seen him cry before. And it was over me!"

"Wow," I said sarcastically. "Very heartrending."

Elena sighed. "Are you angry?"

I kicked up some sand—I no longer cared that my shoes were totally ruined. "No," I mumbled. "Whatever."

I glared at Steve, who was loping up ahead. I remembered how excited Elena had been when they met—and how excited I'd been for her. Elena was funny. Smart. Creative. Wry. Introspective. She deserved a great boyfriend. And then, when I'd seen Steve flirting with that girl in the diner, my heart had broken for her. But as I'd watched Steve shoveling in his omelet and home fries, his whole personality had seemed different. He was blunter. Brasher. Not the polite, sweet, caring guy he portrayed to Elena. It was all an act, I realized. He was being for Elena what she wanted to see. But that wasn't who he really was. Of course he'd come to her crying—he knew she'd melt. But had he really been sad?

We pushed past the last set of trees and came to a rocky edge. About ten feet below us, a frothy sea swirled. Beyond the shore, a dozen enormous boats bobbed, each lit by romantic, twinkling lights. I drew in a breath, startled. So there *were* yachts here.

I gazed in wonderment. They looked like floating castles: smaller than cruise ships, but somehow even more luxurious. I squinted hard, wondering if I could make out celebrities on board, but the light was too dim, and the distances to them were too great. *Still.*

"Come on." Steve started down at the natural rock stairway to the shore. I wasn't a fan of descending a slippery rock wall at dusk, but Elena was already climbing down, and I didn't want to get separated. The rocks were slick, but there were handholds by each step. At the bottom, I looked up at the rock face, wondering if this was where Eric, the guy I'd met outside the convenience shop, had gone climbing today. It was certainly beautiful here. He was right—this island was special.

An inflatable motorized raft roared up to us, and a man in a white sailor outfit ushered us aboard. Elena, Steve, and I climbed on. "Sit over here, Adri," Elena said, patting a spot next to her. But I mumbled an excuse about not wanting to get splashed, opting for one of the seats in the middle. Elena was making an effort, but I couldn't quite forgive her yet.

The motorboat wove around anchored yachts, each one larger and grander than the last. I peered up at them, awestruck . . . and then a little disgusted. They were almost *too* opulent. I couldn't help but think about all of those stranded people on the concert grounds. What would happen to them tonight?

Finally, we approached a boat that was so modern, so sleek, and so *huge*, it probably could be a country all its own. I gaped as the boat jetted up to it and was tethered to the side. There were four levels of decks and glass. The boat's name, *Lady Luck*, was painted along the hull in letters at least six feet tall. Through a window, I could see a bar, a spiral staircase, a huge table seemingly set for twenty, and paintings on the walls. I'd never seen a house this grand, not even Elena's.

She met my eyes and grinned excitedly. Her smile said, *Told ya it would be amazing!* The smile I returned was uneasy. This boat was great and all, but I was only here to keep her safe.

A few men stood at the pool's edge, watching us arrive. One of them was Zack Frazier; he was dressed in a beige jacket, jeans, and sunglasses. The other guy was heavier, had a dark beard, and carried a martini glass in his hand.

"Welcome!" Zack called out as we docked.

"Ahoy!" the second guy bellowed.

The boat driver helped us off the raft. It took me a moment to get my sea legs, but I stumbled up a flight of stairs to an upper deck. Once there, I took in a huge, sparkling pool with little bubbling hot tubs in alcoves. Multicolored tile work glittered like diamonds. A beautiful woman in a bikini, seemingly straight out of the Solstice promotional video, lay on one of the chaises listening to something through a pair of headphones. Two other bikini-clad girls danced together to music a DJ was playing near a rock wall planted with an array of succulents. On the other side of the pool, a long table held a spread of every type of food imaginable: lobster, crab cakes, a sizzling pile of chicken wings, salads, fruit, desserts, and even the sushi Elena was desperately craving. Who was all that *for*? Besides the girls, the yacht appeared empty.

Elena shivered with glee. "This is like something out of a James Bond movie. I'm like, *pinch me*!"

"It's . . . *something*," I said quietly, eyeing the mounds of sushi.

"Welcome, ladies." Zack kissed Elena on the cheeks, and then, to my surprise, kissed me, too. I awkwardly moved away, a little skeeved out by his intimacy. "I'd like to introduce you to my very good friend, *and* the owner of this yacht, Mr. James Marx."

The bearded guy propped his sunglasses on his head and shook our hands, looking straight into our eyes.

"Hello," I said shakily, realizing I recognized him. Was this *Captain* Marx, aka one of the biggest music producers on the planet? He'd been on tons of singing competition shows. He was best friends with Jay-Z. He'd discovered Lavender, too. So did that mean if *he* was here, her performance was still on?

Butterflies swarmed my stomach. I was ready to ask him gushing questions about Lavender . . . but then I noticed the cavalier expressions on Steve's and even Elena's faces. Maybe I should play it cool. "Nice to meet you," I added.

"Welcome to my yacht." Marx had a booming, everyone-stop-talking-and-pay-attention-to-me sort of voice. His eyes sparkled with mischief. "Any friend of Zack's is a friend of mine. Drinks, everyone?"

"Yes, please!" Elena piped up. "And maybe some of that food over there?"

"Absolutely. Be my guest."

Elena filled her plate, and, reluctantly, I did, too.

Everything was beyond delicious, and I ate ravenously. Next, we moved to the chaises set up around a marble firepit. The bikini-clad girls were still dancing, paying no attention to us; I wondered if Marx had hired them just for decoration. I noticed Steve sneaking them flirty glances. My heart lifted when Elena followed his gaze and frowned. Steve's attention snapped back to her. He took her hand, leaned into Elena lovingly. I gritted my teeth.

A waiter in a Hawaiian shirt passed around martinis, and I took a glass, thinking it would be rude to decline. I set it on the table, watching as some of the liquid sloshed over the side. Then I noticed that Marx was looking at me. My skin began to prickle. "Oh," I said quickly, mopping up the spilled martini. "I'm sorry."

"Don't worry," he said. "I was looking at you because I know who you are."

"Me?" I let out an incredulous laugh. "Uh, I don't think so!"

"You're the person who's been asking questions about the festival all day." His tone was playful, but something about the statement seemed accusatory. "Checking up on security, food, medical staff . . ."

Steve looked startled. "*That's* where you were today?"

I felt my shoulders draw in, but I made an effort not to wilt under their intense gazes. "Shouldn't we have the right to ask questions?" I said calmly. "And, well, the festival *does* seem a little disorganized." I glanced at Zack. "With all due respect."

Zack waved his hand. "It's fine. A few things came in later than we expected, but by morning, everything will be ready. Almost all of the geodesic domes have been built, and they're very comfortable. And catering should show up tomorrow."

Elena made a face. "I don't want to sleep in a geodesic dome."

Steve pulled her close. "You won't have to, baby."

Then Zack added, "And as for security, don't worry. Everyone will be safe. Today was a rough start, but it's truly going to be an event worth waiting for. You'll see."

"You have to trust Mr. Frazier," Marx added, clapping a hand on Zack's shoulder. "He is a master. He leaves no stone unturned."

"And what about all those people back at the festival site right now?" I asked. "Are they okay? Do they have shelter?"

Steve looked at me with surprise. "Are you sure you should care about them, Adri? Elena said some of the girls were rude to you."

"I still want them to be safe," I said. "Especially if it rains. People are people."

"It's all good," Zack said. "Everyone's in domes or tents. Not ideal, but this is our first go-round—and like I said, it'll all be worked out by tomorrow."

"Okay," I said slowly. Maybe they were right—it *would* all come together. Despite myself, I began to relax. I even reached for my drink and sipped, staring out at the other yachts twinkling on the water. They were filled with celebrities, or influencers, and wealthy moguls—and *they* hadn't bailed yet. They must have confidence in Zack, too.

I looked up, realizing something. "Do you have Wi-Fi on this boat, Captain Marx?"

"Call me James," Marx said, and then nodded, gesturing to the doors that led to the yacht's interior. "It's spotty—the closer you get to the router, the better chance you'll have of picking up a signal. Go right ahead. The password is Lady Luck, all one word, ninety-five."

I thanked him and excused myself. Through a set of glass doors was a sleek seating area. A grand piano stood in one corner, and a giant head of an elephant—no joke—hung in the other. I recoiled at the thing, horrified that someone had killed and mounted something so beautiful. I took a few steps away from it, almost feeling like it was casting a negative energy into the room.

With shaking hands, I pulled out my phone. I only had 9 percent battery remaining, but a window popped up listing that a Wi-Fi connection was available. I clicked on it, then typed in the password Marx had given me. His signal must have been stronger than the one at the convenience store, because texts started to flood in immediately. There were so many from my parents that I couldn't read all of them, but they grew increasingly fraught as the day wore on. Guilt tugged at me. Strict and irrational my parents might be, but I didn't want to worry them. Hayden had texted, too, along with a few other concerned friends. Even my *sister* had texted me— definitely a first.

I'm okay, I wrote back again, even though I'd alerted them earlier, too. *No cell service, but all is safe. Be home in a few days.*

I sent them off with a *bloop*. Then I noticed that Hayden had replied earlier to the text I'd sent him. *Call me when you can!* he wrote.

I hastily dialed. Hayden picked up on the first ring. "I'm so glad you're okay!" he cried. "I've been trolling message boards all day, asking festivalgoers if they've seen you!"

"Wait, really?" I felt flattered that he cared enough. Then I realized that we lived in an age where a whole day of no cell service was call for alarm. "Everyone's fine. Things were hot and confusing when we got to the site, but it's all been worked out now." I explained I was on a yacht—a real yacht! And that the other festivalgoers had shelter, food, the works.

Hayden was quiet. "I guess those reports I saw were wrong."

"Why?" I asked, feeling a prickle of concern.

"No—it's fine. There was a broadcast saying that the festival organizers left everyone high and dry tonight, but again, barely any news is coming out of Myla. It's probably a rumor."

"Probably," I said, feeling shaky. *Zack and Marx wouldn't lie to us, would they?*

Hayden said something I couldn't make out. "You're breaking up!" I called, pressing the phone closer to my ear. "What's that?" But then the call went dead. I stared despondently at my phone. The Wi-Fi icon disappeared. I guess the service was spotty after all.

Wind pressed up against the windows, and all at once I felt the barometric pressure drop. The dancing models rushed inside, squealing, just as the first raindrops started to fall. I looked at my phone again. *Searching*, the Wi-Fi bar read. I wished I'd had a few more minutes to talk to Hayden. I knew he'd be on my side about all of this—Elena, Steve, the terrible conditions here, my investigating. But even when I turned Wi-Fi off and then on again, retyping the password and reconnecting to the router, I kept getting the same message: *Cannot Connect to Internet*. I settled on videoing a panoramic shot around the ridiculously plushy living area, figuring I'd send it to Hayden when I again found a connection.

The rain was still pelting the deck, but my group was safe under an awning. I peered outside, noticing that Elena was curled up in Steve's lap. She leaped up when she saw me coming toward them. "James said we could sleep here, Adri," she said. "Isn't that awesome?"

"There's plenty of room." Marx folded his hands over his ample stomach. "I don't want to send you back out to shore in this weather."

I couldn't help but look at Zack. "Are you *sure* everyone on land is safe?"

"It's being handled," Zack said. "I talked to my crew before coming back to the boat. There should be enough shelter for all of those who reserved lodging."

I really wanted this to be true. It would mean that there was shelter for us as well, which we'd need tomorrow. At the same time, I got Marx's point about not heading back in a storm. I looked at Elena again. I couldn't leave her. I doubted anyone would take me back in this storm, anyway. "Okay," I said.

"I'm relieved we're not going back across that water again tonight." Steve stretched out his legs. "Those rumors I heard about that thing surrounding Myla—it gives me the creeps."

Zack glanced at Marx, then rolled his eyes. "Those rumors aren't true, dude. Don't be stupid."

"What rumors?" Elena asked innocently.

Steve turned to her. "You didn't hear? There's a local legend that talks about a spirit that lives on the island. The spirit's been around for years—disrupting the crops, conjuring up storms, and eating the natives."

"The Mylans," I corrected him. "And what do you mean *eating*? Some kind of monster?"

"A big sandworm, they say," Zack said. "With shark teeth. And a thousand eyes. And two tongues! The locals do a human sacrifice every so often to keep the thing happy. The monster is attracted to glowing objects, so the sacrifice is strapped with phosphorescent items and thrown into its lair."

I cocked my head. "That sounds a little insensitive. The Mylans seem smarter than to make ritual sacrifices." I thought about how Plantain Girl's buddy in the convenience store said the Mylans rode goats to work. And then how Paul thought I was questioning his staff as some sort of judgment against this island and its people.

"No, I've heard that rumor, too," Marx said. "Some of the people around here are quite backward. It's remarkable."

Backward? I hated the way they were talking. "None of the Mylans told *me* about a monster thing that eats people. Or human sacrifices."

"Of course they didn't." Steve looked worried for me. "They're probably hoping Solstice guests will *be* the sacrifice."

My mouth fell open in shock. I thought of the woman in the convenience store who'd given me the Wi-Fi password. Did the Mylans really think that?

But then Marx hooted with laughter. "He's kidding, Adri! About all of it!"

"The creature isn't real!" Zack cried.

"You should see your face!" Steve added. "Oh, Adri, it was like you saw a ghost!"

And then everyone started laughing—even Elena. I turned away, angry and defensive and humiliated. I was the butt of a joke to them. The loser.

I jumped to my feet. "I'm going to bed."

"Aw, Adri!" Elena jumped up, too. "Don't be angry!"

"We're not laughing at you," Steve said. "Honest."

I tried to smile. "I'm really tired. Thanks for letting me stay. Really."

"I'll come, too." Elena cast Steve an apologetic look. "G'night, babe."

I almost wanted to tell her she didn't have to come. It was obvious she wanted to stay with Steve. But it felt like a little victory, to take her away from him.

Hawaiian Shirt Waiter doubled as a bellhop and showed us to our suite, which was bigger than the entire downstairs of my house and seemed polished to a shine. A massive, king-size bed with at least a hundred pillows sat in the center. A wall of windows was to the left, leading to a long veranda. The bureau and end tables were some sort of expensive lacquer material. The carpet beneath my feet was the softest I'd ever felt. The en suite bathroom had a shower that could fit at least five people and had twelve—I counted—showerheads. I worried that I wouldn't have pajamas to change into—I'd ended up stashing my luggage in the trailer by the stage just like everyone else—but then I noticed that the closet doors were flung open, revealing robes, silk pajamas, slippers, socks, and even gym clothes and bathing suits.

"Whoa," I whispered as I ran my fingers against the soft fabrics. "This is something."

"I know," Elena said solemnly.

Then she turned to me, her hands clasped at her waist. Her expression was so plaintive, like she was about to cry. "Adri, this Steve thing . . . I can tell you're still upset. Are you thinking that I tricked you into coming just so I could be with him?"

The wooden hangers clicked softly as I looked through the clothes. "I don't know," I murmured, pulling down a gray silk pajama top and matching pants. "Maybe."

She touched my shoulder. "It was a coincidence. My dad got me the tickets. I invited you. And then, at the last minute, Steve said he was coming, too. I didn't tell you because I was afraid you'd back out."

"And you wouldn't be able to come and see Steve," I said bitterly.

"No! I didn't want you to back out because I wanted to do this with *you*." Elena clasped her hands together. "I was heartbroken when you ran off today. We lost a whole day together. This is our trip. If you want me to tell Steve to give us some space—if you want me to stay away from him the whole trip—I'll do it. I swear."

The tenderness in Elena's voice made the hard crust over my heart dissolve. "You don't have to do that. But thanks." I really didn't want to be angry. And I appreciated how she'd just offered to give up Steve for me.

Elena settled onto the bed, squishing the pillows at the headboard. I pawed through the goodie bags of toiletries and sleep masks and candies on the nightstands. Next, Elena hopped off the mattress and opened the sliding door to the veranda. Warm, tropical air gusted in. The rain had stopped. We stepped outside to the veranda and stared out at the horizon, astonished at all of the stars we could see in the clear, unpolluted air.

"Not to talk about him anymore, but if Steve weren't here, we wouldn't get to be on this amazing boat," Elena said softly.

"I *guess* that's true," I conceded.

"In the morning, we can watch the sunrise. And I think that's Lavender's yacht right there." She pointed at some twinkling lights out at sea.

"What? No way." There was no way to tell one yacht from another, but it was nice to imagine.

We stood for a moment in silence, letting the breeze billow our hair. I imagined lapping waves below, invisible in the darkness. "We should send Lavender a message in a bottle," I murmured, gesturing to the nearby boat. "Lavvy, we love you!"

"Let us show you the dance we made up to 'Rose Gold'!" Elena giggled.

"Remember that?" I cried. I started doing the moves Elena and I had created one weekend last year when we were bored out of our minds. To my delight, Elena remembered every step, too—and suddenly we were moving like we were part of Lavender's formation onstage.

"Over here, Lavender!" I cried, moving closer to the sliding glass door. It was possible Lavender was looking out her window at this exact moment and *saw* us. It was possible she'd invite us over immediately and demand that we be part of her tour. Suddenly *anything* felt possible.

When the dance was finished, we collapsed in giggles on the mattress, sunburned, exhausted, and friends again. "I'm sorry," I said.

"Are you kidding? *I'm* sorry," Elena argued. She clasped my hand. "Oh, Adri. We're still going to have so much fun."

Thuds from upstairs rocked the ceiling, followed by hoots of laughter. I wondered how long Zack, Marx, and Steve would stay up partying. Had those snotty models returned, too? Would Steve's eyes wander—or worse? I considered warning Elena, but I didn't want to ruin the mood.

Instead, I said, staring at the whirling, stainless steel ceiling fan, "Do you really think there's a monster out there?"

Elena didn't answer for a long time, her expression inscrutable. But finally, she shrugged, yawned, and burrowed under the covers. "Nah. The only thing that's going to eat us on this island are the bugs."

9

I AWOKE TO THE SOUNDS of quick footsteps and low voices. When I opened my eyes, I was disoriented—bright morning sun streamed through the window, and I was lying on top of an impossibly soft white comforter. I sat up quickly, rubbing the sleep from my eyes. Oh, right. I was on a music mogul's yacht. Because of course.

Elena lay on her side, her chest evenly rising and falling. I glanced at my phone, which was charging on the bedside table. Wi-Fi hadn't returned, meaning I still didn't know if my mom had written me back, but I did see that the clock on the home screen read 6:23 a.m.

The footsteps rang out again, and I looked at the ceiling. Were those the guys up there? Had they ever gone to bed? I'd heard thumps and laughter long into the night.

I stumbled to the bathroom and washed my face with the kale-cucumber scrub that had been set out for us. The voices echoed clearly off the tiled walls. First came Marx's baritone, then Zack's higher-pitched whine, and then Steve's mid-range voice. He kept saying what sounded like, "But, but . . ."

I paused. They sounded worried.

Curious, I threw on a robe and slipped out of the suite. The hall was empty, but a grand staircase led straight to the upper level, where I noticed several figures pacing. Marx stood against the windows, staring out at the sea.

"Colin? Yeah, hey. James here," Marx said into a cell phone. I wondered how it had service. "Listen. I hear there's been an . . . incident."

He paused, apparently listening to whatever the person was saying on the other end. I curled my hand around the cold brass bannister. *Incident?*

"We need to cover this up fast, or we're toast," Zack added.

"Cover it up?" Steve sounded panicked. "How are we going to do *that?*"

More footsteps. It sounded like they were moving toward the side of the ship. I crept halfway up the stairs just in time to see Zack disappearing around a corner. What the hell had happened? Was someone hurt? Was it about the festival? Had someone else pulled out? Was there a disaster on the field? The storm hadn't rolled in last night like we'd thought—we'd barely gotten any rain. But maybe something else had happened. Maybe something with the people on the mainland? I remembered what Hayden had said last night: *I guess those reports I saw were wrong.* Or was it Marx and Zack who were wrong. Or *lying.*

"Shit," I heard Zack whisper. "Shit, shit, shit." His voice rose in fear.

"Get yourself together, man." Marx's voice was sharp. "We can't have you falling apart."

This sounded *big*. Stealthily, I tiptoed the rest of the way up the stairs and scampered for cover behind an enormous leather sofa. I stayed close to the wall, edging my way toward their voices. When I dared to look around the corner, I saw the three guys climbing down a ladder to the same inflatable raft we'd used last night. Marx's phone was still glued to his ear, and his brow was furrowed. Zack's face was ashen. Steve lingered on the side of the boat like he didn't want to go along, but Zack hurriedly gestured for him to climb aboard. The outboard motor revved, and the raft shot away from the yacht, creating a whitecapped ripple in the otherwise still water.

I stared at it, the tips of my fingers tingling. Something was happening—and it sounded like they didn't want any rumors to get out. I glanced over my shoulder, contemplating waking up Elena, too—but if I did, I'd lose sight of where the group was going.

I looked around. Last night, Marx had said there were kayaks in a storage closet next to the pool for us to use if we wanted. I ran there and wrenched the door open, relieved to see a few large ocean kayaks stacked against the wall. I hefted one out, grabbed a paddle, heaved the kayak down the ladder to the water, and dropped it in with speed and dexterity I hadn't really gotten to flex since my brief stint on the crew team in eighth grade. In the distance, I could just make out the raft speeding to shore. I began to paddle as hard as I could.

The water was warm and fairly calm. I recalled what the flight attendant had said about jellyfish, but luckily I didn't notice any. I wasn't the most athletic person—I'd only joined soccer one year because I knew athletics looked good on college applications—but I'd always been strong, and I was surprised at how good it felt to paddle through the waves. It gave me an outlet for my nervous energy.

A wave ferried me to shore. I caught sight of where the crew had abandoned the boat on a beach littered with seaweed. I pulled the kayak up the sand about a hundred yards away and hid it in some bushes, not wanting Zack and the others to spy it and realize I'd followed them.

I tiptoed closer, taking refuge behind any tree I could. The waves lapped at the sand soporifically. A colorful bird with an elongated beak squawked overhead. I heard something slithering in the dunes and prayed it wasn't something poisonous.

"Oh my God," someone hissed, his voice rising over a dune. My body stiffened in alert.

"Oh my God," the voice said again. Steve. "Oh *shit*."

"Calm down." Zack sounded frantic. "We can't panic."

More footsteps. I crouched behind a tree trunk, my heart thudding fast. They weren't far from me at all—

maybe only a room or so away. I stayed low, trying not to breathe. With every step, their voices came closer and closer until, finally, I spotted them over the dunes. They stood on a sandy patch of beach, the waves slurping at their feet. Above them, cliffs loomed, medium-brown limestone. Zack, Steve, Marx, and two guys in Solstice T-shirts stared at something on the ground, but their bodies blocked my view.

A shark. It had to be. A dead shark, which would cause panic among the concertgoers. As if there wasn't enough panic already.

Zack stepped back, his face twisted and gray, giving me a better look. I stared at the object on the shore, expecting to see a gray fin, a slash of sharp teeth, a powerful tail. Instead, I saw a human hand curled stiffly into the sand. Attached to that was a wrist, and then an arm, and then a pale, shirtless torso lying facedown. But it was stiff and unmoving. Like a mannequin. Like a corpse.

The breath left my body. No. *No.* I felt my legs trembling, my throat closing, and I tried as hard as I could to remain quiet. I couldn't look away from the lifeless figure. His feet splayed out in a ballet pose. He wore industrial shoes with serious treads. Why did I recognize them? In horror, I realized: because they were climbing shoes. I'd talked to someone who was wearing climbing shoes just yesterday.

I stepped forward, pushing aside more leaves. I had to know for sure. Mustering up all my courage, I forced a

119

closer look at the body. The face was turned away from me, so I could only see the back of the head. There was dark, curly hair that ended at the nape of the neck. On his back was a small tattoo of a mountain peak—the very same design I'd noticed the day before.

A sob rose within me, mixing with fear. It was Eric Jedry. The friendly rock climber I'd met outside the convenience store.

He was dead.

@TheRealZackFrazier: It's a new day, party people! Who's ready to GREET THE SOLSTICE?

@TheRealZackFrazier: We have an amazing lineup: Hip-hop band Luscious is playing at noon, and then we have a great singer-songwriter named FoMo—if you haven't heard him yet, get ready to SWOON—and then, stepping in for Blankface is our new headliner, LAVENDER.

@TheRealZackFrazier: I hope you're as excited as I am for the festivities.

@TheRealZackFrazier: And as for the minor snafus: Because of the weather, some of our deliveries didn't make it in time—NOT OUR FAULT! But fear not: We're going to be up and running by noon—food, drinks, bathrooms, the works.

@TheRealZackFrazier: So get ready to party down! I'm game if you are!

Replies:

@CC22blather: Are you for real? I can't get in touch with my friend and I'm scared shitless because of the news reports of the storms! Get ready to greet the Solstice? How about get ready to answer to a jury—cause you're going down, scammer!

@TheRealZackFrazierPR: @CC22blather Whoa, whoa, whoa! This is Zack's PR point person, Marissa. We know you've heard some scary news about storms. And we're doing everything we can to solve the cellular connection problem. But everyone at Solstice is FINE.

@TheRealZackFrazierPR: @CC22blather Things are awesome here. We've got top-shelf tequila, good vibes, great weather—it's all good!

Comments are closed.

10

DON'T PANIC. *Don't panic. Don't panic.*

My stomach roiled. Goose bumps prickled over my skin. I felt like I was going to faint. Eric was dead. *How?* Had someone at the concert done this? It scared me senseless. But I couldn't run. For one thing, they'd see me right away. For another, this was intriguing. There was something so strange about the way Zack, Marx, and the others were wringing their hands and swearing. They looked so pale. Almost . . . *responsible.*

"He must have been walking on the rocks above and slipped," Marx said loudly and authoritatively, almost like he knew he had an audience. "Stupid adrenaline-junkie kids. I bet he'd been drinking, too."

He wasn't! I wanted to scream.

"So does that make us responsible?" Zack sounded nervous.

"'Course not. You put up a warning not to go too far from the site, didn't you? And you're not liable for anyone once they wander away from the concert site. This kid left at his own risk. He should have known better."

"This doesn't look good, though," Zack insisted. "We need to come up with a plan to make sure the press doesn't find out we lost a guest."

"Didn't you make connections with the police on the west side of the island?" Steve asked. His voice was hushed. And his nice-guy act was gone.

Zack shoved his hands into his pockets. "I did . . . weeks ago . . . but they haven't been returning my calls. I need to think. I don't want to sound any alarms." He gazed warily into the sky. I wondered if he was looking for the helicopter that had been circling the day before. I'd heard it was an aerial photographer, hired by Solstice to snap pictures of the event—though could that be right? Why would Zack spend money on a photographer who would gain physical evidence of this place's lack of bathrooms?

"Where's his shirt?" Marx asked.

Zack shrugged. "I guess he wasn't wearing one. Half the kids at the festival were shirtless."

Yes he was! It was red!

Then Zack looked at Steve. "Go get our man. His home is just over the dunes. He'll know what to do."

"Me?" Steve looked nervous. "*Alone?*"

"It's not far. There's a clearing, and you'll find his place."

Steve still didn't move; Marx shoved him toward the path. "There's no monster in the woods, idiot! Go!"

I could feel a mosquito sucking on my arm, but I didn't move to slap it. The air was thick with tension. It felt like they might break out in a fight.

Finally, Steve lowered his shoulders and disappeared into the woods. I wondered who he was going to fetch. I looked at the body on the sand again. I was no medical expert, but if Eric had fallen off the rocks, wouldn't his bones be a little more broken? Nothing was twisted or snapped, the way my brother's leg had looked when he fell off his bike when he was ten. I remembered how boastful Eric had been about his climbing skills, too. He spoke with authority and confidence. Not the kind of guy who'd misstep.

Then again, maybe I was just being contrary: Just because I didn't like Marx or Steve or even Zack didn't mean they were wrong. Because why *else* would Eric be dead now besides a fall? Unless someone *pushed* him. Or . . . or unless it was that evil monster thing Zack and Steve were talking about last night. I pressed my nails into the rough bark of the tree. There had to be another explanation. This island was small, rural, and tropical, but that didn't mean it was ruled by mythological beasts.

New footsteps sounded. I ducked down, out of view. Steve reappeared. A second figure followed him, and as he stepped into the clearing and laid eyes on the body, his limbs grew stiff. "Oh my God," he said in a quiet voice.

It was Paul, the guy from yesterday. There were dark circles under his tired eyes, but his cargo shorts were spotless, and his dreadlocks hung down his shoulders. I hadn't noticed them yesterday—I guessed he'd bunched them into his hat. He wheeled around and gaped at Zack. "How did this happen?"

"He . . . fell," Zack said.

"*Fell?*" Paul snorted like he didn't believe it.

"These guys found him," Marx explained, gesturing to the guys in the Solstice shirts. "They were boating back to the other side of the island to pick up some supplies and saw him from the sea. More guests are coming in today. We can't risk anyone else seeing this."

"But what's he doing over here?" Paul's voice was wild. I had to admit I was enjoying how rudely he was speaking to Captain Marx. "You *know* people aren't supposed to wander away from the festival site. We had an agreement."

"We can't keep control of everyone," Marx said almost cavalierly, rolling his eyes. "What were we supposed to do? Put up a barbed-wire fence?"

"If it would have prevented this, then yes!" Paul's voice rose. "I told you something like this might happen if you held this concert here. I *told* you."

"Calm down," Marx said, but then Paul took a step closer, and he wilted a little. "Look, the guy probably had too much to drink. He was probably trying to show off and slipped. We just need to get the body out of here. Then we'll figure out everything else."

"Okay, fine." Paul squatted and moved to roll Eric over. Marx lunged forward. "Don't *touch* him!"

"Why?" Paul looked up in alarm. "You think I'm going to destroy evidence?"

There was a strange expression on Paul's face that I didn't at first understand. But then it hit me: doubt. He didn't believe that Eric had fallen.

But what *did* he believe?

Marx and Zack came up with a plan: They would wrap Eric in a tarp Zack had brought from the ship to hide him, hurry him away, put him in a closet on a ferry, and then *what?* I waited to see if they were going to say anything about contacting Eric's parents to tell them the tragic news, but they didn't seem particularly concerned. It gutted me. I thought of what my parents would do if I'd been the one who fell—especially if they didn't learn of it right away. It felt irresponsible. Callous. I noticed, too, that Paul stood back from the group, arms tightly crossed, not participating in the plotting. "Come on and help," Marx finally growled when they began to wrap Eric in the tarp. Paul did so reluctantly, glowering at the others.

Then my skin started to prickle. I could tell someone was watching me even before I saw who it was. I moved only my eyes, not my head, toward Steve. He was no longer gazing at the body but into the trees—and right at me. The corners of his mouth tugged into a frown. His stare was unblinking and angry. I stood so still, not moving, not breathing.

Steve's eyes narrowed. His lip curled in a way I'd

never seen before—and I was sure Elena hadn't, either. But a few seconds later, his gaze returned to the men and the body. Still, my heart thumped all the same. Steve knew I was here . . . and that I'd witnessed something I wasn't supposed to see.

11

THE MEN WRAPPED ERIC in a tarp and carried him off. The job required everyone's participation, which left no time for Steve to come after me. It was only after I'd gotten safely away I felt I could breathe a little easier. I crouched against a palm tree as fat, traumatized tears started to fall down my cheeks. What I'd witnessed was inhumane. Those guys were choosing their concert's PR over basic human decency.

I wasn't sure what to do next. Elena would be worried when she didn't find me on the yacht, yet my arms were too tired to paddle back there. Maybe I should just head to the festival—despite the fact that I was still wearing linen pajamas. But was the festival safe? I was beginning to believe that Zack Frazier and Captain Marx weren't just careless and slapdash . . . they truly didn't care about our lives.

And I kept thinking about the peculiar expression on Paul's face. He didn't believe the theory that Eric had fallen. Was some sort of conspiracy happening? Were these guys hiding something from us?

I shouldn't have been shocked that the festival site looked no different than it had when I left it. The tents were only half-erected. The field was packed with dazed-looking, half-asleep people holding their shoes in their hands. Some donned garbage bags as rain gear. There were a few piles of people still sleeping, using their cashmere hoodies as blankets and calfskin steamer trunks as pillows.

The field was muddy and slippery; I stumbled twice just crossing to the customer relations tent, which had only an unoccupied table. A few of the electronic gadgets used to check people's tickets sat on the table, unclaimed. They were waterlogged, probably nonfunctional. I spied Indigo, the same guy in board shorts who'd ushered us to the festival grounds the day before. He was heading in the direction of where the buses had dropped us off. "Indigo?" I called out. He turned warily. "Are those shuttle buses running?" I asked.

Indigo checked the large sports watch on his wrist. "Yep, one will be back from another airport run in about ten minutes."

I was shocked. Did he mean more people were on their way *here*?

"And what about going *back* to the airport?" I asked Indigo. "Is that possible?"

The corners of Indigo's mouth curled up like I'd told a joke. "Yeah, it's possible. But you'll have to get in line."

He gestured over the dunes to the lot where we'd been dropped. A huge mass of people were milling around, hands on hips, staring impatiently at the horizon. There were more of them down there than would fit on three buses. How long would it take to shuttle them back? When would it be my turn?

"Put me on the waiting list," I said weakly. "A-and my friend, too. Adrianna Sanchez and Elena Sykes." I needed to tell Elena what had happened with Eric. Surely she'd want to leave, too.

A crackle of feedback pierced the air. The speakers on the stage were, astonishingly, working, and someone stepped onstage. A barrage of boos rose up and then some angry chants. I drifted back to the festival grounds to see what was happening. The crowd was thick around the stage, but I pushed to the front to get a good view. Zack Frazier stood in the middle, microphone in hand, waving his arms to calm the crowd. It was startling how relaxed he looked. Jubilant, even—almost not the same guy who'd been standing over a dead body an hour ago.

"Greetings, marauders!" Zack's voice boomed. "Welcome to Solstice!"

More boos. Someone screamed, "Where's my suite?!"

"Where's my private jet?" someone else said.

"Why did we have to ride a *school bus* to get here and sleep on Hefty bags?"

Someone threw what looked like an empty water

bottle at Zack's head. Zack ducked, his smile faltering just a tad.

"People, people! I apologize if last night wasn't what you're normally used to." His mirrored sunglasses reflected the irate mob. "I'm still trying to sort out what happened and why our shelters didn't arrive on time. To make up for it, all drinks are free today. All food, too."

There was a smattering of applause, but most people still looked pissed. I pulled my fully charged phone from my pocket, deciding to record the mob. Of course, seeing my phone's full bars of energy gave me a pang of guilt. It was likely everyone else's phones had been dead for hours. I felt naïve for trusting Zack Frazier that everything was okay back at the concert site, and for sleeping so soundly on zillion-thread-count sheets.

"I'm in credit card debt because of this!" someone yelled from up front.

"I could have been in Capri!" someone else said.

"Where the hell are the bathrooms?" a girl shouted from the left of the stage. "Way too many people have seen my butt!"

A raucous cheer rose up. A bunch of people started to chant: "Privacy! Privacy!"

I kept recording. This was interesting video footage for Hayden—or maybe the whole world.

Zack smiled wanly. "Rest assured that by tonight, everything will be up and running. I have a great team putting together final details. Again, I am deeply sorry for the inconvenience, but I promise you, this still will be the concert of a lifetime."

"Liar!" someone screeched. "You're playing us!"

"You'll be hearing from my lawyer!" cried another voice.

"My father's a senator!" someone else screamed.

A new figure stepped onstage. Steve edged toward Zack and whispered something in his ear. Zack nodded, his expression inscrutable. Steve stepped away, but not before he looked out into the angry crowd. For who? Eric's friends? He'd mentioned he'd come with a big group. Did they even know yet?

But then I felt the heat of Steve's gaze on *me*. I shrank behind a tall guy in a melon-colored polo shirt, but I could still feel Steve's gaze cutting through like a laser beam. Was he angry because I'd witnessed a Solstice boondoggle? Or was he worried I'd stumbled upon something even scarier?

I hurried toward the bus line. The bus had arrived, and another guy in Solstice board shorts jumped off, a stormy look on his face. He eyed the crowd with annoyance. "There's no point in going to the airport," he grumbled. "The flight computers are all messed up. Nothing's going out today."

A gasp rose up. One girl shouldered her duffel anyway. "At least there's sparkling water at the airport. I'm *dying* without my LaCroix."

"And *organic food*," someone else piped up. "Well, fingers crossed."

"And air-conditioning!" came another voice.

And safety from Steve, I thought nervously.

Everyone crowded around the gangplank. People peppered the driver with questions, and he just shrugged. "I don't know when the systems are going to be back up," he said. "But one thing's for sure: Everyone's flights are going to be delayed, if not canceled."

My chest tightened. Elena had booked us on a flight that left Monday afternoon; it cut things close, but we'd be getting in Monday evening, so I'd be able to go to my internship the next morning. Would I be stuck here for *days*? It was petty to think about losing my internship in light of a boy lying dead on the other side of the island, but at the same time, I couldn't stop picturing my parents' heartbroken expressions. I couldn't let them down after sneaking off to be here.

But then something else hit me: I couldn't go without Elena. She had our tickets. I had little money of my own. My debit card was linked to a bank account that had about two hundred dollars in it. I hadn't brought another credit card because I'd snuck out.

I glanced back to the festival area. Zack was still on the stage, bellowing about the amazing acts on the roster. Steve stood in the wings, his hands on his hips, his narrowed eyes scanning the crowd.

I felt a tap on my shoulder and jumped. It was the same

youngish man from the little market the day before—the one who'd said he liked my attitude. Today he had on a ball cap and was pushing around a cart filled with ice-cold beers and water. "Have one," he said, pushing it toward me. I cradled the cold water in my hands, then pressed it to a pressure point in my neck, feeling my veins throb.

"I remember you," the man said, looking me over.

"I remember you, too," I said, appreciating his warmth.

"Name's Mosley," he said. "Everything okay? You look like you've seen a ghost."

I opened my mouth. *Close, but not quite. It was actually a body.*

He reached into his ice-filled cart and handed me a beer. "On the house," he said, his brow wrinkling. "You need it."

12

I KNEW ELENA WAS PROBABLY FRANTIC over my whereabouts, but it turned out that I didn't have to kayak over there—I was just about to wend back over the dunes when I heard her cries. Elena, freshly showered, her long hair curled and sprayed, her makeup perfectly applied, ran for me across the muddy field.

"You ditched me!" she squawked. "What happened to our plans of sneaking onto Lavender's boat?"

I licked my lips. "Is Steve with you?" I blurted. There was so much to tell her that I didn't even know where to start.

Elena frowned. "No. Why?"

I looked over her shoulder. A bunch of intrepid, hippie-esque twenty-somethings sat on a tarp, talking and laughing. I was glad to see that someone was taking the less-than-ideal conditions in stride.

"I haven't seen Steve all morning," Elena went on. "One of Marx's guys brought me over." She cocked her head. "You all right? You look upset. Is it because of the toilets? Zack said they're coming soon."

I pulled her to a small, cleared patch of land that was much more private. "I witnessed something really weird," I said, my voice quavering. "And . . . I'm scared. I think we have to leave this island. *Now.*"

Elena's eyes grew large as I told her about Eric's body on the beach. I explained how cavalier Zack was, and how the men had covered him with the tarp and hefted him into the woods like an old carpet. I also told her how livid Paul got when he discovered that someone had strayed from the festival site. "He said they had some sort of *agreement*. And that he'd warned Zack that this sort of thing might happen if people left the festival site. It was like he was speaking in code."

For a moment Elena was speechless. "*Or* he was simply saying that this is a dangerous island with some scary rocks. And that people are likely to fall, especially after drinking."

"But I'm not sure Paul believed that Eric died from a fall."

Elena searched my face. "Did he say what he *did* believe happened?"

"That kid died by a fall," boomed a new, bright voice. "It's tragic, but that's what happened."

Steve's hands were stuffed in his pockets. He had the appropriate somber, sober expression of a person who'd witnessed a terrible death, but I could also see the slight twitch and tremor of barely concealed rage when he glanced at me. Uh-oh.

Elena reached for him, her face slack with fear. "So it's true? Someone died?"

Steve ran his hand through his thick brown hair. "Yes. In a freak accident. I guess he drank too much, decided it would be fun to hop along the rocks, and then . . . slipped." He shut his eyes. His mouth wobbled. *Oh God,* I thought. *Is he going to fake cry again?* "A festival worker discovered him and called us there to help."

"Help?" I snapped. "You rolled him in a tarp. How is that helping?"

Steve turned to me, his jaw dropping. "What were we supposed to do, Adri? Carry his body over our heads through the festival grounds like a trophy?"

"Have you contacted his family?" I challenged. "Or did you just dump him on the ferry to sort it out later—*after* the festival?"

"Adri," Elena warned. "I'm sure they're handling it."

Steve blinked slowly. "Of course we contacted his family." He put his hand territorially around Elena's waist, but his gaze was still on me. "Adri, I'm worried about you. It wasn't safe to leave the yacht alone. It's a good thing only I spotted you in the bushes, because Zack and Marx might not have just let you go."

I swallowed hard. Steve was acting concerned . . . but I could tell this was a veiled threat. Still, I didn't back down. "A guy is dead." I pointed over my shoulder in the direction of the little market. "I *met* him right there.

He was an experienced climber. I think something else happened, *and* I think you know what it is. That's why you're acting so strangely. That's why you rolled him up and made him disappear."

Steve shrugged, then looked at Elena. "It's not true. This island has some risks. Unfortunately, someone didn't heed the warnings."

Elena nodded. "It makes sense, Adri," she said. "There was a lot of drinking yesterday. And no one knows the lay of the land here. That guy probably had no clue there was a huge cliff in front of him. He'd probably been out walking in the dark. Steve isn't covering anything up. And they haven't announced the death because they don't want anyone to panic."

Steve crossed his arms over his chest. "We're on an island. If too many people find out what happened— even an accident like this—morale will drop. I mean, what do you want Zack to do?" He looked at me with insouciance. "Cancel the festival?"

I shrugged. "Wouldn't you want someone to cancel a festival if *you'd* been the person to fall off that cliff?"

Steve waved his hand. "People often die at these things. At the OG Woodstock festival, a guy on a tractor ran over a kid in a sleeping bag. And then there was this Pearl Jam show in Denmark where at least five people died by crowd suffocation. Coachella, someone had hypothermia. And at Bonnaroo—"

"Okay, okay," I interrupted, a little disgusted. "You

think that Top Ten Music Fest Deaths is going to convince me you're right?"

"I'm just telling you the reality, Adri," Steve said, his eyes still round. He almost looked sorry for me. "And consider what *we* had to go through. I feel traumatized by seeing that body. And I had to carry him, tell his friends . . ."

Here came the wobbling chin again. "Baby," Elena said, reaching for him. Steve fell into her, and they hugged tightly.

Oh brother. I'd had enough. I turned on my heel and marched away, feeling tears sting my eyes. Talking to Steve was useless.

Then I heard footsteps behind me. "Adri . . ." Elena was at my side. She grabbed my hand, urging me to slow down. We looked like an unlikely pair: I was so grimy from my kayak trip to the beach, still wearing the pajamas from the yacht, and Elena so preserved and festival-ready in her sundress and strappy leather sandals.

"Look," Elena said. "I get it. It's terrible that someone died. And I'm sorry it was someone you connected with. We could have a prayer vigil for him later tonight—what about that? But it's not *Zack's* fault. You're overreacting. Panicking. And if people overhear you . . . it could spell disaster."

"Don't worry," I said tightly. "I won't say anything—because I'm leaving. I'm not staying on this island tonight."

"Well, of course you're not." Elena's smile was shaky. "You'll stay on the yacht again. With me."

"There's absolutely *no* way I'm staying there," I insisted. "I don't want to be anywhere near Zack Frazier or Captain Marx. They're everything that's wrong with the world. If they value their business over human life, that's . . . *disgusting*."

Elena planted her feet in the mud. "Adri, you must have misinterpreted. And there's a difference between valuing human life and not wanting to cause a scene in a field of ten thousand concertgoers!"

I glowered at her. "Does it not matter to you that I *witnessed* what happened?" I whispered. "Are you that snowed by Steve's act?"

"Steve isn't acting! He had to deal with something awful this morning!"

"Yeah, I know! I was there! But why won't you even listen to my side of it?" I shook my head. "Are you that desperate for a boyfriend?"

Elena's eyes flashed. "You're one to talk, hanging out with Hayden Collins."

A prickle went through me. "What's wrong with Hayden? You think he's from a 'bad' neighborhood? He doesn't drive a BMW? He's on *scholarship*, just like me?"

Elena's mouth dropped open. "Is that what you think matters to me?"

"*Isn't* it?" I shot back.

Elena was about to say something but then changed her mind and shrugged. "What's the point of explaining myself? You're not going to listen."

I scoffed. "What's that supposed to mean?"

There were two blotches of pink on Elena's cheeks. It took her a few moments to speak again. "You just do what you want and think what you want, Adrianna—always. I don't matter to you. What I care about, what I think—you think I'm beneath you."

"What!" I couldn't believe it. "Why would you say that?"

"A lot of things. Little things." Her jaw was set. "Like with school. And that new job you just got. You don't think I'm good enough to do the things you do."

"What?" I blinked, flabbergasted.

"And I tell you Steve apologized, but you don't care—you're going to hate him just like you've always hated him instead of giving him a chance out of kindness for *me*."

"I'm being kind by warning you!" I roared. "You can do so much better than him!"

"Are you saying that because you truly don't like him . . . or because you've stereotyped him? The way you stereotype *everyone*?" Elena snapped.

I staggered back as though she'd punched me. Then I spun on my heel, my cheeks blazing. *I don't stereotype people*, I thought fiercely.

I needed Elena to believe me—I wasn't overreacting. And I didn't want to be in this scared headspace alone. But how could I make her trust anything I said now? According to her, my outlook was flawed. I saw only what I wanted to see. I saw rich white men looming over

141

a young man's body and of course thought of greed and conspiracy. Because I was stereotyping? Or because it was true? And how could I prove it?

And then it hit me. I knew how I could prove it. I would do what I did yesterday: I would investigate. I would report.

Except this time, I would figure out how and why Eric died.

Myla Breaking News:

1 hr ago

"IT'S HELL" AND "SCAM OF THE CENTURY": KIDS TRYING TO ESCAPE SOLSTICE FESTIVAL STUCK ON AIRPORT TARMAC, OTHERS STILL TRAPPED ON ISLAND.

EAST MYLA ISLAND: Reports are trickling in from the Solstice Festival on Myla Island, which is mostly unreachable by cell signal despite festival organizers having promised "unlimited Wi-Fi hotspots," "luxury accommodations," and "a weekend you'll never forget."

It *has* been a weekend concertgoers will never forget—just not in the way they expected.

In interviews with several groups that were able to board a shuttle from the festival site back to Myla Airport, travelers were shocked by the "primitive" conditions of the festival, including limited food, little drinking water, filthy restrooms, and no sleeping accommodations. "Quite a few of us had to sleep on the ground—*in the rain*," said one young woman from Scottsdale, Arizona. "There were no blankets, no pillows. I paid for a three-bedroom suite with a wraparound balcony and strawberries and cream in bed."

For 23-year-old Chase Hutchins of Annapolis, Maryland, the sign to leave was when he contracted a strange rash on his leg after a walk through some thistle overgrowth to get to the actual concert site. There was no first-aid station on the festival grounds, and when he asked a Solstice worker if someone could arrange for him to go to a medical clinic

143

elsewhere on the island, he was very forcefully talked out of it. "I have an Amex Black card," Chase said. "I could probably buy that island if I wanted. I knew there were medical facilities on the *normal* part of the island, and I just wanted to rent a motor scooter to *find* them. But I was being held captive." Hutchins was able to receive proper medical care when he returned to Myla West.

But some still remain on the island, waiting for the festival to start. One woman said she was "praying" for those who'd remained—"to Buddha, a bunch of crystals, and even Cthulhu!" It is unclear which bands are still committed to performing, but currently, more than nine acts have dropped out, citing the poor conditions.

Zack Frazier, the organizer of Solstice, could not be reached for comment.

13

THE HASHTAG FOR THE SOLSTICE FESTIVAL had officially become #SolShitFestival. People were writing it on their arms and legs. It was sharpied on a flag fashioned out of someone's boxers. I also noticed it in shaky letters on the dry dirt. I had a sneaking suspicion some guys had spelled it out in pee.

I rustled up some lunch from the food truck—which, to my surprise, offered granola bars, apples, and lemon Dannon yogurt along with greasy French fries and sweating cans of Coke. *We're not starving,* I wanted to say to the weak-acting droves who passed by, whining. Yet I was rattled to be here, too. Just for different reasons.

The first thing I did to get to the bottom of Eric's death was head to the little roadside market outside the festival site where Eric and I had met. This didn't prove super easy, because the moment I stepped over the festival-ground border, a Solstice worker jumped in my path. "Miss? Miss? Where you headed?"

I stared at the guy's longish brown hair, his thick

eyebrows, stern face. What did he know about the body found on the shore? *Did* he know? Or would telling everyone cause mass panic?

"I need to go to the bathroom," I said. "The porta-potty lines are too long." This wasn't even a lie. The porta-potty lines were criminal.

The worker shrugged. "Fine. But don't, *under any circumstances*, go near the water. Okay?"

"Why?" I placed my hands on my hips. I'd been *in* the water, kayaking to the shore. I'd been on the beach where Eric's body was found. What had I avoided? And was this a warning because of what had happened to Eric?

The worker turned away from me without answering to handle two drunken boys who'd begun throwing half-hearted punches. A screech of feedback came from the stage—it seemed that at least one of the acts, a singer-songwriter named FoMo, was going to have a go at performing. There were no cheers, though. Most people were beyond caring.

The little convenience store was overflowing. Even before I went inside, I tapped my Wi-Fi icon, hoping to use their server, but, unfortunately, it was unavailable. The younger woman who'd been at the register caught my eye as she trundled in from hauling trash to the dumpster. "Mosley is a softie, and he gave the Wi-Fi out to a bunch of other people. Who told *their* friends, and *their* friends—anyway, they flooded the system. We had to turn it off for a while. It'll be on again soon—but people will have to take turns logging on."

I nodded and fiddled with my phone, wishing I could send Hayden another update video. Then Elena's words popped into my head. *You're one to talk, hanging out with Hayden Collins.* She *was* judging him for having less than her. I couldn't believe it.

I also couldn't believe she thought that I found her beneath me. It was so far from the truth—and the total opposite of how I really felt. I found *Steve* beneath me—and beneath Elena, too—but when had I treated Elena that way? I listened to her opinions. I cared about what she said. Unless the conversation turned toward Steve—but that was only because I didn't think he was right for her. How had she misinterpreted that?

Or was I being shortsighted? *Did* I tune her out? *Did* I act haughty and superior? Did I stereotype people—including Elena? I scoured our conversations, and how I presented certain things, and the comments I made. Elena had said, specifically, work and school. Sometimes I glossed over what I was working on in my honors classes by saying, "Oh, just random, boring, smart-people stuff." Maybe I shouldn't have.

And there was that comment after my first day at the law firm—Elena suggested that maybe she get a job at the firm, too, so we could spend the whole summer together. I'd written back, *The office definitely isn't for you.*

I'd said it because the place wasn't for *me*, either . . . Had she thought I'd dissuaded her because I didn't think she was smart enough to work there? Or that *I* deserved the job more than she did?

All this time, I'd thought Elena was confident and untouchable. But maybe I was wrong. And maybe I'd said things that poked at insecurities I didn't know existed.

"Yo!" said a voice on the stage, jolting me from my thoughts. I could just make out a guy in glasses with a guitar strapped over his shoulder peered into the crowd. "Um, Blink-182 couldn't make it, but I'm FoMo. It's really, really great to be here."

"Is Lavender coming?" an olive-skinned girl with two pink ponytails near me screeched.

Her friend looked at her in surprise. "You didn't hear? Lavender backed out, too. This morning."

Pink Ponytails looked chagrined. "Then what the hell are we still doing here?"

There was a lump in my throat. My favorite artist was no longer coming. I wasn't surprised Lavender had bailed, but still, it filled me with disappointment and despair. If I were her, I wouldn't play this venue, either.

As FoMo Whoever-He-Was started to play a few jangly chords—I pitied him; he was playing for probably the angriest audience in the history of audiences—I made my way into the little market. Inside were the same three Mylan locals working—the two smiling women and Mosley, who'd given me the water and beer earlier today.

He brightened when he saw me. "You're looking much better now!" he sang. "Out from the heat!"

"Yes, I'm feeling a little better," I said, and then asked carefully, "So this is a long shot, but do you remember a guy coming in here yesterday? He had on a red T-shirt with a mountain-climbing logo. Glasses. Pretty fit. Friendly."

Mosley scrunched up his face. "Why? He lost?"

"Um, actually, there was an accident," I said, deciding to take the risk.

The Mylans exchanged glances. My heart sped up. *Did they know?*

The younger woman with the Afro swished her hand. "Of course there was an accident. The festival is a disaster waiting to happen."

"I'm surprised people aren't dead." The older woman tut-tutted, making a face.

This wasn't the answer I wanted.

"Is there someone I could talk to?" I asked. "Police? Maybe someone from the coast guard?"

"What's a coast guard?" Mosley asked, cocking his head.

I blinked. "Th-they protect the waterways?" But maybe people of Myla had some other infrastructure. It felt weird that I didn't know.

"I'm just messing with you," Mosley said teasingly. "Of course we have something like a coast guard, but it's called the Royal Mylan Defence Force. It's not a very big faction, though. And the water is safe—if you're okay with jellyfish."

"Oh." I felt uncomfortable after falling for his joke—like it said something bad about me that I believed it. "And the police?" I asked. "Surely *they're* here . . ."

The older woman narrowed her big brown eyes. "If you ask the *other* concert guests, we just rely on voodoo magic to make our problems disappear."

"Auntie." Mosley touched the older one's arm. "Cut her some slack."

The door burst open and in walked the same Solstice worker who'd apprehended me at the festival border. The guy's eyes clapped on mine. "There you are," he said sharply. "Best if you headed back now, okay?"

I wanted to make a scene—this random guy couldn't tell me what to do. But maybe keeping a low profile in my investigation was smart. Heading out, I shot Mosley what I hoped was an apologetic look, feeling like I could have handled that *way* better. The women were snickering.

Back within the festival borders, my mind thrummed, tuning out FoMo's whiny song about how his girlfriend drowned in the Gowanus Canal. I couldn't give up. Maybe Eric's friends were still here. Surely *they* would have some details. I didn't remember anyone being with him yesterday, though I was pretty sure he mentioned he'd come with a group.

I looked around the crowds to see if there was anyone

who seemed more worried and distraught than normal. The problem was that *everyone* looked distraught: We were all sunburned, exhausted, hungry, dehydrated, and out thousands of dollars—*and* without easy transport home. I saw a lot of pacing. A lot of crying. I approached the fringes of a few groups who looked particularly in agony, speaking softly, "Do you know someone named Eric? Is there an Eric in your group?" Everyone shook their heads.

Then I heard footsteps. A girl in a red ball cap covering her long, blond hair faced me. Her shoulders were sunburned, and she carried a battered Gucci handbag that was covered in splotches of mud, and there was a hesitant look on her face. "I just overheard you," she said. "Do you mean Eric Jedry?"

My eyes widened. "*Yes!*"

"Who are you?" she asked suspiciously. "How do you know him?"

I licked my lips. "I spoke to him a little yesterday—he said he was going rock climbing. He seemed really nice." I paused. "Do you know him?"

"I'm Pearl. Eric came with me and a few other friends." Then she stepped closer, her gaze darting. "But I thought Eric was—" Then her mouth clamped shut.

"It's okay," I whispered, cutting her off. "I *know*. I know he's dead."

"Someone's *dead*?" a voice next to us said, and I jumped. A guy I hadn't noticed before was sitting on the ground, drinking one of Zack's free cocktails and eavesdropping.

Pearl stared at me in fear.

"You sure you heard that right?" I said, staring pointedly at his cocktail as I steered Pearl away toward an unpopulated patch of grass.

"How do you know?" she whispered, when we were out of earshot. "Who are you?"

"It's a long story," I said. "I happened to see the guys who found him. But . . . what did they tell you? *When?*"

Pearl swallowed. "The police contacted us about an hour ago after they'd ID'd his body. They tracked who he'd come with through flight manifests and the Solstice ticket sales."

"So the police know, then?" That was kind of a relief.

She nodded, her eyes glistening. "I need to get out of here. I'm having a panic attack. I put my name on the ferry list, but it's taking forever. I need to call my mom. I need to process what's happening, not in this nightmare of a concert."

"I know," I said. The anxiety was stifling. I kept seeing Eric's limp body whenever I closed my eyes.

"Eric was the *responsible* one of all of us." She choked on another sob. "He can't be . . . *gone!*"

Yes, I thought. *Yes, yes, yes*—I'd thought Eric seemed responsible, too. "So he didn't get drunk yesterday?" I asked.

"No way." Pearl shook her head emphatically. "Eric

never drank. He didn't even come to this festival for the music—he was interested in the landscape. Rock climbing."

"He told me he was an experienced rock climber and that he was going out to climb since the festival didn't seem like it was starting up anytime soon. But the organizers are sure he died from a fall."

Pearl chewed on her lip. "That's what the police said, too, but I don't know how that could be possible. He was *so* careful when it came to climbing. And the rocks here? They're nothing compared to what he's used to." Then she breathed in sharply. "You know what's weird? They wouldn't let us see his body. Not that *I* would have looked—but my friend Andrew wanted to. Just to . . . see, I guess."

"How might he have died if he didn't fall?" I hated that I was asking this question. "Do you have any theories?"

"No." She bit her lip. "I mean, what are the options? A sudden heart attack? Instant poisoning from a snake? A murderer on the loose?" Her eyes widened. "What if it's one of the other attendees?"

A chill went through me. I suddenly remembered Paul's words when Zack warned him not to touch the body: *Why? You think I'm going to destroy evidence?*

"How late did you see Eric last night?" I asked.

Pearl's eyes lowered. "He went on a hike at about three, but then came back around dinnertime. We had one of those cheese sandwiches from the food cart." In another time, I thought, she'd probably be harping on

153

those cheese sandwiches and how gross they were and the injustice of it all. But she was too numb.

"And then what? Eric went out again?"

"He knew other people from our town who'd come, too. Eric said he wanted to look for them. Say hi."

"Who were these other people?"

"I don't know. I'd never met them. James . . . something. And a girl. Kylie? Kayla?"

"Did the police talk to them, too?"

Pearl shrugged. "I told them that they were probably the last people who'd seen Eric alive, but they didn't even write down their names." She paused contemplatively. "If someone else is involved, if someone *knows* something, shouldn't the police be doing everything possible to figure it out—even if it ends up being an accident in the end?"

I nodded. That sounded reasonable. But what if the police were in Zack Frazier's pockets? What if Zack spun the situation to the cops that Eric died from a fall and nothing more? But . . . *why*? Simply to avoid bad PR? That seemed like a lot of hoops to jump through.

A guy in a windbreaker with big bags under his eyes burst through the crowd and touched Pearl's arm. "It's our turn for the ferry," he said. "We have to hurry."

Pearl gestured to me. "This is Adri. She met Eric yesterday. And she knows about Eric and . . . you know."

The guy's face pinched with pain. "Oh." He closed his eyes, almost looking like he was going to cry, but then, in that I-need-to-be-strong thing guys sometimes did, powered through it. "You wanna come with us?" he asked. "I could probably convince the driver to let you jump the line."

It was tempting. I didn't feel particularly loyal to Elena. At the airport, I might have cell service. The money in my bank account could at least pay for a youth hostel until my flight left . . . or, at the very least, I could sleep at my gate. On the other hand, I felt committed to following this mystery through—even if it meant sleeping out in the elements. After talking to Pearl, I was more convinced than ever that something with Eric's death was very, very wrong.

"Thanks," I decided. "But I'm on the list for a later boat. Good luck, though. And I'm really sorry about Eric. It's . . . unthinkable."

The two of them collapsed into each other, and more tears dripped down Pearl's face. They staggered down the path that led to the water. I envied that they were leaving. I didn't envy the emotional storm that would confront them when they got back home—all those questions, the painful funeral, a family now without a son.

Sweat pooled on my back. I looked around the concert site. FoMo had finished up onstage—to tepid applause. As he stepped off, no roadies appeared to turn off amps or wind up cords. Now what would I do? I'd stalled again. Maybe I could try to find this other group of people Eric spoke to last night, but Pearl hadn't given me much to go on—just a guy named James. Could I wander through the crowd, calling his name? Could I climb onstage and yell it through a microphone? *All Jameses come forward! Is anyone named Kayla or Kylie?*

Suddenly the mood shifted. People stood straighter, spooked and alert. I glanced toward the stage, thinking a new band was coming on, but it was dark. I heard whispers around me and saw hands cupped around mouths. One by one, a rumor began to ripple: I heard gasps; I saw shocked expressions; one girl even looked like she was about to faint.

I tapped a tall Asian girl on the shoulder. "What's going on?"

Her mouth made an O. Then she stood on her tiptoes and whispered in my ear. "Somebody *died* this morning. On the beach. Some people are saying his throat was slit."

Her friend shook her head. "*No*, I heard he was in *pieces*. Hacked up by . . . *something*."

My limbs turned to stone. All around me, Eric's death was breaking news. Was it *because* of me? Had that drunk guy on the ground heard us . . . and repeated everything? And how had these rumors started?

The news was spreading fast, whipping through the site like a line of dominoes falling over. I could see people whispering, then looking around in alarm. Soon enough, it would reach Steve . . . and Elena . . . and Zack. Elena would hate me even more. And the guys? What if Zack Frazier did something drastic to punish me for telling?

I needed answers—*fast*. And suddenly it hit me. There was someone else who wasn't on Zack Frazier's side. I even knew where he lived—well, approximately anyway.

Paul. I needed to find him.

14

I ONLY KNEW WHERE PAUL'S TRAILER was in rela-
tion to where I'd hidden the kayak on the shoreline—
Zack had shouted out that he lived down a path not far
away. So I made my way back to the site of Eric's death,
taking several wrong turns and slogging through a marsh
to get there. The kayak I'd used was still nestled in the
brush. The sand where Eric had lain was eerily vacant—
smooth and flat, as though someone had combed it clean.

The trail Marx had pointed to through the dunes
for Steve to take was overgrown with thistle and other
weeds. After walking through my fifth swarm of gnats,
I was starting to get antsy. It was so silent here. Twigs
snapped and cracked beneath me, sending my heart racing. I glanced around fearfully, realizing that if someone
was following me, it was so wide open that I'd be a sitting
duck.

I took a few more steps forward, then noticed a small
red structure one hundred feet ahead. I hurried for it,
then halted behind a giant palm. In front of me was
a cabin, weathered by age, with a satellite dish sitting

crookedly on the roof. Next to it sat a yellow motorbike and a rusty pickup truck whose tires had been stripped bald. Farther from that was what looked like a firepit. And surrounding the perimeter was a booby-trap-like contraption of bells and metal objects strung from the trees. It seemed like a makeshift burglar alarm, perhaps alerting Paul if anyone was in his territory. I made sure to step over the low trip wires and avoid banging into any of the bells. Either Paul was terrifically paranoid, or he was really, really afraid of something in the dunes.

My stomach gurgled, and I realized I hadn't eaten since my snacks from the food truck hours ago. As I glanced up at the swath of sky, I was struck with horror. The sun was setting—soon it would be dark again. I had a feeling I wouldn't be offered the luxury suite at Captain Marx's tonight—not after fighting with Adri, and especially now that the rumor about Eric's death had spread far and wide—and I was one of the few people who had known about it.

A front porch light snapped on inside the cabin. I let out a little gasp and jumped back. Was it on an automatic timer, or was Paul in there? I pulled out my phone, praying that maybe this spot in the island would pick up a cell signal. Of course not.

I pressed forward, tiptoeing across the scorched lawn and walking up the little house's front steps. The door had big scratches at the bottom as though something with giant claws had once fought very hard to get in.

Shaking, I rapped my knuckles on the wood. My heart was pounding so hard it was the only sound I heard in my ears.

After a minute, the door hadn't opened. I bit my lip, then knocked again. "Paul?" I called out weakly. "Mr. . . . ?" I'd never been told his last name.

Still no answer. What possessed me to turn the knob, I still don't know, but that was what I did. To my surprise, the door was unlocked, and it swung open, revealing a surprisingly tidy little room. A single dish sat in a metal sink. The oven sparkled. A quilt lay over the back of a small couch.

"Paul?" I called out tentatively. "Sir?" No answer. It was safe to assume he wasn't home. Still, it felt very wrong that I was in his trailer. Paul didn't seem like the kind of guy who'd take kindly to trespassing

Yet something kept me rooted to the carpet. I looked around. The tiny TV had a small layer of dust on the top. There were stacks of newspapers on the coffee table, scattered papers. I glanced down at a thick book opened facedown. It looked more like a photo album or scrapbook than something that was professionally published, with a canvas cover and a handwritten title on the spine. *A History of Unusual Deaths of Myla Island.*

My stomach turned over. *Unusual deaths?*

I opened the book. On one page was a newspaper clipping from 1965; the article told of a man named Jacob Tretheway having washed ashore on Myla. It was presumed that he'd drowned, but there were "strange bite marks" on his legs, torso, neck, and shoulders. Beside the article was a black-and-white photo of Jacob Tretheway himself. He wore a long-sleeved plaid shirt and had his arms clasped at his waist. His eyes looked hollow, and he wasn't smiling, but maybe that was just the style of pictures at the time. *Jacob Tretheway, August 15, 1923–July 7, 1965*, read someone's wobbly hand-printed letters. *Champion swimmer.*

Feeling my stomach roil, I turned to the next page. A handwritten letter was pasted on the left-hand side. *Dear Annabel, I'm writing to tell you the bad news. It got Sidney. We tried to keep him safe, but there was nothing we could do.*

The letter went on to describe what Sidney had left to Annabel in his will—several acres of land, some money, a mahogany music box. An article from a Mylan paper was pasted next to the letter. ACCIDENTAL DROWNING ON MYLA ISLAND read the headline, and it went on to tell the story of how Sidney Robinson, thirty-two, had been found on the shores of the east side of Myla Island after a fierce battle with the sea.

I looked from the letter to the article; it took me a moment to realize what was bothering me. In the letter, the writer didn't say Sidney drowned—it said, *It got Sidney.* What was *it*? The ocean? Maybe it was custom to think of the ocean as an entity, in the same way sailors called ships "she"?

The stories intrigued me—and also made me very

uneasy—so I pulled out my phone and snapped pictures of the pages. But the sun was setting quickly outside, and there wasn't much available light to read by—I didn't dare switch on a lamp. I had to get out of there. But as I moved toward the door, a flash of red off to the right caught my eye. I peered into the bedroom, seeing the edge of a neatly made bed. A red T-shirt was heaped on top of a bureau. It seemed familiar. The yellow logo on the front read EVEREST.

My heart stopped. *No.* This wasn't . . .

I lurched for it. The mountain-peak logo Eric had displayed on his chest winked at me teasingly. What was Paul *doing* with this? I picked it up between two pinched fingers. There was something caked on the shirt, almost the same color as the fabric, thick around the neck and then around the hem. A sharp, metallic scent entered my nostrils, and I dropped the shirt in horror.

Blood.

15

I DIDN'T REMEMBER leaving the trailer, but suddenly I was standing on the grass, breathing hard, repeating over and over to myself, "Oh my God, *oh* my God."

I could still smell blood in my nostrils. I could still see the thick red streaks along the neckline. I hadn't seen the blood on Eric's body from my hiding spot in the bushes, but then he'd been facedown. I'd only looked at the twist of his limbs, the lack of breakage. Why hadn't I peered closer at his face? And where did all that blood *come* from?

Paul?

I replayed the scene on the beach in my mind. Solstice workers had found Eric's body, and then Marx and Zack had come along, and then Steve had run to get Paul, presumably because he was their local contact and knew how things worked on Myla. Paul had *acted* surprised— and suspicious—but maybe that was a ruse?

Though I wasn't sure that made sense. Why would Paul hurt a Solstice guest? On the other hand, what was he doing with the T-shirt? I remembered Marx asking where Eric's shirt was, then Zack replying that Eric probably wasn't wearing one. *If* Paul hurt Eric, maybe he swiped it from him beforehand? *Or*, what if Marx and/or Zack knew full well that Eric *did* have a shirt, but it was so saturated in blood they stripped it off him so the police wouldn't see it? And maybe they forced Paul to hide it for them. Maybe they'd muscled Paul into falling in line.

Crack.

The sound came from the north side of the property. The sky was almost pitch-black, and the dim light on the front porch barely reached to the bottom of the steps. I stood with arms outstretched, trying to make out a distinct shape in the darkness. To my horror, I saw a tall figure emerge through the trees. *Paul*. He clomped across the yard and up the stairs to the trailer. I stared down at myself, fully aware that the only thing really hiding me was the darkness. I held my breath. Tried not to move a muscle.

Paul tried the doorknob and frowned when it easily turned. He whirled around, a suspicious look on his face. My heart banged in my ears. Did my eyes glow in the darkness, like an animal's? Crickets chirped. The wind whistled. The night was thick and muggy, and I could feel the sweat seeping into my shoes. Paul scanned his yard for a long time, a scowl on his face. But then, finally, he opened the door, went inside, and slammed it shut.

I hurled myself into the bushes, scrambling as fast as I could down the path. I needed to get far from that blood-soaked shirt. I needed to tell someone—though *what*, I wasn't sure. That there was a conspiracy, I guess. That Paul was covering up something—which might reveal his guilt or get him to confess that Zack and Marx were monsters.

Something stung my leg. My left foot sank in the sand, and my ankle twisted. Groaning, I limped on in the dark, using my phone's flashlight app to dimly light my path. I listened for sounds of the Solstice festival, but I heard no thrums of a bass line, no pounding drums. After what felt like hours of walking, the stars glittering overhead, I finally found myself behind the giant food truck. The site was very close by, but the field was eerily dark. My heart lurched with fear. Maybe everyone had evacuated the island while I was checking on Paul. Maybe they were all *dead*, somehow, in some sort of chemical warfare attack. Steve. Zack. *Elena*. And now I was left here all alone. I'd never get home.

But then I heard murmurs. The sound grew louder as I stepped away from the truck, and it built into a dull, scattered noise of a panicking crowd. And then there everyone was, rising up before me like zombies, in huge clusters on the festival grounds. I spied a pair of glowing yellow board shorts with the Solstice logo emblazoned down the leg.

"Calm down, everyone!" the guy was yelling. "It's just a power outage! No biggie!"

I wanted to laugh. No one was dead. They were just drowned in darkness.

A firework issued a high whine, popped into the air, and exploded into sparks. People cheered, and another one went up closer to the stage, flying dangerously close to the speakers. Someone had built a big bonfire, at risk of burning out of control. The fire glowed orange against people's faces, and they looked almost savage and feral. Not far away, a cluster of people chanted what sounded like "*Zack Frazier's a fraud. Zack Frazier's a fraud.*" And behind me, from where I'd come, I heard a groan. I whirled around to see that the food truck was . . . *rocking*.

"You got it!" a voice called. "Just a little bit more!"

More voices sounded from behind the giant vehicle, and that was when I understood—people were trying to push it over. I jumped out of the way. The last thing I wanted, after all this, was death by food truck.

I grabbed an arm of a tall guy in an Under Armour tee drinking a beer. "Why are they trying to knock that over?"

"Haven't you heard?" I caught a sharp scent of body odor. "They've run out of food. Not even those shitty cheese sandwiches. It's mutiny now. Every man for himself."

I blinked. "But there's got to be food *somewhere*." The west side of the island could bring some, couldn't they? I thought, too, of the sumptuous buffet laid out on Captain Marx's boat. Why weren't *they* helping?

"I heard a rumor every act left, too," the guy's buddy, who wore a Rasta-style hat and long, fringed shorts insisted. "And they're going to leave us here to rot."

"I'd rather be that dude who was found on the beach," Stinky Armpits spat. "At least he's over the worst of it."

A shrill screech sounded from the stage. Someone held a torch in one hand and a bullhorn in another; as I looked closer, I realized it was Zack himself. His voice didn't really carry through the bullhorn. I pushed closer to the stage to hear what he was saying.

"Hey, everyone!" Zack bellowed almost cheerfully, the torch throwing great licks of fire around his face. "We're working as hard as we can to restore the power! And the next band will be on shortly! *Greet the Solstice!*"

"Is he *serious*?" murmured a voice. "He's still trying to put on the show?"

"*What* show?" someone else said. "I thought there were no more bands left."

I stood on tiptoes and canvased the faces lit by the bonfire flames. *Elena.* I needed to find her, make sure she was okay. I needed to tell her, too, about what I'd found in Paul's trailer. I whipped my head back toward the stage—I could climb up there and tell Zack first. But Zack was no longer there. It was like he'd disappeared into the ether.

My stomach knotted with dread as I fought my way around piles of garbage, puke, drunk people passed out on the ground, and a second bonfire that people were jumping over, their bodies inches from being incinerated. Suddenly there was a booming crash behind me, and I turned just in time to see the food truck tipping over on its side. A hideous cross between a snarl and a cheer rose up. Then figures began to climb on and in the vehicle.

"Wait!" a voice cried. "Get ahold of yourselves!"

Steve. He stood by the semi that held our luggage. People were shaking it, maybe wanting to knock it down, too.

Steve grabbed a guy's sleeve as he tried to pry open the semi's back doors. "What the hell are you doing?" he yelled.

"We just want our luggage!" a guy was screaming, his face inches from Steve's. "Stop holding it hostage! The revolution has begun!"

"Step back!" Steve threw his body in front of the semi. Behind him, I saw a small, delicate-looking blond girl curled up on the grass. At first I thought it was some chick Steve had picked up at the concert, but then I realized—it was *Elena.* She looked so different from when I'd seen her this morning. Smaller. More fragile. Terrified.

I ran toward her, my arms outstretched. Elena looked up just as I was approaching and made a little relieved bleat. We collided, shaking and crying.

"I was so worried about you," Elena whispered.

"I was so worried about *you*," I said back. I stepped away and looked her up and down. She looked strung out, almost. And she was shivering. "Are you okay? What happened?"

"Nothing. I just . . ." She bit her lip. "This is bad, Adri. This concert. I don't think it's going to get any better."

"You just figured that out?" I blurted, despite myself. But I wasn't trying to be snarky. I was just happy she was okay.

Before I could say anything else, thunder crackled above. The mutinous crowd fell silent, and all heads tilted upward. Like a light switch had been flipped, the rain began to pelt down from the sky. It was so heavy and forceful, like giant balls of hail. And it was so *cold* with the sudden drop in humidity. The ground was instantly saturated.

Everyone wailed. I tore my hoodie from my waist and draped it over my head, not that it served much purpose. Elena pulled down the bill of her ball cap; water dripped off the front. People ran for cover—except there *was* no cover save for a few tents the workers had set up the day before and the puny, pathetic customer relations tent by the path that led to the ferry. Fights broke out over tiny swaths of shelter. Two guys thudded to the ground in a muddy wrestling hold. It escalated quickly, and soon one of the guys was on top of the other, his hands clasped around his neck.

I lurched toward Steve, who stood guard by the semi. "Do something!"

He rounded on me, looking both surprised and furious at my presence. Rain dripped off his eyelashes, his lips, the ends of his hair, and he had to be as freezing as I was, but I could see the heat rising into his face all the same.

I pointed to the boys fighting on the ground. "Break them up! They're going to kill each other!"

Steve glanced at the fighting guys, then back at me. "*You* do something, Adri. This is your mess. You started this nightmare by spreading the rumor about that dead guy on the beach, and now everyone's gone apeshit."

"Steve!" Elena cried. "Don't talk to her like that!"

I pointed at Steve. "Uh, first of all, I didn't go around *telling* people. And second of all, are you seriously going to blame all of this on *me*? Don't you think this concert's complete lack of organization is why everyone's panicking?"

"No. *No.*" Steve's face was gnarled and ugly. He pointed a soggy finger at me. "We could have fixed this. We had it under control. But the panic—it's because of *you*. You should have never come. You ruined everything."

"Steve!" Elena cried. "Whoa! Settle down!" She looked truly flummoxed. I wanted to tell her that *this* was Steve's true personality. The mask was off.

Steve rounded on Elena, sticking out his lip. "What? I'm just saying what we're all thinking."

I gasped. *Was* that what Elena thought? But Elena shook her head fast. "No," she said. "You're not."

A second figure stepped behind Steve and clapped a hand on his shoulder. Zack Frazier had a poncho on, but he still looked wet and miserable. "Reel it in, man," he said sharply. "This isn't Adri's fault."

Steve snorted. "Are you kidding me? You want *me* to reel it in?"

"Reel. It. *In*," Zack growled.

Steve glared at him through the driving rain. "And what if I don't want to, big shot? What are you going to do?"

Whack! It happened before I even realized what went down: Zack's hand flying out through the darkness and connecting with Steve's jaw, the sound of bone on bone, and then Steve falling sideways and landing with a *plop* in the mud. Elena screamed. She fell to her knees and started working on Steve's face, dabbing at the blood on his lip, trying to shield him from the rain.

I pushed my soggy hair out of my eyes. Oh dear. Steve was going to be extra pissed now. And Elena was going to take his side again.

"Ow," Zack said, cradling his fist. He glanced at me sheepishly. "I didn't realize that hitting someone *hurt*."

I blinked hard. "You didn't have to do that."

"Yes, I did." He shrugged. "My cousin's been getting on my nerves for days."

I tilted my head up to the sky. The rain had slowed, stopping as quickly as it had started. Someone had broken up the guys fighting on the ground, though now they all sat in the mud, drenched and pissed.

Zack was still looking at me. "None of this is your fault. You're not the only one who knew that boy died. My workers did, too—and they've been gossiping about it all day. So did the boy's friends. I should have known it was something we couldn't keep under wraps."

I nodded, surprised at Zack's levelheadedness.

"And you're right." Zack's bright blue eyes met mine. "This show—it's a disaster. Of course that's why people are panicking. *I'm* panicking. Nothing is where it's supposed to be. Nothing has come in on time. Food . . . shelter . . . it's like no one got my messages, and a couple of people have outright *lied* to me, saying things were delivered when they weren't." He glanced over at Steve, who was still twisted on the ground, milking his injury for all it was worth. "My cousin owes you an apology. You have nothing to do with why everything's gone downhill. He should never have said that."

I tried to conceal my surprise. Maybe, just maybe, Zack wasn't the rich, entitled, clueless jerk I thought he was. Maybe he wasn't even the enemy. He just sounded overwhelmed and frazzled. But not . . . *evil.*

But then, who *was* evil? I thought again about the T-shirt in Paul's trailer. And then I shivered. Did I dare tell Zack? I needed to tell *someone.*

I stepped closer, feeling my heart pounding again. "There's something you should know," I murmured. I cleared my throat, looking at Zack. "That Paul guy you hired? I stumbled on his trailer in the woods." It was easier to describe it like that instead of something I'd purposefully set out to do. "I needed to use the bathroom, so I went inside. And then . . . I found something. Eric's

172

shirt. It was covered in blood. It was like he was . . . *hiding* it."

Zack's eyebrows shot up, but he didn't seem that surprised. Then he leaned closer. "As I recall, Eric didn't have a shirt on when we found him."

"That's right," I said.

"Which would mean that Paul encountered him *before* we did," Zack said, brow furrowed.

Or this is all a setup, I thought. But Zack looked so earnest.

"Regardless, this is evidence, and it's serious," Zack said. "Maybe this wasn't an accident after all."

I felt a gush of relief that he was taking me seriously. Zack was going to deal with this before it got out of hand. And suddenly I felt almost . . . *safe*.

But then I watched as his face clouded, and then closed, and then shifted into a look of dismay. "What?" I cried. "What's wrong?"

His hand flew to his head, and a shower of raindrops dripped onto his shoulders. "Shit," he said. "Shit, shit, *shit*. I just realized we can't go to the police." His voice was empty and haunted. "Because you know whose family is the head of law enforcement on this island?"

"Who?" I cried.

I saw doom in his eyes. "*Paul's*."

16

"WHAT DO YOU MEAN PAUL'S?" I cried. "He's a police officer?"

Zack raked his fingers through his hair. "No. But his father is. And his father's father. His family has long roots on this island. Paul's father would never accept that Paul killed a man, even if we had empirical proof. He'd look the other way, and he'd force his deputies to do the same."

"So what are we supposed to do?" I threw up my hands. "Paul holds the answers!" I stepped closer to Zack, feeling brave. "Eric's family will want to know what happened. They'll argue against the theory that he got drunk and fell off a cliff. They're going to demand an autopsy and bring forth evidence that he was an experienced rock climber. We can't conceal this forever. Otherwise it's a way worse PR nightmare than what's happening already."

Zack peered around the dark festival site. The rain had stopped, and now people stood in miserable, shivering clumps. Suddenly another fight erupted, this time between two girls wearing waterlogged Chanel fanny packs. The girls fell to the muddy earth with a *thump* and started rolling, every few seconds letting out screeches and expletives. A Solstice worker timidly tried to pry them apart, but one of the girls lashed out at him, slashing his forearm with her perfectly manicured, square-edged nails.

Zack stepped forward to stop the fight. The girls looked annoyed, but then, when they saw who was standing above them, flew into a rage. "*You*," one of them said. "*You* are the devil."

"Please," Zack said, raising his hands in surrender. He looked so small all of a sudden. Okay, yes, Zack *was* evil for duping everyone into attending this festival . . . but what if he'd been duped, too? What if he was telling the truth about all the details being in order just days before the festival beginning? What if he was legitimately baffled about why no food or toilets or lodging or anything had shown up when people had assured him everything was taken care of? Maybe Zack was a victim.

He turned to me, suddenly looking more resolute. "Let's go, Adri. We're going to go over Paul's father's head on this—to the authorities."

"Okay," I said. "Should we take a bus there, or . . . ?"

Zack squinted at the sky. Thick clouds obscured the moon. "We probably wouldn't make it with this bad weather. But we could try calling them from Marx's yacht." He took my hand. "You'll explain to the police what you saw in Paul's trailer? What you know about Eric?"

Looking back, I realized how bizarre the moment was: A billionaire genius was holding *my* hand, needing *me*. But I gave Zack a shaky nod. "Of course. I'll do whatever you need me to do."

"Good." Zack's gaze was steely. "But listen, let's try and keep this between us right now, okay? No panicking. No telling anyone else—people are already up in arms about the death as it is." Then he glanced at Steve and Elena. "And let's not tell *them* yet, either."

Steve leaned against the luggage semi, muttering. Elena rubbed his back and cooed in his ear.

"I don't know how your friend can take it," Zack said quietly. "My cousin can sometimes be a real douche."

I wanted to grin. Zack was totally speaking my language.

"He always overreacts," he went on. "He's irrational, and he takes things out of context. And he already doesn't like Paul—he gets wind Paul might've killed someone, and he might try and be the hero and kill the guy himself." He rolled his eyes.

I offered a wary smile. "Sure. The secret's safe with me."

But as if on cue, Elena looked up at us, a suspicious crease forming on her brow. She glanced from Zack to me and then to Zack again, then broke away from Steve and padded over, using a soggy piece of cardboard as an umbrella.

"What's going on?" she asked me. "You guys have weird looks on your faces."

"Um, nothing," I mumbled. I didn't want to look at Zack for fear I'd give something away. "Zack wants to go back to Marx's boat. To, um, make a phone call. About the state of the festival. Do you want to come with?"

Elena kept staring. I could tell that she knew I was keeping something from her. I prayed she wouldn't interpret this as me acting superior. I didn't want to go down that road of misunderstanding again. So I leaned closer and murmured, "I'll explain everything soon, I promise."

"Well if you're going back to the yacht, I'm coming, too." She marched back over to Steve, grabbed his arm, and whispered something into his ear. At first, Steve shook his head, zinging an angry look in my direction, but then he heaved a dramatic sigh and started walking toward us.

"I can barely *breathe*," he said through gritted teeth to his cousin. "Because some asshole decided to punch me in the face."

We started across the field. Every few steps brought another agonizing vignette of festival hell. More drunk people. More cold, scared, despairing people. We came upon a girl squatting on the ground and clutching her arm, a look of worry in her eyes.

"Are you all right?" I asked her. I crouched down and used the flashlight app on my phone to look at her arm. She had a huge wound—from what, I have no idea. Blood seeped to her elbow and into the grass. She stared at it almost numbly, like she was maybe in shock.

I pointed it out to Zack. "We should get her to the medical tent."

The girl scoffed. "I already went there. All they had was *rubbing alcohol*."

I felt Zack wilt. "But . . . they told me they'd have more supplies by tonight. They *promised*."

The girl twisted her mouth. "I guess it's a promise they couldn't keep."

Zack stepped back, the agony clear on his face. He extended a hand to help the girl up. "Go see my buddy Allen." He pointed out a Solstice worker a few paces away who, unlike many of the others, seemed to still be doing his job, talking to the festivalgoers with his hands on his hips, handing out water bottles. "I gave him some emergency gauze for his backpack. He'll dress the wound. I'll call a real doctor and get you cleaned up."

The girl nodded and headed toward Allen. Zack stared at her receding back and shook his head. It was one thing to think a YouTube star had duped all of us, but it was another to understand that he'd been duped, too. Zack had really tried to make this place safe . . . and it had blown up in his face. Had Paul orchestrated this? Maybe he'd called up all the vendors and told them *not* to deliver? But why would he have such a vendetta against Zack in particular? It just didn't make sense.

We made it to the edge of the stage, where the trail down to the water's edge picked up. As I turned, I noticed a bunch of concertgoers had followed us—probably wondering where the great Zack Frazier was going, because obviously he was too good to suffer on the concert grounds with everyone else. They looked at me suspiciously, too, and I could see the annoyance in their eyes. I felt a flood of guilt. It *wasn't* fair that I got to leave. I was no better than anyone else, yet I was going to a yacht where there was real food, private bathrooms, even cell service.

I bit my lip, wishing I could offer someone in the crowd my place on the yacht—the girl with the arm wound, maybe, or a tall, skinny guy who was sitting on the ground, rocking back and forth, seemingly traumatized by everything that had happened. They deserved it. But then I remembered: I needed to be on that phone call with the police. I was the only one who'd seen what was in Paul's trailer. I glanced at Steve, hoping that he'd have empathy for the suffering crowd and offer to switch with someone, but—surprise, surprise—he pretended like they weren't there.

We turned, heading for the little stairway that would lead to the craft that would take us to the yacht. But just as Zack started down the steps, we heard a scream. Torchlight bounced off branches, the sparse grass, our faces. Three people ran over their dunes, their cries so disjointed and harried it was hard to tell what they were saying. They awkwardly carried something in a tarp. When they set it on the ground, still screaming—I could now make out the words *oh my God, oh my God*—the tarp fell heavily with a thud.

My heart thudded, too. There was something so *familiar* about that shape under the tarp. When I looked at Zack's expression, his face was a mask of horror.

We moved away from the steps. Zack pushed to the front of the crowd, ordering the Solstice workers to keep everyone else back, too, but it was too late—seemingly the whole festival had stampeded over to the fallen bundle in the tarp, desperate to know what was under there. The boys who'd carried it from the woods were trying to tell a story, but they were so overwrought, their words came out in mangled pieces: ". . . we found him . . . I don't know how . . . all the *blood*."

Something large and heavy clogged my throat. I stared down at the object on the ground as someone handed Zack a torch. Zack stood over the shape and started to lift the tarp away. The moment I saw the creamy swath of skin, a few tendrils of hair, a few curled fingers, the palm soaked in blood, I knew. I sank to my knees, my scream mingling with everyone else's.

It was another body.

17

I WHEELED AROUND, frantically searching to make sure Elena was okay. She stumbled for me, her face contorted with terror. We held each other, screaming, and I suddenly knew, unequivocally, that she finally believed there was something very wrong with this festival. I didn't have to convince her anymore. She was seeing it with her own eyes.

"I think I know who might know something about this," I whispered, my voice dry.

"What?" Elena's eyes were large and round, visible even in the darkness. "Who?"

I glanced back at Zack, who stood over the body.

"Madison!" someone screamed over and over. The name echoed from one person to another like a game of telephone: *Madison, Madison, Madison.* Someone named Madison was now dead, and no one knew why.

Solstice workers made a wall behind Zack to keep people from mobbing the scene, but people panicked all the same. Some were crying. Some were screaming at Zack, begging for answers. Some were trying to take a swing at Zack. This was chaos, I thought. Pure anarchy.

"Adri." Elena shook me. "What did you mean? Who knows something about this?"

"I think . . . Paul," I answered, squeezing my best friend's hand. "The local guy who's been helping with the festival. I think he knows more than he's letting on."

Elena backed up from me, her eyes wild. "You think he's *killing* people?"

A sick feeling welled in my stomach. "I don't *want* to believe it. But I think Paul has some answers." Then I made the mistake of staring at Madison, who wore a green romper and an armful of bangle bracelets and was facedown, just as Eric had been. Her fingers were bent and twisted. I could see the blood on her neck, face, and arms. The same blood was evident on the T-shirt of Eric's that was now crumpled up in Paul's trailer.

Why was that shirt *there*?

"I want to go home," Elena cried. She dug her nails into my skin. I could feel her wet tears on my bare arms. "Adrianna. We *need* to go home. Now!"

"I know." I hugged her tightly. "Let's get to the yacht, okay? Zack wants to call the police. Maybe we can call your dad, too."

Elena nodded. "Maybe he can get us a helicopter."

Steve, having overheard us, snorted sarcastically. "You think it's going to be that easy? *Everyone's* trying to leave. *Everyone's* booked a helicopter. Face reality, Elena."

Elena wheeled around and stared at him. "I don't see *you* offering solutions!"

I reared back, startled by her venom. Steve looked shocked, too—and then hurt, and then pissed. But there was no time to be petty. Everything suddenly felt so serious.

Zack trudged back to us, a beleaguered look on his face. "Okay. I have some people guarding the . . . body." He said the last word reluctantly, a sick look washing across his features. He pointed toward the shore. "Let's get to the yacht. We need to make that call, *now*. We can't have anyone else hurt."

I glanced over his shoulder and watched as a few Solstice workers cordoned off the area where Madison's body lay. The boys who'd carried her corpse over the dunes sat curled up on the ground; a few Solstice workers crouched next to them, treating them for shock. It was the most kindness and care I'd seen in the workers since we'd arrived. A few more workers wrapped Madison back in the tarp, and then lifted her and marched off toward the semi that held everyone's luggage. They were taking her to the ferry, I presumed, but they weren't just going to walk right through the grounds, were they? If there was anyone at the concert who didn't yet know about the murders, there wouldn't be in a few minutes. But maybe the Solstice workers didn't care anymore. We were all in this nightmare together.

I caught up to Zack, who looked wrecked. "Are you all right?"

He shook his head. His eyes were glazed. He barely

saw where he was going, stumbling over a jutting log. "I'm just having a hard time believing Paul could do this."

"Well, maybe he *didn't*," I said. "Maybe someone planted the shirt in his trailer?"

Zack just looked at me emptily, as though he didn't really believe that theory.

"How did the kids find . . . Madison?" I asked.

Zack let out a ragged breath. "They were her friends, part of a group she came with. She went into the woods to pee, they said. But then . . . she didn't come back after a really long time. It was dark; they thought she might have lost her way . . . God." He shut his eyes. "One of them said she heard a strange sound, so she rushed off to see what was going on. But then they found her on the ground. She wasn't breathing."

"A strange sound?" My heart was pounding so fast. "Like . . . what?"

Zack shrugged. "They didn't say. There are so many questions. That's why we need to get to the boat—we need to reach out to the police, *all* police. The other thing, with the boy—it could have been an accident. It *looked* like an accident. But this? You don't just drop dead walking down a trail."

"Did they . . . *see* someone? Some*thing*?"

Zack started down a gradual incline and shook his head. "It was too dark." Then he peered ahead. "What the hell?"

He pointed down the stairs to the shoreline. The narrow beach was already packed with people. Tons of concertgoers were already in the water, too, swimming out to the yachts that were moored in the pitch-black sea.

My mouth dropped open. It was so late at night. The ocean was so dark. Didn't they realize it was dangerous?

"Damn it," Zack said under his breath, perhaps thinking the same thing I was. He raised the bullhorn he was still holding to his mouth. "*Everyone in the water! Come back in! You'll die out there!*" He shined his flashlight across the sea. The heads still bobbed. No one listened.

Zack gritted his teeth. "They have to come in." He glanced pleadingly at Steve. "Can you run back to the festival site and grab some more workers? We need as much help as we can get to bring everyone back to shore."

Steve sniffed. "I'm not going back there alone."

"Steve, come on!" Zack sounded exasperated. "We need five or six more guys. You really want to be responsible for dozens of people drowning?"

One of Steve's shoulders rose indifferently. "I mean, it was their choice to go in. Didn't you have them sign waivers saying we're not responsible for what they do when they're off the festival grounds?"

"This isn't about the *legality* of it!" Zack slapped his arms to his sides. But then, glowering at his cousin, he brushed past him, sideswiping his shoulder. "Forget it. I'll do it myself."

He glanced over his shoulder at Elena and me, then pointed toward a copse of palm trees. "Marx's Zodiac is over there. It's not hard to drive. Get out there, get on a phone, and call the police."

Elena and I nodded and ran for the palms. We found the Zodiac and dragged it across the sand. Steve helped, breathing heavily. We pushed the Zodiac into the waves and climbed aboard. Steve was about to crank up the motor when I heard splashes behind me. At least six kids tried to clamber onto the raft, but they added so much weight to the thing that it began to take on water.

"What the hell?" Steve bellowed. "Get off! This is private!"

"Please," a guy said. His face was shadowy in the darkness, but I could see how wide his eyes were. "Please let us on. We can't stay here. We're so scared."

"No, man!" Steve said. "We're going to a private yacht. Sorry."

"Steve," I said through gritted teeth. "Let him on!"

Steve glowered. "We need to save ourselves. He'll make the raft too heavy."

"We could at least *try*," I urged. We couldn't just leave people behind. Not with a murderer on the loose. It was unthinkable.

Steve's shrug seemed to say, *No way*. He cranked up the motor. The boat lurched sluggishly forward. But then more people swarmed out of the woodwork, splashing through the waves to get to us, trying to climb onto the boat, too.

"Wait!" I cried when a kid grabbed on to the boat's

sides, intending perhaps to just be dragged through the water to the yacht. "You're welcome to take shelter, but we have to make multiple trips, okay?"

Steve shot me a look. "Hell no. I am not making multiple trips!"

He peeled the guy's fingers from the side of the boat, but the guy just gripped tighter. "Don't leave me here with that thing over the dunes!"

Elena and I exchanged shocked glances. *Thing over the dunes?*

"Just wait on the shore for the next trip," Elena begged him. "Your legs will drag into the motor. You could end up without a foot . . . or worse."

"I'll take that chance!" the guy screamed.

He dug his nails into the rubber, and there was a *pop*. I instantly knew what had happened. The part of the raft he was holding onto lost its shape, deflating into a flat, useless tube. The guy floundered, kicking, sinking, horrified at what he'd just done.

Steve stared at the puncture in the boat, then at me. "*See?*"

The raft seemed to deflate at once. Everyone tipped into the waves.

The water was shockingly chilly. I felt a wave drag me under and fought to the surface. Elena bobbed up as well, spluttering and coughing. She paddled for me, panic in her eyes, and we clung to each other, breathing hard. A wave crashed over us, seemingly out of nowhere. Just as we were recovering, another came. Elena pointed toward the twinkling lights out at sea. It seemed like there were quite a few *less* than yesterday—no surprise—but we thought we could make out Captain Marx's *Lady Luck*'s distinctive light pattern among the group.

"I think we can swim for it," she said.

I shrugged. It seemed like as good a plan as any—as long as we could get past these initial breakers. "Let's go."

Elena and I started kicking as hard as we could, fighting against the current. I glanced over my shoulder and saw Steve swimming behind us, too. But then, as I was switching to breaststroke kick, I felt a sharp pain on my calf. Fire jolted through my hip, and then the bottom of my foot. I stopped and screamed.

"What the hell?" I peered into the dark water. "Something just bit me!"

Next to me, Elena was screaming, too. "It's in my suit! Something's in my suit!"

"It's jellyfish!" a random voice shouted from a few yards away, staring in horror at something in the water. "I see one! There's a jellyfish bloom!"

Steve was screaming, too, as though a whole swarm of jellyfish had taken up residence in his swimsuit. "I can't stand it!" he cried. He turned for the shore. I tried to keep swimming, but my legs were throbbing in pain, too. There was no way I could go on, either.

Moaning, I headed back to shore. So did Elena. A big wave carried us in, dumping us onto the sand. We washed up on the beach, wailing and dripping and clutching our stinging limbs. I expected to see Steve next to us, but the beach was empty. After a few deep breaths, I caught sight of a figure running for the very last boat, bobbing in knee-deep water.

"Let me on," a familiar voice said. People shoved over, and the figure climbed in. "Okay, go," he said. "*Go.*"

I had to do a double take before I understood what I was looking at. "Elena," I whispered, pointing. It was *Steve*. He faced the horizon, the torch flickering against his face, his jaw set in a line.

"Steve!" Elena cried. "Hey, Steve!"

Steve seemed to look through us. The shock of it was worse than the plunge into the water. Elena's lips pressed together like she was trying hard not to cry. I placed a hand on her shoulder. Steve's canoe drifted past the waves. Moments later, it disappeared from view.

"Elena . . . ," I started. But I had no words.

Shivering, I glanced over my shoulder at the dunes. We were the only people left on the beach. Had everyone else truly gotten onto a boat? Had some powered through the jellyfish stings to the yachts? Would Elena and I have to hike back up those slippery steps and through those imposing woods . . . *alone*?

"We're sitting ducks," I said, tears clouding my vision.

"What are we supposed to do?" Elena asked. "Should we just stay here all night? Someone's going to come for us, right?"

"But why would someone come for us?" I asked. I stared at the lapping waves. They looked so innocuous from here. Certainly not riddled with stinging, angry creatures.

"Can we hide in a tent, maybe?" Elena suggested. "Perhaps someone will let us bunk with them."

I shook my head, not certain that was a good solution, either. "But that means we'll have to go over the dunes again. I'm not sure I want to do that."

"Then we're out of options!" Elena cried.

"I don't know." I wiped the tears from my cheeks. My chest felt like it was going to explode, I was hungry and exhausted and shaky with fear, but I had to try to power through it. I stared toward the dunes, realizing that Zack hadn't returned with reinforcements yet. What if something had happened to him? What if he was dead now, too?

Then I had a thought. "Maybe we try to find Paul. And . . . talk to him."

Elena stared at me. "But what if he's the one murdering people?"

"We don't know that," I argued. "We don't really know anything."

"Adri . . ." Elena blinked hard. "That sounds like a terrible idea."

"But it's the only idea we have. And besides, Paul knows this island. If it *isn't* him, he could help us get to safety." I stood up and gazed around, then seized a big, sharp stick from the ground and handed it to her. "We can't let anyone else die, Elena. We have to figure out what's going on."

Elena stared at the stick as though it was covered in radiation. I found another stick just as sharp and pointy and gripped it in my fist. "Come on," I said, starting up the steps. To my relief, she followed.

We hurried through the brush. It was slow going, having only a phone app for a flashlight—but after our plunge into the water, I was thrilled my iPhone still *worked*. No one jumped out from behind any trees or swung from any vines, though, so that felt like a win.

The night was eerily silent. For a few minutes, the only sounds I heard were our footsteps and Elena's halting breaths. Then she said, "I'm sorry, Adri."

"Sorry for what?"

"What I said about Hayden. And Steve. And . . . everything else."

I shined my flashlight app on the ground, careful of jutting roots. I didn't know what to say.

"Hayden . . . he seems really nice," Elena said sheepishly. "I only said it because I was angry. You're right about Steve—it being an act, him not good enough for me. I *know* you're right. I think I knew way before he abandoned us in the boat." She punctuated this with a laugh, but it actually sounded like she might burst into tears.

"Well, I'm sorry, too," I said. "I never meant to make

you feel . . . *less* than me. I mean, God, El. That's ludicrous!"

"You're just so smart." Elena's feet sloshed through the mud. "And determined. And ambitious. I feel like a silly girl who likes clothes."

"You're way more than a silly girl who likes clothes."

"But seriously, I get self-conscious around you. Though I'm wondering if I project that self-consciousness onto things you say, twist them around and hear them to mean something they don't."

I glanced over my shoulder at her, unable to conceal a smile. "Has someone been going to therapy?"

"No." Elena ducked her head. "But I *should*. The relationship with my dad makes no sense. It's super dysfunctional. We never actually talk. He never shows me he loves me except by buying me things." She sighed. "Which, actually, is what Steve does, too."

"It's easy to fall into old patterns," I said gently, shining my light on a tree stump in our path. "I mean, look—I *wanted* to like Steve. Honest. But when I saw his true colors . . . You're amazing, El. Smart, gorgeous, funny. You should have someone who's just as good."

"Thanks," Elena said quietly.

We crunched through wet leaves a few moments more, and then I said, "So you like Hayden?"

"I only know him through study hall, but he seems really sweet. Quiet, you know—mysterious, maybe?

But actually, he seems like a good match for you. He's serious . . . but he also seems to have a fun side."

"He's the one who convinced me to come with you to this," I said miserably.

Elena chuckled sadly. "Well, don't hold *that* too harshly against him."

Above us, the sky was a deep blue black and glittering with stars. I felt so disconnected from the world, but very much a part of it at the same time. It was so jarring that, even when it felt like the world might end, even in such chaos, everything felt so *normal*, minute by minute—the ache in the bottom of my feet, the conversation I was having with Elena, the same stars above our heads.

We reached the road, and I looked right and left, my heart pounding in my ears. I could hear the panicked wails of the festivalgoers through the darkness. Someone yelled through a bullhorn, "We need *order*. You cross over the border, and your *life is in your hands*. Do you understand?"

Then I saw a glint of silver ahead. The roadside market stood a few paces away, its windows shuttered for the night. It startled me. I was so disoriented—I hadn't realized we were on *this* side of the festival grounds. Then I realized something else: The only vehicle parked in the lot, plain as day, was a stripped-down, rusty pickup truck. Where had I seen one of those? My heart froze as I realized.

Outside Paul's trailer.

I grabbed Elena's arm. *"That's Paul's truck,"* I whispered, shakily pointing at it. So Paul *was* creeping around the Solstice property? Or was he just doing his job as the coordinator?

"And *look*," Elena whispered, pointing to the back of the van. Smoke rose from the tailpipe in thick, gray curls. The parking lights shone red. My heart flipped over. Was someone *inside*? This seemed like an unbelievable stroke of luck—perhaps we could speak with Paul right now.

We tiptoed over, sticking just inside the tree line, ducking behind trunks and giant shrubs. I turned off my flashlight app and prayed we wouldn't stumble over any logs or encounter any snakes in the brush. My fingers trembled, making my walking stick wobble. I heard Elena's nervous breathing. The van's windows were tinted, so I had no idea who was in there. What if Paul was armed? What if he *was* a killer?

"Everyone!" a voice burst behind us down the trail, much closer than I'd expected. "There's shelter this way! You can lie low there!"

Elena and I froze and exchanged a confused look. It was a man's voice—a *familiar* voice—but not Paul's. We squinted through the thick vines, but it was too dark to see anything. There were sounds of panicked murmurs and quick footsteps; a flashlight beam zigzagged off trees. Did someone else know Paul was dangerous, maybe? Perhaps we should fall in line with the people in the woods?

I glanced at Elena. By the conflicted look on her face, I could tell she was thinking the same thing. That voice sounded so comforting and sure. It certainly seemed like a better plan to follow a crowd to safety than to lurk outside a murderer's van.

"Maybe we should . . . ," I began.

"Yeah," Elena interrupted. "Let's go."

We pivoted on our heels and headed in the opposite direction. Forget Paul—we needed safety.

But then something felt wrong. Something pulled me backward. A hand clapped over my mouth, and I murmured a protest, first figuring it was Elena, trying to warn me. The hand pressed in harder, blocking up my nose. I swung around, desperate and confused, startled by Elena's sheer strength. That's when I felt someone's elbow knock into me—and I realized Elena was *next* to me. It was someone *else* holding both of us, his hands clapped over our mouths, his strong arms keeping both of us from our ambush.

I swung around, desperate and terrified. And that's when I saw the face. My heart froze in my chest. My insides went to liquid. Holding me tight, only an inch away, was a face I least expected.

Paul's.

Myla Breaking News:

STRANGE OCEAN ACTIVITY ON EAST SIDE OF MYLA ISLAND

EAST MYLA ISLAND: Reports from several sailing vessels have come in about strange ocean activity near the eastern part of the Island. Currents have been very "erratic," according to boat captains—not behaving in their normal way whatsoever. A longtime sailor remarked that it felt like there was an unusual "pressure" under the water. "Sort of like a fault opening up," he said. "Sort of like there was going to be an earthquake . . . except there was no earthquake activity reported." And local fishermen have reported that an alarming number of fish have turned up dead in the water over the past twenty-four hours. "Almost like the water has been poisoned," Carmine Lorde, who runs a commercial fishing fleet, mused. "Except we ran tests. Water's fine."

Given that the Solstice Festival is taking place on Myla Island, the royal guard advises that no one venture into the waters around Myla until tides normalize. This includes any boats leaving the island for the Myla International Airport—meaning the young guests who are stranded at the poorly planned Solstice Festival might just be there even longer than they expected.

(This is a developing story.)

Comments:

@jofrank22: That's what you get, snowflakes. How are you liking Solstice now? 😀 #nocleandrinkingwateratSolstice #tenthousanddollarshithole #4billiondollardisaster

18

I FOUGHT HARD against Paul's grip. His palms felt rough. The muscles in his beefy arms flexed as they pinned me to his chest. Elena struggled, too, her eyes full of fear.

"*Stop squirming*," Paul said through clenched teeth. "*Just stay still!*"

"No!" I said against his palm. But he wouldn't let up. *This is it. Maybe he* is *going to kill us*. Maybe Paul knew we suspected him. He needed us out of the way before we warned anyone else.

I shut my eyes, desperately wanting to feel some sort of peace, some sort of spiritualism before I died. Even a lack of fear would have been nice—but I was too aware of Paul's breath on my neck and my pounding heart.

Paul yanked us behind the pickup. I glanced around desperately, praying some other Mylan might be witnessing this, but the road was empty. I didn't even see any concertgoers milling about. I tensed, certain Paul was going to do something awful. A horrible sense of guilt pounded over me, too—if only I'd run away, if only I hadn't tried to be the hero, but now I was going to get myself killed as well as Elena.

I wanted to reach out to her, tell her I was sorry. But Paul had a hand over my mouth. I couldn't speak—I could barely breathe.

A few moments of silence passed. Paul had us pinned to the back of the truck, my tailbone pressing into the bumper. For a while, he just stood there like he was waiting for some sort of signal. He still held us very tightly. We squirmed and struggled, but that just made him even more determined to keep us steady. I managed to exchange a glance with Elena. I hated how petrified she looked. I couldn't let something bad happen to her. I needed to warn someone of this. I needed to scream.

But strangely, I *heard* a scream next . . . and it wasn't my own. Elena and I stopped struggling, confused. Another scream sounded down the wooded path. Then another. Then came the strangest, most savage growling sounds I'd ever heard. It was a dinosaur-like roar that rocked the whole earth, sending branches shooting upward, and dirt spiraling, and my ears ringing. And after that, a hideously loud bird screech, the kind a pterodactyl might have made, the noise so shrill and dissonant it set my teeth on edge.

A chill went through every cell of my body. The sound definitely wasn't human.

Paul struggled to keep his balance, but his clamp over our mouths loosened. He, too, stared in horror toward the sounds coming from the woods. And the roars grew louder, harmonizing with the screams. After that, there was a loud gobbling sound—like a fairy-tale giant was smacking its lips. I got a whiff of blood. I heard a gurgle of what sounded like an enormous digestive tract. And then, moments after it began, there was . . . *nothing.*

Insects chirped peacefully. The wind blew. The world was so silent it almost hurt my damaged eardrums.

Paul lifted his hand from my mouth, and I darted away from him. But when I turned back to look, I was surprised by his expression. He didn't seem angry that I was trying to run from him. He was still staring down the path with a mix of horror and determination. "We've got to go," he told us. "*Now.*"

"Go?" I planted my feet. "With you? Yeah, right."

But then another roar rose up, its force shaking the trees. My heart stopped. My knees buckled. It was louder than any lion, any bear, any animal I'd ever visited at the zoo. The sound was so loud, it kicked up its own windstorm. And the roar rose and fell in pitch, almost like whatever creature was making it was trying to sing a song. Once again there were crunching noises and that awful intestinal gurgle. And then, once again, silence.

Paul yanked me by my wrist, then turned to grab Elena, too. "It's getting closer!" he screamed again, gesturing to his truck. "Get in!"

I did what I was told—whatever was happening in the woods chilled me to the bone. Was it a huge robot-machine engineered for killing? A giant tiger only seen on Myla? A reanimated T. rex? I didn't want to find out.

I climbed into the car, Elena scrambling behind me. Paul gunned the engine and turned onto a residential road. Houses whizzed past, then fields of tethered goats, then an old, rickety child's playground that looked like it hadn't been used in decades. I didn't see any people, which made the whole experience seem even more alienating and post-apocalyptic. I kept looking over my shoulder, wondering if I'd get a glimpse of whatever had made that sound running for us on six legs, blinking its twelve eyes, waggling a forked tongue. I heard another screech in the distance. The sound sent panicked birds flapping from their nests.

Paul glanced at something on the dashboard and winced. "I'm on empty. We're going to have to get out."

"*What?*" Elena shrieked.

"Come on. It'll be okay." Paul stopped the truck at a dead-end road and threw open his door. Down a grassy slope, there were more dunes to cross, but that meant the water was close. "Let's go," Paul urged. We scrambled into the woods and then across the dunes, coming upon a beach. The moon glittered on calm water. We couldn't see any waves, and there were a few smaller fishing boats tied to buoys about fifty yards out.

Through stinging eyes, I stared back in the direction we had come. I didn't hear any more roars. Nor did I hear screams. It almost made me wonder if I'd imagined the whole thing.

I swallowed hard and glanced at Paul. He returned my gaze and softened just a little, seemingly sensing my fear. "Be glad I caught you back there," he said gruffly. "You were being led straight for it. Just like everyone else at that silly concert."

Elena was panting from running. Pieces of blond hair fell into her eyes. "Running straight for *what*? That awful roar we heard? What was that? Some kind of monster?"

Monster. I thought, suddenly, of the legend Zack and Marx had told us on the boat, the Myla creature that demanded human sacrifice. But no. No *way*. And yet, with every crash of a wave, every swish of wind, I braced myself, readying for another roar, another scream. My nerves twitched. I wasn't sure I was afraid of Paul anymore. Perhaps he'd just saved us from something terrifying.

Paul's dark eyes narrowed. "Never mind. If I told you what you should be afraid of, you wouldn't believe me," he finally said. "Now come on. We can't stay here. We have to go before it tracks us down."

19

"THIS WAY." Paul held a flashlight along yet another series of dunes. We were running parallel to the ocean now. "It isn't far."

Elena and I tramped across the uneven ground. The dunes were dark and uneven. I had no idea where we were going. I was sweaty, starving, and without hope, and marching, probably, toward certain death. For some reason, I kept flashing to the AP History class I'd taken last year—how boring it had been, and how badly I wanted to be sitting at my desk in the back row right now, diligently taking notes, never imagining I'd be on a foreign island, running from some sort of mythological beast.

I stared at Paul's bobbing head as he navigated the path. He pushed aside branches for us, pointed out jutting roots with his flashlight. What did he mean about the danger in the woods, anyway? Why would we not believe what it was? It had to be a person he was talking about, right? And yet, those noises we'd heard in the woods—they didn't exactly *sound* human. Did tigers live in the Caribbean? I wasn't sure *that* made sense.

I swallowed hard, wishing I could catch Elena's eye. I felt guilty for putting her in this predicament. I felt annoyed at myself for picking a fight with her about Steve. I felt bad for her because Steve had screwed her over. But mostly, I just felt scared—we were literally running for our lives. It was still very likely we'd end up dead.

We reached the familiar clearing I'd visited just hours before. The same yellowish light spilled across Paul's front porch, but now that the moon was higher in the sky, I noticed a carefully tended garden off to the left, a paved back patio with a grill, and a few outdoor chairs. Such ordinary things gave me some comfort. I mean, *we* had a grill at home—the same brand, even. Perhaps Paul really was who he said he was.

"Let's get you two some water," Paul said as he climbed the steps to the front door. He pushed it open and snapped on some lights, then glanced over his shoulder at us to usher us inside. But Elena and I couldn't move. He put his hands on his hips. "What's the deal? We need to hydrate. Then again, if you'd rather die of thirst out here, be my guest."

Elena and I huddled together. I could tell by the stiffness of her body that she felt as uncertain as I did. There were still a lot of questions that needed to be answered.

I cleared my throat. "Um, Mr. . . . Paul? I know you

have the shirt that belonged to the boy who was found dead. I saw it in your trailer."

Paul turned slowly. He looked shocked. "What were you doing in my home?"

"I . . ." I waved my hands, my thoughts too scattered to explain. Elena was staring at me like she thought I wasn't thinking straight, but I needed Paul to know where we all stood. "It's a long story, but it doesn't change that it's in there—and I saw it. So why do you have it? Did you . . . *hurt* Eric?"

Paul leaned against the side of the trailer, and all of a sudden he looked so young—barely older than we were. "You think *I* had something to do with Eric's death?"

"I just don't understand why you have his shirt," I said, feeling knocked a little off-kilter. It wasn't the response I expected. "Nothing has been explained to us. Not just with the shirt, but with the details about Solstice, too. And why people are dying. And that noise in the woods. I can't deal with not knowing things!"

Paul plopped down on the stoop and folded his arms around his knees. He stared at us, his thick eyebrows knitting with concern. A few beats passed. Crickets sawed away in the trees. "I get it. It sucks to be in the dark."

"You got that right," I grumbled, cautiously.

"As for me." Paul pointed to his chest. "I'm a marine biology student at the University of Myla. My family has lived on this island for centuries. We live on the other side of the island, though—the inhabited side. The *safer* side."

"Safer?" Elena's voice trembled. "Why is it safer?" Though as soon as she said it, I realized it was obvious why this side wasn't safe. Those noises over the dunes said it all.

"I've been curious about this side of the island ever since I was a kid," Paul went on, nervously picking at his nails. "There were unexplained deaths a few decades ago, and then more a few decades before that—people would come over here to hike or swim or whatever, but they'd never come back. And then their families would go looking for them, and they'd find them lying on the shore . . . *mangled*. And these were good swimmers. Strong, young people. It was baffling. They had body parts missing. Huge gashes on their limbs. Like something . . . *ate* them.

I sucked in my breath, remembering the scrapbook I'd found in Paul's trailer. *A History of Unusual Deaths of Myla Island*. Those newspaper clippings. Those strange drownings. The picture of the man I'd looked at: His caption had said *champion swimmer*.

"So were they . . . shark attacks?" Elena asked.

"That's what a lot of people thought—but I don't think so, no."

"Then . . . what?"

Paul raised a finger. "Hang on. I'm getting to that. Anyway, I'd heard these rumors all my life, and I knew not to come over here unless I wanted the same thing to happen to me. It was just a part of life—an old warning you knew to obey, except it seemed that no one really asked why these deaths happened, or what was the cause."

"So, few people live on this side of the island?" I shifted nervously. "I saw houses, though. A playground."

"And they looked quite old, didn't they?" We both nodded. "They're all uninhabited now. A few brave souls still have houses here—they can certainly get property for dirt cheap. You may have met a few of them in the general store." I nodded, thinking of the group with the Wi-Fi password. "They don't buy that something really strange is going on out here. But most people believe. I mean, no one dared to build hotel complexes, or restaurants, or snorkeling schools, or things you find on other islands in the Caribbean. No one wanted to take the risk."

I narrowed my eyes. "So why would someone hold a music festival here?"

Once again, Paul held up a finger as if to say, *I told you, be patient.* "Like I said, no one was looking at the cause of these strange deaths. But when I got to college last year, I started to poke around. I thought about the water around Myla—its ecosystem. It's pretty unique here—especially on this side of the island. See, around most islands, the ecosystem is pretty balanced—there are consistent levels of certain fishes, mollusks, plants, et cetera. But the ecosystem in the ocean surrounding this side of Myla is different from anywhere else in the Caribbean—and no one knows why. For example, you know conch? Those big shells kids put their ears to and think they hear the ocean?"

"Yeah," I said incredulously, not knowing why we were suddenly getting a marine biology lecture.

"Well, we have way too many on the ocean floor. More than we can handle—and everywhere else in this part of the Caribbean has a shortage! Conch eat up all the algae, which is usually a good thing—we avoid red tide, anyway—but it doesn't leave any algae for the *other* species that also eat it, which throws everything out of balance."

"Why are there so many conch?" Elena asked.

Paul pointed at her. "Good question." The corners of his eyes crinkled as he smiled, and Elena smiled, too, and for just a second, the mood almost felt casual and friendly. "Because of what's *missing* from these waters. Nurse sharks: the conch's natural predator. But again, no one could figure out why that was—there are nurse sharks elsewhere in the Caribbean. And while that seems like a good thing that there aren't sharks on Myla, it's actually very unnatural. They might not tell you this on *Shark Week*, but ocean ecosystems need sharks. The conch population needs to be controlled—but given the rumors that these waters are dangerous, divers are too afraid to get all the conch out." He twisted his mouth. "But anyway, I started to think. What could be keeping the sharks away? They have lots of food here; it's a good habitat; the water is clean. And then it hit me: What if there was something in the water that was scaring the sharks away? An even *bigger* predator than the shark, using intimidation to mark its territory?"

"Like . . . what?" I said slowly, not knowing what might be above a shark on the food chain.

"I started to wonder. Maybe this predator was something we'd never seen before. Some kind of . . . *thing*— which is also responsible for these strange deaths we've seen over the years."

I frowned, something sparking in my brain. "So it *is* the legend? Zack mentioned it—some sort of monster on the island, and the Mylans offering human sacrifices to keep it away?" I clucked my tongue. "It sounded condescending. Insulting to the people on the island." I figured that Paul, who seemed so proud of Myla, would find the legend offensive.

"Yep, it underestimates our sophistication for sure. We'd never dream of offering people up as sacrifice," Paul agreed. "But there is some truth to the story."

"Truth how? There *is* a monster?" I could feel my body tensing up. "What is it? Loch Ness?"

"We *heard* it," Elena reminded me. "It sounded way bigger than Loch Ness."

Paul nodded. "We did hear it. Mylans call it Diab. Creole for *devil*. Something that can shape-shift. That's the epitome of evil."

We stared at him, slack jawed.

"But I've never seen it," Paul added. "Those who *do* see it don't live to tell the tale."

I let out a nervous laugh. He had to be pulling our leg. "But this doesn't explain why you have Eric's T-shirt," I said, trying to keep my voice from trembling.

"I'm getting to that," Paul said. "So anyway, for a long time, little has happened on this side of the island. Like I said, a few intrepid people have built houses here, but they know full well they're living somewhere where danger might strike at any moment, given the historical accounts of strange deaths by Diab. They're either prepared to take that risk, or they're in denial that it could be true, but deep down, they know the threat is there. But then, suddenly, this mysterious buyer bought this half of the island last year. Our government was happy to give it up—especially for the handsome price the buyer paid. But then we heard rumors that this buyer was going to hold an extravagant music festival over here. Which seemed"—he wagged his head back and forth like he was trying to choose his words carefully—"irresponsible."

"Wait, who's the buyer?" I interrupted.

Paul shrugged. "Some shell company. The government couldn't trace it to one person—and believe me, they looked into it. But it was like the company was run by a hacker—every time the authorities thought they hit a lead on who the buyer was, it ended up being a false identity . . . or a dead end."

"Whoa," Elena said.

"So anyway, this music festival was suddenly scheduled. And that's when the videos about it started popping up. Everyone was talking about it. We had no idea how the festival organizers were going to pull it off, considering nothing was developed on this side of the island. They didn't reach out to our side, either. They didn't ask for help, security, medical supplies, even tents. We figured they were sourcing that from the west side, but something about it was just . . . strange. And that's not even considering the dangerous element over here. Diab. It seemed like a recipe for disaster." Paul waved his hand in the direction of the path, where we'd come from. "And, obviously, that's exactly what's happening."

I shifted my weight. "Did you warn the people who were organizing the festival about the monster?" I cringed at calling it a monster. Monsters didn't exist . . . did they?

"Sure I did. I told Zack Frazier about Diab over and over. I had a whole presentation about the deaths and the ecosystem and the rumors and the evidence that the creature is real. But he just laughed. He brought up the obsessed people in the US who believe in Bigfoot, who go *looking* for him—there are whole shows about it, apparently! And Zack went ahead with the plans anyway. Not that there *were* many plans—as you saw, the festival is a disaster. My people and I did what we could, but we didn't have much to work with. I still don't know if they even bothered to organize any of it or if all their contracts just fell apart at the last minute. But the concert is going to go down as the biggest wreck in music-festival history."

"But why would you join a festival crew if you knew it was doomed from the start?"

Paul scoffed. "I joined so I could keep people safe. I trained my people to make sure kids didn't wander away from the festival boundaries—from what we've learned, Diab doesn't like open spaces, instead preferring the dunes, the rocks, the wooded areas, or the water. I emphasized to Zack that we must *never* let people wander away. But he just shrugged me off. And then people *did* wander away. I should have guessed they would once only one food truck arrived and there were no shelters. When I saw what happened on the cliffs, I screamed to Frazier that I knew something like this might happen."

I nodded, remembering when he'd said that on the beach, as the men loomed over Eric's body. *What were we supposed to do?* Zack had asked. *Put up a barbed-wire fence?*

"But he didn't seem to hear me, not even then. He thought that kid just got drunk and fell." Paul rolled his eyes.

Sweat prickled the back of my neck. I'd *known* Paul didn't believe that Eric had fallen. Now I knew why.

"So that's how Eric died?" I said quietly. "By Diab?"

Paul nodded solemnly. "I think so."

"And that second death? Madison?" My heart started to pound. "The monster got her, too?"

Elena let out an incredulous whimper of fear. I stared into the sky, marveling over the fact that I was looking at the very same stars that shone over my house in Atlanta. How had I wandered into a world where there was a . . . *beast*? Some kind of magical, monstrous thing that could move from sea to land, gobbling up humans? How could this be real?

"Anyway," Paul said quietly. "After I saw Eric's body on the beach, I found his T-shirt snagged on a rock, and I grabbed it. I want to test it for DNA. I want to see what the creature that did this to him most closely resembles, genetically." He looked at us pleadingly, real truth in his eyes. "I didn't kill Eric! I'm just trying to keep you guys safe! This concert never should have come here. And now people might die. The concert organizers don't seem to give a shit."

Elena let out a whimper, and in the moonlight, I could see a crystal teardrop running down her cheek. "What are we going to do?" she cried. "How can we stay away from that . . . *thing?*"

"We'll figure that out." Paul reached out his arm hesitantly, like he wasn't quite sure of himself, but suddenly Elena flung her body at him, burying her head into his chest. He awkwardly wrapped his arm around her shoulders and let her sob. "It's okay," he said. "I'll make sure you don't get hurt."

I watched as he comforted her, his posture so different from the brittle, angry man I'd thought he was.

This was a guy, I realized, who was brittle and angry not because he resented all of us for being on his island but because he was fighting a losing battle of keeping all of us safe. I really *did* believe he was going to do everything to make sure we wouldn't be hurt. But once again, I considered everyone else on this island—they were all so exposed and vulnerable.

I cleared my throat, and Paul looked up. "What about the people still at the festival?" I asked quietly. "What's going to happen to them?"

Paul's face clouded. "I don't know," he admitted. "But now that Diab is back, I'm afraid it won't be good."

Myla Breaking News:

WHERE IS ZACK FRAZIER?

EAST MYLA ISLAND: One day into the Solstice Festival, with multiple acts canceled and rampant complaints of unsafe conditions, and Zack Frazier, festival organizer and major YouTube personality, has gone missing.

Some sources last saw him trying to calm an angry crowd that was demanding answers about why they'd paid tens of thousands of dollars to attend a concert that had fallen apart. A few festivalgoers who returned to the United States say *they* last saw Mr. Frazier on a raft leaving Myla East—"looking pretty desperate and angry." But since then, Mr. Frazier has not been heard from. Meaning there is no one to answer for the atrocity that is the Solstice Festival. Has Frazier run away from his self-made disaster? Where will he turn up next?

(This is a developing story.)

Comments:

@boomer92: Such a wimp. I've lost all respect.

@KNArdley_O: Unsubscribe, unsubscribe, unsubscribe!

@45bb: Anyone else watching the active weather and ocean map over Myla? What's with that weird swirl on the eastern side? Some sort of underground tornado?

> **Reply: @KNArdley_O:** Who cares??

@HaydenATL: Adri? If you're reading this, please give me a sign you're okay. I should have never encouraged you to go to that festival. I'm so sorry.

20

PAUL GAVE ELENA AND ME big glasses of water and made us peanut butter sandwiches. We hovered in the doorway, glancing cagily into his space suspiciously. I noticed the same stack of newspapers on the coffee table.

Paul noticed me looking and pointed at them. "I pulled out all the research I'd done on the Diab—but I never found exactly what I was looking for. I think it was stolen."

I took another bite of my sandwich, trying to hide my skepticism. I couldn't fathom who might want to sneak into Paul's cabin and steal random research about a monster that may or may not be real.

Then again, Diab *had* to be real, didn't it? Because what *else* explained those savage noises? I glanced at the coffee table. The scrapbook was still there, facedown as I'd left it. Suddenly I wanted to leaf through every page. I wanted to read about all of these strange deaths. I thought of the way someone had phrased what had happened in one of the letters I'd read: *It got Sidney.* It. Diab.

Paul disappeared into his bedroom and came out with

Eric's T-shirt in his outstretched hands. "I still want to test this for DNA, but I haven't had time with managing the festival and making sure no one else goes off the grounds. But you see this mark here?" He pointed to some dark smears near the collar. "It's not human. It might be some kind of ink."

Elena swallowed. "You think it's from the . . . Dia—whatever? It's a giant squid?"

"That can also walk on land?" I asked incredulously.

"I don't know, but other historical accounts of similar deaths found nonhuman material on the bodies—the same color as this, too. Maybe Diab ejects some kind of liquid when it's angry or eating. There isn't much record of finding this stuff in the woods or rocks after the monster disappears—but then, when Diab's around, usually people are so *afraid* to venture anywhere outdoors, so there isn't much research to go on. Once I get around to testing it, I'll have a better idea." He set the shirt down gently on his table. "But that's not important right now. The important thing is to figure out how we're going to make sure everyone's safe."

He stared at us as though expecting we'd have some sort of answer. I looked helplessly at Elena. She opened her mouth, then let it fall wordlessly shut.

My gaze drifted to the small window. It offered a clear view through the trees, straight to the water. I could just make out the tiny, twinkling lights of the remaining yachts bobbing in the distance. I was so surprised by their presence I had to do a double take.

"I can't believe yachts are still here," I gasped. "Don't they realize that some sort of person-eating . . . *thing* is on land?"

Paul crossed his arms and followed my gaze. "They probably don't. They're farther out than you think—I doubt they heard the screams. And it's not like anyone can broadcast what's happening with all the cell service being out on this side of the island."

"Yeah, what's *with* that?" Elena asked, and then straightened like she had a thought. "Do you think the festival organizers deactivated the cell tower or something? So none of us could report to the world how horrible the festival is?"

"I wouldn't put it past Zack Frazier," Paul muttered.

I shifted my weight. Before Zack disappeared, he'd seemed so earnest. Like he really was trying to do good. I didn't know what to believe.

Elena crossed her arms over her chest. "Maybe we should find Zack. He has access to Captain Marx's yacht. That'll get us closer to the other boats, and we could figure out a plan to reach them. They could help rescue people on the island. Get everyone out of here."

"That's a good idea," I said, though I felt hesitant. Last Zack and I had talked, he'd thought Paul was behind all of this. What if we found him, and Zack did something to Paul? On the other hand, surely he'd heard the noises from the monster in the woods. Surely he understood that *that* was the thing killing people, not Paul.

Elena and I tried to remember where we'd seen Zack last. "Maybe he's still at the concert site?" I suggested.

We started on the path back to the festival. As we walked, I thought more about how much disdain Paul had for Zack. I'd gotten a different picture of the guy—someone who seemed genuinely shocked that his careful plans weren't working out like he'd hoped. Had he really brushed off Paul's warnings so cavalierly? The very same guy had worriedly checked out a concertgoer's wounds, looking deeply guilty, as though he'd caused the injury himself. It seemed like we were missing a piece of this puzzle. I just didn't know what it was.

I felt only marginally safer with Paul with us as we traipsed over the dark dunes. The air inside the woods was eerily still. I kept thinking I heard mysterious noises—gurgling, growls, clicks, lip smacks—but it was possible I'd contrived all of it, paranoid that Diab was watching.

Elena stepped over a large, deep puddle that had been left from the flash flood earlier in the day. "So why is the creature only local to Myla? Like, why does it never go anywhere else in the Caribbean?"

"I'm not sure," Paul answered. "That's what I've been studying—it has to be something with the ecosystem. Or maybe Diab feels safe here. Maybe this is its territory."

"Do you think there's more than one of its kind on earth?"

"I don't know. I don't know if one has just lived a long, long time . . . or if there were two Diab and they spawned another—but whatever the case, it's been part of the Mylan lore for centuries."

"And no other biologist is interested?" I felt water seep into my sneaker as I took a soggy step into a shallow puddle. "But I thought scientists loved discovering new species."

"We've kept it really quiet," Paul admitted. "We don't want to be inundated. Of course people would love to study Diab. But we worry that if they came, studied the thing, tramped all over the island, and then left us *alone* with it again . . ."

"It might anger the creature?" Elena guessed. "And it would lash out at the locals even *more*?"

Paul twisted around and grinned at her. "You're a smart one. Mylans need to protect their own, you know?"

Despite it being too dark to see, I could feel a small, sudden shift in the atmosphere. "I get it," Elena said bashfully. I could tell she was smiling.

We could hear the hubbub at the festival site before we actually arrived. As we pushed aside the palm fronds, a figure in a Solstice T-shirt suddenly stepped in front of us, wielding what looked like a canoe paddle over his head. He raised it up like he was ready to smack us, and we cowered back. Elena let out a scream.

"Whoa, whoa!" Paul cried. "It's just us!"

The guy's wild eyes adjusted. I recognized him—this was Indigo, the same cheerful guy who'd ushered us off the ferry on our first morning here. But now his eyes were sunken. His mouth wobbled. His shirt was torn at the front, revealing a big bruise on his torso, and the veins in his arms bulged in a way that seemed almost grotesque. Slowly he lowered the oar. "Paul. What the hell are you doing out here? Haven't you *heard*?" Indigo glanced around as though making sure no one was listening in. "There's something over the dunes," he whispered. His voice trembled with fear. "We heard . . . screams."

Paul gave Indigo a level look. But once the guy's back was turned, he exchanged a glance with Elena and me. People were figuring it out. Of course they were. And this—mutiny, barbarism, defending oneself with boat oars—was what was coming out of it.

As we walked across the field, there was evidence everywhere that things were starting to . . . *deteriorate*. Girls were in screaming matches with one another over bottles of water. People lay hoodies, shoes, and even spare pairs of underwear flat on the ground to mark their territory; I noticed a guy inadvertently step inside someone's circle and the circle's inhabitants went ballistic, two of them attacking him around the waist. People sat in huddled groups, gazing wildly into the woods. Some clutched makeshift items as weapons: belts, metal water bottles, a stiletto-heeled shoe.

They all knew—I could just tell. Everyone had heard those screams. I wondered if anyone had dared to venture away from the festival site to see what had happened. I don't know if *I* would have.

Paul put his hands on his hips and scanned for Zack. I did, too, taking in the tipped-over food truck, the abandoned customer service table, the looted stage—several amps had been smashed. I didn't see Zack anywhere.

"Maybe he went back to Marx's yacht?" I suggested.

"He *should* be here," Paul grumbled. "He *should* be trying to save people."

"He was," I said. I kept thinking about how gently Zack had helped the hurt girl. "He came back to grab reinforcements—he was worried about everyone in the ocean."

Another shriek sounded from the woods. I froze. Elena grabbed my arm tightly. It was so dark in the trees that it was hard to know what was going on. I listened for monster sounds—roars, screeches, that horrible gurgling. Nothing. But there were no more shrieks, either. I still felt a little clench in my chest. What had just happened?

"Come on," I said. "We should go to Marx's boat regardless of whether Zack's there or not. We'll beg him to let us on. We can broadcast to other boats over his radio."

"On an open channel. Good idea," Paul said, nodding. He rubbed his chin worriedly. "But I've already tried to convince Marx about the creature, too. He laughed in my face even more than Frazier did. What makes you think it's going to be any different now?"

Elena straightened and started rummaging in her pocket. "I have something."

She tapped the screen until she got to the photos app. The last image was a video still of what looked like a dark, abandoned road. She hit the triangle button and a video began to play. It didn't take me very long to realize that she'd shot this when she and I were cowering behind Paul's van. For a few seconds, nothing moved in the video, but suddenly a shriek rang out. And then another, and then another, and a horrible, sloshing, slurping *gurgle* of an enormous thing—a Diab—swallowing down a body without even bothering to chew.

We stared at it until the video ended. Paul looked visibly shaken. Elena cleared her throat. "I hit record because I knew *something* sketchy was going down," she said, glancing guiltily away from Paul. At the time, we'd thought the sketchy thing was him.

"This is great," I said. "Marx will have to believe us."

But as we turned toward the shoreline, that eerie gurgle echoed in my mind again and again. I had a feeling I'd never forget that sound for as long as I lived.

Text message log:

To: Gigi

From: Mom

Sent: 10:04 p.m., Friday, June 19

Honey, please write back when you get this. I've heard scary rumors. Please tell me you aren't one of the kids in the water trying to swim to the yachts. There are so many random tweets flying right now that I don't know what's true and what's a hoax—I think that's how the Mylan officials are seeing it, too. Please send word if you can! I'm so scared for you.

To: Mama

From: Avery

Sent: 10:23 p.m., Friday, June 19

Mom IDK if u will ever get this but i'm huddled under a tree and haven't eaten in days and there's some kind of multi-eyed giant octopus in the woods and if i die i'm sorry for all the shit i put you through because i've totally been an asshole and u don't deserve it. love u so much.

> *(Message unable to send)*

To: Juliana

From: Rob

Sent: 10:37 p.m., Friday, June 19

Hey, it's Rob—we met at Coachella? Listen, this is going to sound totally random, but I'm here at the Solstice Festival and I'm pretty sure none of us are going to survive and I just want to say that I'm in love with you and I should have told you that night but I was too afraid . . . and now I'll never get the chance. Live life to the fullest.

223

You never know which day's gonna be your last. I always thought that was just random BS they put on Hallmark plaques for above your stove, but boy is it TRUTH.

(Message unable to send)

21

MOONLIGHT RIPPLED ACROSS the water. The tide was out, but the waves were choppy, and we could see heads bobbing out at sea. Hysterical voices rose in the air. It was all the people who'd climbed onto the boats earlier. They didn't know where to go. All I could think of was Paul's research about the creature in the water. The strange ecosystem around Myla Island. The fact that sharks, even huge ones, were too afraid to enter this territory because of . . . *the thing.*

I bit hard on my thumbnail, cracking it down the middle. "What's going to happen to them?" I asked nervously. "I mean, what if the creature decides to go for a swim?" I wondered, too, what they thought they were going to accomplish in the ocean. They seemed so far from the yachts. And it wasn't like salt water was suitable for drinking . . .

"They might be okay," Paul said. "Historical accounts show that the Diab goes on a feeding frenzy for a bit, then quiets down for a little while, then feeds again." He glanced back over the dunes, where we'd heard the screams. "It might be full right now. But probably not for long."

Elena walked toward the shore. "Maybe we should just swim for the yacht?"

"Wait," Paul reached for her arm. "You can't. The jellyfish."

Elena gritted her teeth, and I could tell she was remembering the stings we'd received only hours before. "But we have to get out there," she said. "Maybe I can just deal?"

"I can deal, too," I offered, impressed by Elena's bravery. "They're just stings. It's not going to kill us."

Paul looked conflicted, then glanced around the beach, as though searching for something with which to make a boat. Suddenly footsteps sounded in the soft sand. I straightened, on full alert. Branches began to rustle, and my vision went spotty. *Diab?*

"Yo!" said a familiar voice as someone burst through the trees. "Need to get somewhere safe?"

I slowly opened my eyes. It was Mosley, the guy from the market, and he was dragging a Zodiac raft with a small outboard motor. He wore a rainproof jacket and a canvas hat, but he might as well have been wearing angel wings.

"Man," Paul said emphatically, slapping his hand. "You are a *lifesaver*."

Mosley glanced over his shoulder toward the dunes. "You having some trouble at the concert, eh?"

"You think?" Paul muttered sarcastically. "We're heading for one of the yachts. We need to call for help." He helped Mosley get the raft into the water, then shook his head. "I asked them one thing: to keep everyone on the festival grounds. I *tried* to warn them."

"Aw, man, kids never listen to instructions," Mosley said gently. Then he looked at us. "Climb in."

I climbed into the raft, feeling the warmish water wash over my aching jellyfish stings—definitely *not* the most pleasant feeling.

"It'll be okay," Mosley said as we pushed out to sea. He sounded almost cheerful. "Tell me where to go. I'm your captain."

"This way," Elena instructed, pointing toward the boat with the blue lights. She looked at Mosley gratefully. "Thank you so much."

"No problem!" Mosley grinned. "Anything to help."

There was something jarring about his tone, I felt—so sunny when everything seemed so bleak. Then again, Mosley's boat was a huge break. We were in the water now. We'd be at the yacht soon. And after that, we'd be able to call for help . . . and save everyone from Diab.

"So I think it's definitely back," Paul said after we got over the initial breakers and were on calmer water.

"What's that, brother?" Mosley asked absently.

"*You* know."

A small, tense beat passed. The outboard motor sputtered a little. Mosley's expression didn't change. "You believe that nonsense, Pauly boy? I thought that was just something you were into when you were younger."

Paul pressed his lips together. "You mean to tell me you didn't hear that growl in the woods? You didn't hear the screams?"

"Nah, I was over on the other side of the island," Mosley said as we crested another wave. "I just got back here about fifteen minutes ago. Saw you guys scuttling down to shore, figured I'd see what's up."

"Wait, you don't believe in the Diab?" I interrupted. "And you're *from* here?"

Mosley shrugged. "Not everyone from Myla is as cuckoo as Paul here. Generally, I only believe in things I see." He nudged Paul playfully, as though he was his little brother. "Don't buy everything this guy tells you! He's a real manipulator, this one!"

Paul opened his mouth, then shut it again. The fury on his face was obvious. So was the sinking in my stomach. What if Mosley was right? *Was* Paul pulling our leg? I thought of the screams I'd heard, the roar. Could it have been from something else? Was this some sort of elaborate . . . scam?

But then something hit me. Mosley's voice: It wasn't just familiar because he'd spoken to me in the market and at the festival. I'd heard it more recently than that. Like . . . earlier tonight. There was no way Mosley had just gotten to this side of the island only fifteen minutes ago. It had been Mosley in the trees, calling out to that big group of people.

There's shelter this way, a voice just like his had said. *You can lie low there.*

The voice had sounded so assured, comforting, confident . . . but by the screams that followed, Mosley had led the group straight into the jaws of the creature.

I glanced at Paul, not wanting to give away what I'd just put together. If it *was* Mosley, why had he just lied to us—about his whereabouts, and about believing in the creature?

"Those are interesting flashlights," Elena said suddenly, pointing to something in Mosley's bag.

Mosley looked down sharply, and I caught the look that flashed across his face. "Oh." He secured the flap of the bag, which set off alarms in my head. I hadn't gotten a great look at what was in there, but they sort of resembled glow sticks that were passed around at concerts. It seemed like an innocent thing to be carrying—maybe Mosley thought he could sell them to people at Solstice.

But why was he trying to hide them?

But suddenly something popped into my head: When Zack and Steve had told the legend of the creature on the island, they said the thing was attracted to phosphorescent light. As in . . . *glow sticks*. Was that why Mosley had a bunch of them? Was this what he'd used to lure the creature to the people in the woods?

The boat suddenly felt dangerous. Without moving my head, I flicked my gaze toward Paul. He was staring at Mosley's knapsack, too, his eyes blinking fast. He'd also figured it out. But he wasn't sure what to do.

Blue light shone on our faces. When I looked up, I realized we were only yards from Marx's yacht. Relief filled me—I wanted off this boat with Mosley as quickly as possible.

A few of Marx's men scrambled down the stairs to the launching dock and threw us ropes. Paul grabbed one, and they pulled us in. I stood, ready to disembark, but suddenly I felt someone shoving past me—and Mosley was off first.

"Excuse *you*," Paul said under his breath.

Mosley's knapsack bobbed against his back. I eyed it warily, imagining the glow sticks inside. Mosley stuck out his hand to a worker on the yacht, and the guy greeted him warmly like they were old friends. But the smile melted from Mosley's face as he stared at the landing just above the launching deck. A second man was standing there.

"Why did you bring *them*?" this second man called.

I followed Mosley's gaze, my heart lurching in my chest. There, in the shadows, stood Captain Marx. His arms were at his sides. His face was calm, in repose. Something lay next to him. Something big. Something *limp*. Something I was used to by now, considering I'd seen it two other times already today. *A body.*

Elena gasped. I felt Paul stiffen. I squinted hard, taking in the person's twisted fingers, spiky brown hair, and plastic glasses, now askew across his lifeless face. I clapped a hand to my mouth and let out a weak wail.

It was Zack Frazier.

22

"ZACK?" I SCREECHED IN HORROR. Then I stared at Marx. "What the hell! What happened?"

"Is he . . . ?" Elena cried, staring at Zack's lifeless body. But she didn't have to finish the question. He *was*. "Oh my God. Oh my *God*."

"Mosley," Marx said sharply, interrupting us. "Why. Did. You. Bring. *Them?*"

"I . . ." Mosley glanced at us, then at Marx again. "Shit. I thought you *wanted* them here."

Marx blinked impassively. "And why would you think that?"

Marx was just standing there, staring at us, his face eerily . . . *neutral*. It was almost like he didn't notice there was a dead man at his feet. I thought of Marx and Zack clinking glasses the night before. I thought of their camaraderie, their closeness, the way they'd bonded when they found Eric on the shore.

But now Marx was acting like Zack was a crash-test dummy. Not even human.

Marx glanced at Mosley, raising his chin in a silent

command. Mosley nodded, opened his knapsack, and tossed a glow stick—it *was* a glow stick!—into the water. And then, as though Zack Frazier's body was an annoying bit of trash, Marx kicked it, hard. Zack rolled over the side of the yacht, making a loud splash in the sea, just inches from where the glow stick bobbed.

"No!" I cried out, pivoting toward the waves. I wanted to jump in. Save Zack, somehow—even though I knew, intellectually, he was dead.

Paul grabbed my arm hard to pull me back. Just in time, too, because suddenly there was a great rumbling beneath us. The boat started to shake, and the current became so rough I nearly toppled overboard. White foam swirled around Zack's corpse, bubbling and bubbling, and then, like a geyser, something exploded from the deep.

Something gooey.

Something muscular.

Something bigger than any shark or whale I'd ever seen.

Something that took up the whole horizon, its body covered in scales and lesions, its mouth huge and filled with many layers of teeth, its eyes oozing from multiple parts of its head. It emitted a stench I couldn't fathom—of rot, of blood, of decaying bodies, of bacteria, of dead teeth, and of some kind of musk that was the pure odor of a predator. Long tentacles jutted from parts of its body, lashing out for us. And then it turned in the air powerfully, as though it could fly, and, for a moment, one of its large, glassy, oozing eyes fixed directly on me. I could see my slack, terrified face reflected in its eyeball.

"*Diab!*" Paul screamed.

My brain couldn't quite process what I was seeing. I screamed. *Everyone* screamed. And then the thing roared, making that awful pterodactyl howl, and as it turned, its shape seemed to morph—becoming more fishlike, more linear, like a snake. It's tentacles literally *disappeared*. One eyeball jutted out like an appendage. The monster stretched its mouth wide, revealing a thick, meaty, terrifying tongue.

Finally, it pounded back into the water with a groan, setting off a tsunami that nearly upended our boat. A funnel of water trailed behind it as it burrowed back to the bottom of the ocean, though its smell lingered like a fog.

And when I looked again, the glow stick was gone. So was Zack's body.

The scream froze in my throat. Next to me, Elena was too stunned to sob. I stared at Paul in horror only to find that he'd leaned over the side of the raft to throw up.

"What *was* that?" I wailed. My brain couldn't process what I'd just seen. I kept picturing the thing's eye fixing on me. It seemed like it was sizing me up in an almost human kind of way. And when I looked at my hands, they were covered in ooze. I shrieked and wiped them on my shorts. From the thing? Was it *poisonous*? How did this even get on me?

"Oh my God, oh my God, oh my God." Elena trembled on the raft's floor, her arms wrapped around her knees. I crouched down next to her and slung an arm around her shoulder, for my benefit as much as hers. I stared emptily up at Marx and Mosley, who now stood side by side on the upper deck, their mouths twisted into smirks. It was like they weren't even afraid of the thing. How was that *possible*? And then it hit me: This wasn't the first time they'd seen it. They were *used* to Diab— had it trained, even.

"You did that on purpose!" I cried. "You let it *eat* him!"

"Of course they did." Paul's voice was gruff and ragged as he stood back up and wiped off his mouth. "That was their plan all along."

Marx glared. "Watch it, Paul. Don't say something you regret."

I looked from Paul to Marx. *That was their plan all along?* I tried to work out what had happened. Zack must have gotten to Marx's boat after we got separated. He was probably still under the impression that Paul was killing people . . . or maybe he *wasn't*? Maybe he'd seen Diab and wanted to call for help. Whatever the case, he'd reached out to Marx . . . and then . . .

Something happened that led to his death. One piece snapped into place: *Marx* killed him. It certainly explained his lack of empathy. But . . . *why*?

I stared shakily at Marx, wondering what his plan was for *us*. I thought of how he'd apathetically kicked Zack into the water. He could have just waited for him to sink, and that would have been that—but he'd signaled for Diab. He wanted to *show* us that he knew about the thing—and that he could control it. To scare us. To say, *Watch your step, or you're next.*

A sick feeling invaded my chest. Those glow sticks in Mosley's bag were like a carrot on the end of a string, luring Diab straight for those people back on land. Maybe these two had led the monster to Eric, too. Maybe *all* the deaths were Marx's fault.

Was it possible?

I felt the boat shift beneath my feet. Before I knew what was happening, Paul was climbing toward the front of the raft and reaching for the ladder.

"Stop this," he said to Marx as he climbed up. "Stop whatever you're doing. You're killing innocent people."

The corner of Marx's mouth twitched, but he didn't budge.

"You have to save those kids," Paul urged. "You have to get them off this island. You have an *obligation* to do that."

Marx snorted and reached for something in his jacket pocket. "I wouldn't come closer," he warned.

"Oh yeah?" Paul hauled himself up another rung. "Why?"

Marx's hand emerged from under his coat. In it, he held something black and blocky and gun shaped. I cringed. And just like that, Marx aimed the weapon into the sky and fired. Everyone screamed, but to our surprise, out came not a bullet but a phosphorescent flare, exploding into the darkness with a hiss and a whine.

Paul's eyes widened. Marx turned back to Paul, his eyebrows coyly raised. Paul froze, his arms outstretched, his gaze snapping over to the water. Ripples formed on the surface, turning to wavelets, turning to giant breakers. The creature was back. It sensed the flare. I could see it undulating only a few feet down, the length of two yachts put together. My heart pounded. I could feel bile rising in my throat. I didn't feel safe standing on this shaky boat. And Marx was doing just what I thought: showing us he had the creature right where he wanted.

I heard a splash, and the creature's bulbous head popped out for a moment into the air. There were its eyes, searching. It opened its mouth, showing rows and rows of teeth, more than a shark's. The longest, creepiest tongue I'd ever seen—the size of a whole cow—protruded. Elena and I screamed, clutching each other. But then it sank back down into the water, circling some more.

Elena looked at Marx. "Please," she whispered. "Please don't do this to us."

I nodded, too. But then it hit me: We probably weren't going to make it. Marx was unstable—that much was clear. But I couldn't just let Diab eat us without some kind of explanation. I needed this explained to me, even if it was the last thing I ever heard.

"Why won't you help anyone on the island?" I called to Marx. "Why are you trying to *kill* them?"

Marx lowered the gun and looked at me with an almost bored expression. "Haven't you heard that quote from Tennessee Williams? 'Success and failure are equally disastrous.' Sounds like a literary sentiment, huh? Maybe about love, about artistic endeavors, something like that?" He waited a beat. Of course no one answered. "Nope, he was talking about insurance. Which is what I'm thinking about, too. Although"—and now he hooked his thumbs into his belt loops, proudly—"I'd change the quote a little. Maybe to say, *Failure can sometimes be successful. Especially if you've taken out an insurance policy*."

The waves lapped ominously. Wind snapped through my hair, sending a chill down my spine. Then Paul breathed in. "It's you," he said quietly, almost in wonderment. "*You're* the investor. *You're* the one who bought that half of the island. *You're* the one who pushed for that festival."

Marx smiled, not confirming or denying. But I looked at Paul, still not understanding what any of this meant. *Marx* owned half of Myla despite knowing there was a monster that lived here? Why would he do that?

And then it hit me. That one day I'd spent at the law office came in handy, because I remembered something Michael at the law firm—who seemed a million worlds away now—said while I sat in my new cubicle, bored and miserable: the story about the claims adjuster making millions off all those disasters in the buildings that had signed up with him for insurance policies. Sometimes people *hoped* for failures—there was more money in that than success. This was the business equivalent of killing someone when you were their life insurance beneficiary.

I cocked my head, trying to understand Captain Marx's motives. I didn't believe he could be so cruel . . . but then, so many people had surprised me in the past two days. "You're the one who pushed for this festival. And you're the one who orchestrated it to be a train wreck."

Marx looked amused. "*Train wreck* is such a harsh phrase. I prefer *disaster*."

A fire roiled in my belly. "This is why Zack seemed so puzzled about the lack of infrastructure and supplies. *You* never sent them. *Or* medical backup. *Or* security. *You* duped the guy *organizing* this festival—someone who thought of you as a friend."

Marx rolled his eyes. "Zack was a moron. Who makes a living on *YouTube*? He should have been more on the ball. It's people like me who run successful music festivals, not idiot upstarts like him."

Elena looked at Marx, too, seemingly beginning to understand what was going on. "So you knew about the monster all along?"

Marx grinned. "Of course. We all talked about it, remember?"

"But you framed it like it was a silly legend by ignorant people," I pointed out. "You downplayed it to us—including Zack, even after Paul tried to warn him. You didn't want anyone to be worried. You didn't want him to believe—because then he'd cancel the event. But then Zack *did* start to believe. That's it, isn't it? He came out here because he saw the monster firsthand—and he was going to call in the big guns. But you couldn't have that, so you killed him so you could follow through with your plan. The more people who die, the bigger payout you get, is that right? Because now your investment in Myla is worthless. And what pays for that? Your insurance policy."

Marx's smile wavered just a little. I knew I was right.

"How'd you swing that?" Paul challenged. "You must have bought the half of this island for nearly nothing. Were you just figuring that no investigator would dare come over here after they heard the rumor that Diab is real? Did you insure the place for far more than it's worth, saying you were going to build hotels here, resorts, *shopping malls?*" His eyes bugged out. "Someone actually insured you for that?"

"Damn right someone insured me for that." Marx's eyes were steely and cold. "And my lawyers can make a case for all the potential growth I had planned here. The joke's on you."

"Do you even *hear* yourself?" Paul screamed. "The joke's on me? You know, that thing in the water isn't the monster in this story. *You* are."

Marx's fingers tapped on the flare gun. He wanted to use it again. He could aim it right at us, sending Diab and its bovine-size tongue and its brick-size teeth, sharpened to points, straight for this raft. The brazenness of his actions infuriated me. This was a greedy man's egotistical scheme. *Oh, let's just kill some spoiled rich kids. A few dozen lost lives won't matter!*

I curled up my fists. But in that moment, through some sort of invisible signal, Marx's boat lurched away from our raft. Paul shifted forward, losing his balance, scrambling midair to dive for us. He landed on the raft hard, both Elena and I nearly toppling into the water. We dragged Paul fully into the raft and then looked up. The yacht was already too far for us to reach. Marx waved to us, a wide grin on his face.

"Have fun staying away from Diab!" he cried gleefully. "You're gonna need it!"

And then he reached into Mosley's knapsack, brought out a huge handful of glow sticks, and tossed them into the air . . . straight for us.

23

I STARED IN HORROR at the glow sticks as they landed with a *thud* in the bottom of our raft. There had to be at least twenty of them, all bundled together in a neat bunch. They glowed an unnaturally bright yellow and were a perfect beacon for a hungry Diab.

"Quick, douse the light," Paul said.

I yanked off my hoodie and tossed it over the sticks. Only a soft glow emanated through—*hopefully*, it wouldn't attract the creature's attention. Then I looked at the others. "What the hell are we going to do?"

Paul stared at the water. Elena had sunk to her knees and was sobbing. Our boat rippled with a sudden current, and I tipped onto my side, grappling wildly for something to keep my balance. I could feel the creature moving below us. Circling. It still wanted more. It wanted *us*.

Paul pointed toward Marx's receding yacht. "We have to go after him." Then his face brightened with a thought. "Noises," he whispered. "Strange noises sometimes confuse Diab. That's in my research."

"What k-kind of noises?" Elena stammered. "What do we need to do?"

Another great slosh of a wave rose up to our left. We covered our heads as it crashed over us, soaking our bodies, threatening to tip the raft. Amazingly, we stayed upright. As I looked into the water, I saw a flicker of the city-block-size creature, only feet below the surface. A few giant bubbles rose to the surface. I could smell its stench.

Paul revved the small outboard motor. The noise startled Elena and me—but it also seemed to scare Diab, because the water beneath me shifted and then settled. I looked at Paul encouragingly as we zipped forward. "I think it dove down deeper," I said.

Paul nodded. "Sudden noises seem to do that. But there's a problem. We're almost out of gas."

"Then what do we do?" Elena cried.

Paul nodded. "I have an idea." He gripped the steering wheel and revved the engine again, zooming toward Marx's yacht. For thirty seconds, I didn't feel the creature on our tail—the water was calm, easy, unthreatening. But then came a bump. And another. And *another*. I glanced over my shoulder and could see the dark shadow just below the surface once again. The creature might have been afraid of the engine sounds before, but it had gotten over it fast. The smooth top of its head crested out of the water, bumping us again. One of its eyes, positioned eerily on its forehead, tilted upward, seemingly staring right at the boat.

I moved as far away from the back of the raft as I could until I was almost in Paul's lap. "Paul," I said hysterically, gesturing to the water.

"Just hold on." Paul was concentrating on the ocean ahead. Surprisingly, we were almost right alongside the yacht again. Marx was no longer on the deck watching us. Perhaps he hadn't wagered we'd live after his little glow-stick trick? Maybe he didn't think we had the balls to chase him down?

Another bump. Then something slapped the side of the boat. I looked down in horror—it was the creature's *tongue*.

I wobbled forward, crashing into Elena. "Paul!" I screamed. The thing *knew* we were on board. It felt like any moment, it could leap out of the water and just . . . *attack*.

But Paul was still staring at Marx's yacht. After a moment, he stuck two fingers in his mouth and let out a piercing whistle. Elena and I cowered. I glanced to the side of the raft, hoping it frightened Diab, too, but it was still lurking only inches down, almost like it was waiting for the perfect moment to strike.

A figure stepped onto the yacht's deck. Marx stared at us as though we were annoying mosquitos he needed to swat. His gaze flicked to the back of the raft, and the corners of his lips curled into a bemused grin. He saw the creature, too. He knew it was ready to pounce. Marx was probably relishing this, thinking, *Lovely! I'm going to get to see it eat them!*

"Paul," I said, shutting my eyes. I felt Diab rumbling beneath me, gathering its strength. This was how my life would end: in a random ocean, off a random island, on an impulsive and irresponsible trip because I thought my life was too boring. I'd never get to say goodbye to my parents, my sister, my brother. I'd never get to talk to Hayden again. I'd never get to see what Hayden was *about*. I'd never get to be a lawyer or a doctor or a reporter. I'd become one of those people in Paul's scrapbook, another strange death on Myla Island.

I grabbed Elena's hand—she was the only solace I had. At least my friend was with me. At least we were going to do this *together*. Elena met my gaze, her face a mask of desperate fear. "It's okay," I told her gently, squeezing hard. "I love you."

Another lurch from the back of the boat. Marx's eyes up on the deck shone with glee. I heard an angry little voice inside me speak up. *Adri! You're smarter than this! You have a weapon right on board! Use it!*

But I had no idea what my inner voice meant. *Weapon?* What weapon? Still, I opened my eyes, my knees bumping against something hard and plastic on the bottom of the raft. I stared at my wet, crumpled hoodie, remembering what it concealed. I *did* have a weapon. The glow sticks. If we aimed just right, we could toss them back onto the yacht . . . and lure Diab straight to Marx.

I went to grab the sticks under my hoodie. My fingers bumped Paul's—he had the idea, too. This was probably why he'd chased the yacht all along. He gathered the sticks in his hand, but a buzz overhead made us both look up in alarm. "Oh no!" I cried. Marx's yacht had suddenly veered away from us, leaving behind a white, frothy wake. Marx was waving once more.

"No!" Elena screamed.

We felt a *whoosh* from behind. The creature, spotting the glow sticks in Paul's hand, exploded off the right side of the raft, showing a thick, meaty underbelly that was the color of vomit. There was the indentation of something large below its skin, right about where its gut would be. I could make out a hand, what looked like a leg. Oh God—was it *Zack* in there?

"Drop them!" I cried, yanking the glow sticks from Paul's hands and covering them with the hoodie once more. The creature was *still* in the air—that was how huge it was, how high it could get into the sky. I gaped at it again, one large, smooth worm. Where had the tentacles gone? How did it even move through the water? It's body, high in the air, loomed over our tiny vessel. I flattened against the bottom of the boat, certain the moment would be my last.

Water droplets splashed on my arms and legs. I felt a great crash and heard screams in my ears—maybe *my* screams. The boat rocked and tipped, and I was thrown into the water. I felt my body sink down and fought for the surface. I felt something brush past me—it was slimy and strong, slippery and eerily cold—and I realized, *Oh God, the monster. Oh God, it's going to find me.* I screamed beneath the water. I struggled for the surface, but already I was running out of air. I opened my eyes, at first seeing just murkiness, but then I spotted a few pinpricks of light heading right for me. It was the creature's *eyes*—glowing, bulging, *seeing.* I felt my lungs give out. And then I felt hands pull me up.

I coughed and coughed as Paul pulled me back onto the raft. He set me down on the floor and turned me on my side, shouting, "Breathe! Breathe!" I opened my eyes. Elena, also soaked, was lying next to me. Paul was clutching my now-waterlogged hoodie. I could just make out the glow sticks shining underneath.

"Come on!" he screamed, once he realized I was okay. "We only have one chance to get this right!"

I blinked hard, shivering at what I'd just encountered— the monster touching me, its fluorescent eyes coming at me in the darkness. Elena lifted herself to her elbows, looking dazed and traumatized, too. How had the creature missed me? I owed Paul my life. And then I realized something else: The raft was alongside Marx's boat again. How had *that* happened? Had the wave pushed us there? I stared groggily up at the massive yacht. Marx was still standing on the deck, except now he didn't look so happy.

I scrambled to my knees, realizing what we needed to do. I could feel Diab's vibrations below the raft—we definitely couldn't waste any time. I felt my fingers curl around the glow sticks beneath the hoodie. Paul nodded and pulled up so that we were parallel to Marx. The yacht was racing, but the Zodiac held its pace. Underneath us, the creature shook its giant bulk, surely preparing to breach once more—and definitely consume us this time.

Paul, hands tightly gripping the wheel, gave me a final look. I nodded. I was going to be the one to throw the sticks, but I was ready. It would take one carefully positioned toss. Get it wrong, and we'd never live to tell the story.

My heart thundered. My hands shook badly. Elena stared at me with large, round, terrified eyes. But then, suddenly, a strange calm came over me. I could do this. I *had* to do this. There was no way this selfish, self-absorbed, heartless man could get away with all these deaths and exploitation. People needed to know the truth.

The boat was even with Marx now, but I could feel the Zodiac's engine sputtering. We were definitely on empty. I gripped the bunched-up hoodie in my hands. There was a spotlight over Marx's head, and he stared down at me almost daringly, as if to say, *Okay, so you hate me, but what are you going to do about it?*

The engine coughed, then died. "*Shit*," Paul said. He tried to restart it a few times . . . and mercifully, it crackled back to life. We rocked violently with a new series of waves—the creature was ready to make its move. If there was any time to do this, it was now. And so, gathering my strength, settling my nerves, uttering a tiny prayer under my breath, I unearthed the glow sticks from beneath the hoodie, raised them over my head, and let them go.

The bundle flew through the air in a perfect arc. They left a stream of glowing light through the night sky. I saw, too, the creature rise up through the water almost gracefully. It leaped over us, *toward* us, its mouth gaping hungrily, saliva dripping from its jaws. I got a look fully into its mouth: at least *ten* rows of teeth, and that terrifying tongue, and a darkness down its throat. Its multiple eyes landed on me a moment, mid-flight. But this time, I held its gaze. *It's not us you want*, I tried to tell it. *It's Marx.*

The creature blinked, almost like it could read my thoughts. Then its gaze moved elsewhere. It followed the trail of the glow sticks—up, up, up, until they landed perfectly on the deck of the yacht, right at Marx's feet.

Time stood still as Marx stared down at the glow sticks in alarm. He raised his head and saw the creature bearing down on him, its body large enough to crush the yacht, its mouth so huge it would swallow him whole in one gulp. Disbelief registered on Marx's face . . . and then terror. And then time sped up, whizzing ahead as though someone had pushed the fast-forward button on a video. Diab crashed into Marx's yacht with such a force that it knocked the hulking thing on its side with a horrible groan. It plowed across the boat, using its massive bulk to heft itself forward. The tentacles I'd seen earlier sprouted from its head again—just like the retractable awning at my abuela's house—and then it moved, spider-like, across the length of the yacht, taking out whole decks, staircases, pool furniture, chandeliers. I heard breaking glass. Cracking wood. I smelled something burning, and then stomach juices, and then blood. A tidal wave rose up, cascading over us and knocking us deep into the water once more.

I swam to the surface, spluttering. The raft was tipped over only a few feet away, and I paddled for it, struggling to turn it upright again and climb inside. "Elena!" I cried, noticing her bobbing head a few feet away. I grabbed an oar that was floating and stretched it to her. Elena grabbed on weakly, and I pulled her toward me. Coughing, gasping, we both lay on the bottom of the raft, shell-shocked. Then I sat up in alarm. *Paul.* Where was he? Had Diab eaten him?

A snuffle sounded from the direction of the engine. "Shit," Paul said, and suddenly there he was, gripping the side of the raft. I let out a grateful squeal, wanting to hug him. Elena and I helped drag him on board. And then we all sat, shivering, stunned, for a few long moments.

"Is it . . . gone?" Elena dared to ask.

Paul squinted into the darkness where Marx's yacht had been. I followed his gaze . . . but all I saw was water. I glanced at Paul in confusion, then back again. *Where* was the yacht? Had it sunk?

"I—I think it ate the whole boat," Paul finally said. And then he started to laugh. "I guess it was hungry!"

"H-how is that even possible?" Elena said.

"I don't know." Paul was laughing hard now. "But with this thing, *anything's* possible."

I wanted to laugh, too, but I felt way too rattled. I felt the bottom of the raft, trying to sense the creature's vibrations below. It knew we were still up here. What if it was coming for us?

But a few minutes passed. No vibrations. The sea felt calmer than it had been all day. Finally, Paul turned to me, then put his hand over mine. "It's okay," he said. "I really think it's okay."

"Are you sure?" I asked, suddenly feeling tears running down my cheeks.

"If it had just eaten Marx, I'd say no. But it devoured everyone *else* on that yacht . . . *and* the yacht itself." Paul shook his head. "I've read enough historical accounts. Diab goes on a feeding frenzy, but it's like a bear—after it's satisfied, it hibernates. Myla residents won't see it for years."

"*Years?*" Elena stared nervously into the ocean.

"Yep. That's traditionally what's happened, anyway. That's why the strange deaths occur so sporadically. The thing eats and eats, then sleeps." He turned to me and clapped a hand on my shoulder. "You did it. If you hadn't thrown that thing just right, we wouldn't be here right now."

"You did it, Adri," Elena concurred, throwing her body against mine in a vicious hug.

I hugged her back, suddenly feeling all kinds of emotions well over me. Before I knew it, I was sobbing. From the shock of it all, maybe. From adrenaline. From the pure hell of the past few days. But also, I was so grateful we were all okay. We were going to live. We could save everyone else. And Marx was gone. Diab was sated. It was tragic that it had feasted on people—that people were led straight into its trap—but it was over now. I was going to get to go home, after all.

I was so consumed by these swirling feelings that I didn't notice the humming engine or the sudden presence of something very, very large in our midst until it was almost next to us. When I looked up and saw the huge yacht sailing our way, every nerve in my body snapped. Was it Marx? Had the boat risen from the deep?

Except this yacht had pink lights, not blue ones. There wasn't a negative-edge pool on the nose but a vast garden full of lush plants and flowers. I blinked hard as the giant vessel sailed next to us and someone stepped to the railing in a pose eerily similar to Marx's just moments before. "What the hell is going on?" called a voice.

My brain stalled. It was a *familiar* voice. But it *couldn't* be. I had to be dreaming. Maybe I *was* dead.

"We saw something huge rise up from the water!" the voice—female, husky, sexy, inviting—went on. "And then it just took out that yacht! You okay? Why don't you come on board?"

My heart was fluttering wildly. And then the woman stepped into the light, confirming it for me: She was a tall, angular, beautiful woman with large, catlike eyes and a mischievous smile. I was used to seeing her in diva gowns or all-black catsuits that matched her backup dancers and not a T-shirt and jeans, which she was wearing today . . . but it was still her.

Lavender. My favorite person in the world.

My jaw dropped open. "You're still . . . *here*?" I said, immediately wanting to kick myself.

But Lavender just laughed. "Yeah, baby. I'm still here."

24

YOU'D THINK I'D HAVE BEEN more starstruck and fangirly when I boarded Lavender's megayacht, but after the few days I'd had, I was barely fazed. I guess coming face-to-face with a one-of-a-kind, prehistoric-looking, human-eating sea beast named Diab did that to a person.

Lavender welcomed us aboard. When she offered her open arms for a hug, I walked straight into them, thinking, *You know what? I deserve this.* Elena seemed instantly buddy-buddy with the megastar, too, and perhaps that was because Lavender was adorably down-to-earth, downplaying the luxury of her beautiful boat, profusely apologizing that she hadn't set foot on land yet for the festival because she'd come down with a horrible case of the flu. And after she heard what happened, she was looking at Elena and me like *we* were the celebrities.

"So wait. That thing in the water—it wasn't some sort of robot?" she gasped, gawking. Of course she looked beautiful gawking. Her skin was so creamy and smooth. Her eyes seemed to glow luminously, even without a trace of makeup. And her hair—well, everyone wanted Lavender's long, luscious lavender hair.

"Not a robot," I said sheepishly. "But I'm not really sure *what* it was."

"He's the expert," Elena said, pointing at Paul.

Lavender turned and looked at Paul, too. He had a goofy smile on his face. I nudged Elena. Even tough Paul was disarmed by Lavender!

Lavender turned back to me. "Explain how this all went down. I've been worried about everyone on the island. For a few days, my Twitter wasn't working, but suddenly, about a half hour ago, my signal came back. Right around the time I saw that big thing knock over that boat!"

I blinked. The big thing, obviously, was the creature. On a hunch, I pulled out my own phone, which had only 3 percent battery. The screen was cracked, there were a few big dings in the case, but it was still working after all the abuse it had taken—I guess there was something to be said for modern cell phone technology. To my surprise, there were two bars in the upper-left corner. Texts started to ping in: from my parents, from my sister and brother, from Hayden, and then the cycle began again and again, each text growing more panicked.

"Whoa," I whispered. A phone signal felt like a miracle.

"The world is *worried* about Myla," Lavender said. "The people who were able to make it back home, or at least to the west side, have written about the conditions. And then there are rumors about some sort of murderer running rampant? And those rumors mixed with rumors about some sort of *animal* . . . and then I see that thing rise out of the water?" She smiled nervously, tucking her beautiful purplish hair behind her shoulder. "Anyway, I've already called in some of my best people from the children's charity I run. I want them down here. We need to organize rescue efforts. Though I don't know why *I'm* the only one handling it. I mean, where's Zack Frazier?"

"Actually . . ." I lowered my eyes awkwardly. "Zack was killed."

Lavender's eyes bulged. "By that thing in the water?"

"Not exactly," I said. It suddenly occurred to me that Lavender knew who Captain Marx was. They were touted as being great friends. How was she going to handle the fact that this major producer was also a murderer? A *mass* murderer, actually. I swallowed hard.

But when I opened my mouth and the story spilled out, Lavender didn't seem surprised. The corners of her mouth settled into a frown, and she shook her head with dismay . . . then disgust . . . and then astonishment. "My *lord*," she whispered. "You think you know someone. *How* many lives are lost again?"

I tried to tally them up in my head. "Two that we know of on land . . . but there were definitely more." I cringe, thinking of the growls and screams I'd heard on land. "And then Captain Marx . . . and all of his crew. And

Mosley and Zack." I looked guiltily at Paul and Elena—because, after all, I was the one who'd trusted Mosley to ferry us to Marx's yacht in the first place. I wondered how he figured into the whole scheme . . . and *why* he'd led all those people to danger. Marx must have been paying him. And now, ironically, he wouldn't get to benefit from the cash.

"So maybe . . . ten? Twenty?" Lavender was slack jawed. "All by this *thing*?"

"Diab." I glanced toward the water as though it were still lurking there, waiting for us. For all I knew, it might have been. But I was beginning to believe what Paul said about it not being hungry anymore. The ocean felt almost like glass. The air seemed crisper, clearer. I even wondered if the creature's contentment had something to do with the returned phone signal—like its bulk had somehow been blocking the satellite connection.

"You know, Diab might be gone now, but that doesn't mean anyone is safe." I gazed in the direction of Myla, but because of the darkness—and the power outage—I could only see where the land mass interrupted the sky, not any real details. "There's no water. No medical staff. The concertgoers are getting mutinous. There are tons of fights. A lot of people are hurt, sick . . ." I pulled my bottom lip into my mouth. "It's really devastating."

Lavender nodded and started tapping on her phone. "Like I said, we're going to get them out of there. Don't worry, Adri. We're going to help."

Lavender knowing my name sent a tingle up my spine. I grinned. "Thank you," I gushed. "You're saving us all."

Over the next few hours, Lavender was able to reach the remaining yachts nearby and mobilize massive rescue efforts. Her charity team arrived, too—on a fancy seaplane that landed right next to the yacht—and Lavender had them make up the rooms on the ship to serve as emergency stations for all of the sick, dehydrated, and bedraggled concertgoers coming aboard. Her personal assistant made calls to private planes in the area to arrange for flights back to various cities since some of the Mylan systems were down, but once she did, she learned that the Mylan systems had righted themselves again—interestingly, at about the same time our cell signal had come back. Perhaps the monster had been disrupting signals, too? Perhaps Captain Marx knew of this remarkable ability the creature had. Perhaps this total lack of connection and escape had played neatly into his grand scheme of running the festival—and its guests—into the ground.

At about three in the morning, some Red Cross boats set out to collect people from the island. The Mylan police arrived, too, as did the country's defense force. I watched nervously as the vessels cut across the water and followed a line of torches as it wended over the dunes toward the concert site. I momentarily felt worried, but then I remembered—the monster wasn't a threat anymore. And there was no murderer waiting in the trees. The rescue team on the island would be safe from those things, anyway.

"Are you sure there isn't anything we can do?" Elena and I kept asking Lavender, who was pacing the deck of her yacht, phone plastered to her ear. But she shook her head emphatically.

"You two *saved* us," she said. "If it weren't for your bravery facing down that monster in the water—*and* Marx—he'd probably be scheming to blow up the whole island."

Lavender laughed, but I could see the uneasiness in her face. I still hadn't grasped what Marx had done, either. The planning it had required . . . and the sheer duplicity of it all. *Solstice was actually a scam*. Even to Zack Frazier. How many more people would have perished before the weekend was through if we hadn't stopped Marx? How many more lives would have been lost because of his greed?

I wandered back to the chaise lounges on the top deck to sit with Elena and Paul—we were way too keyed up to sleep. My phone flashed with incoming texts—I'd managed to reach out to my parents, telling them I was okay, and they'd sent back *Hallelujah* responses with almost no scolding. I received another interesting text, too: Maybe it was a scam, but it said it was someone from CNN. *Heard you are a writer and already did some digging*

259

on the Solstice situation. Want to write something for us? We'll publish your byline.

I wasn't sure to believe it, though. So I called Hayden. "Oh my God," he said. "I was so worried about you. What the heck is going on there?"

"I'll explain everything in a little bit," I said, over-joyed to hear his voice. Only a few hours ago, I thought I'd never hear it again. "But before that—did you by any chance contact CNN on my behalf?"

There was a pause. Hayden laughed sleepily. It occurred to me that he was awake in the dead of night. "Maybe I did," he said. "But it was before the news came in that people were dying. You should write back to the CNN guy if he's gotten in touch, though. No one could write this story better than you."

I couldn't help but grin. So it *was* real. What did I have to lose? And hell, I certainly had a story to tell.

"You know, Adri," Hayden added. "I'm so, so sorry I sent you down there. You could have been killed."

I licked my lips. It *was* hell . . . but it was also still the experience of a lifetime. Just never in the way I'd expected it to be. "Don't be sorry," I said. "I got a lot of perspective. And now I'm thrilled to be coming home." I hiccupped nervously. "I'm, um, really excited to see you."

I could tell Hayden was smiling. "I'm excited to see you, too."

As I came around the corner to the chaises, Elena

and Paul jumped up like they'd just been caught doing something they weren't supposed to.

"Uh, hi . . . ?" I said, a confused smile spreading across my face. I noticed Elena straightening her blouse. Paul wiped his mouth. I wanted to giggle. I swiveled from Elena to Paul, then back to Elena again. They were an unlikely pair, Paul so rough around the edges and surly, Elena such a sweet, slightly naive glamour girl. But then, who was I to judge? Paul was a great person. He cared about his island. He even cared about the rich teens who'd invaded his island and made ridiculous generalizations about his people. He was *way* better than Steve, that was for sure. I gave Elena a surreptitious thumbs-up. *You have my blessing*, I hoped I was telegraphing. *Go for it.*

As I clomped back down to the main deck, I saw a lantern swinging from one of the very first boats that had come to dock. The little craft was crammed with huddled Solstice guests. They filed off dazedly, barely noticing Lavender standing over them in all of her splendor.

"Found these guys bobbing at sea," one of Lavender's assistants, a bearded guy named Jessie, proclaimed. "I think they were trying to get back to land, but they got a little turned around."

Water dripped off people's clothes and bodies. Some collapsed on the deck instantly And then I noticed a familiar, dark-haired figure pushing ahead of some others like he owned the place. "Hey," Steve sneered to Jessie, his lips turned down crankily. "Where's my water? You promised us water."

Jessie just rolled his eyes, and then helped the next person off. "In a minute, dude. Be patient."

Steve wrinkled his nose like a reprimanded toddler. *Good*, I thought. I knew it wasn't right—I should feel *sorry* for Steve, as he'd been stranded at sea for hours—but it felt like poetic justice that Jessie was ignoring him. And the most poetic justice of all? That soon enough, he'd see his girlfriend in somebody else's arms.

CNN BREAKING NEWS: NINE DEAD ON MYLA ISLAND, MUSIC MOGUL TO BLAME.

By Adrianna Sanchez

MYLA ISLAND: They went to Myla Island to have the weekend of a lifetime. Flocks of wealthy teens and twentysomethings eagerly boarded planes bound for Myla in hopes of spending three days in luxury accommodations, hoping to soak up the sun, eat gourmet food, and listen to their favorite bands.

But that's not how it worked out at all.

The world held its bated breath to hear about the spectacle of the Solstice Festival. It seemed like a dream come true: all the planet's hottest acts on a tropical island, playing to thousands, offering up-close-and-personal private performances, against the backdrop of deep woods and brilliant sunsets. But for the first day, social media was silent. There were barely any tweets or posts about the concert. It was hard to know *what* was happening there. Soledad Carson, from Philadelphia, PA, was a concert attendee. "That's because no one had a cell signal," she said. "Not a single one of my friends. We couldn't call our families, couldn't call each other if we were separated . . . It was scary."

Things got even worse when fans got to the actual concert site. Instead of seeing towering hotels, glittering swimming pools, and a professional stage setup, they were plunked onto a barren field with few public bathrooms, a single food truck, and zero shade. "I got sunburned, like, immediately," said Jordan Lowe, 23, from Los Angeles, CA. "There was really nowhere to escape."

It didn't take long for concertgoers to start grumbling about the conditions. Many blamed Zack Frazier, the mastermind behind the festival—or so everyone thought—though Frazier later stated that he had arranged for proper accommodations to arrive and that he was baffled that everything was late. "It's like people didn't even get my messages," he said.

The line for the ferry to take them back to the airport began to build, but that was when a new complication arose: The systems were down at the airport. Flights were grounded, potentially for days. Combined with sudden, pop-up storms in the area, people were literally stranded on Myla Island with little food, water, or medical supplies.

And then the real trouble started.

Myla is divided into two principalities: There is Myla West, which is fairly developed, with several towns, a capital, and lively commerce. And then there is Myla East, which has long been barren and plagued with troubles. The Solstice Festival was on the eastern side of the island, which baffled many of the Mylans—*and* which was not expressed clearly to interested concertgoers when they bought their festival passes. Because Myla East is its own entity—bought by a front conglomerate two years ago—the western residents had no jurisdiction over what decisions were made with the concert, nor were they consulted for thoughts on how they could help make the concert a success.

Naturally, when concertgoers realized that the festival site lacked resources, they began looking elsewhere on the island for help. Their uneasiness was intensified when it was announced that another concertgoer, Eric Jedry, had died in an accident during a hike on some rocks near the beach. But as it turned out, Jedry's death was not because of a fall. And when the concertgoers headed off over the dunes, they would face the same enemy Eric did: a yet-unidentified creature called Diab that has long been part of Mylan lore.

Able to move on land and sea, Diab is a massive predator and extremely dangerous to humans. It attacked seven concert guests, including Jedry, within twenty-four hours. But not a single festival guest knew of this danger before heading to Solstice. Nor were they warned, when they set foot on Myla East, that they should never, *ever* leave the festival site. Many blame Zack Frazier for this oversight, but there is someone else who was acutely aware of this creature's danger.

Captain James Marx, music mogul.

Marx, 54, is the producer behind twenty-four Grammy-winning albums. He has been touted as the man who launched the careers of dozens of young singers, including Lavender, who was attending the Solstice Festival as a headliner. He was the silent owner of Myla East. And it was Marx, documents show, who persuaded Frazier to hold Solstice on this part of the island—prior to this, Frazier had been considering other locales, including Barbados, Witch's Rock in Costa Rica, and the Dominican Republic. Through emails obtained by this news organization, Marx—though not using his real name but an alias he developed to represent his front company—convinced Frazier that Myla East was untapped, unknown, and there-fore very, very VIP. "It will be like their own private island for a weekend," he wrote. He did not add, however, that it would be their own private island they'd have to share with a monster. Marx's browser history shows that he was very aware of the creature's existence: Many of the pages he recently browsed were of the lore of the creature that lurked on the island.

Paul Mackey, Myla Island resident and student of marine biology at the University of Myla, studies the possibility of the creature and its behavioral anomalies. In early June, Mackey signed on to work for the concert, allegedly because he wanted to make sure the guests remained safe. "I tried to warn Zack Frazier about the thing on our side of the island," Mackey said. "And it seemed like he'd hear me, but the next day, he'd blow it off. It seemed like someone got to him. I only realized later that it was probably Marx." Frazier respected Marx, those close to the business scion and internet genius say. He took his opinions very seriously. And so if Marx said there was no creature and no reason to worry, Frazier believed him.

Even when the deaths started to occur, Frazier, probably at Marx's encouragement, kept a level head and tried to find other answers for why they might be happening. But once the mass murder of six concertgoers in the wooded area outside the concert side occurred, he might have changed his mind. Details are unclear, but several sources saw Frazier run from the concert site and over the dunes. "He was heading toward the yachts," a guest said.

That was the last time anyone saw him alive.

Several concertgoers, including the writer of this article, confronted Marx on his yacht to explain that Diab was real. That was when they encountered Frazier's dead body. "My theory is that Frazier finally believed what I'd been telling him, went to convince Marx, maybe figured out Marx had known it all along, and was killed for it," Mackey, who was among the group that confronted Marx, said. Evidence also shows that Marx had hired a local Myla resident, Mosley Louis, to lead a group of concertgoers through the trees—"toward safety"—but instead lured them straight into the monster's jaws. "Sources say Marx was paying him handsomely," Mackey says. "But I can't believe anyone on my island would do that to innocent kids."

It is believed that Marx was orchestrating the mass deaths on Myla Island in order to claim the purchase of the land as a loss on his insurance. Records show that he had a policy that insured Myla East for 2.3 billion dollars, as Marx expected to develop the land for tourism. With the presence of a monster, however, there was no way any of those plans could come to fruition. He would have made a great deal of money: Marx had purchased the land for a little less than one million dollars. And his plan almost worked, until he, too, perished from the Diab of Myla Island. The giant beast ate not only Marx but the rest of his crew of three, Mosley Louis, and all of the fixtures, furnishings, and materials that made up Marx's 100-foot yacht. No one has seen Diab since.

As for the concertgoers stranded on Myla East: Thanks to great efforts by some of the celebrities and musicians who'd come down to the festival on their private yachts, including Lavender, Wiz Khalifa, and Cardi B, everyone was transported safely off the island, and arrangements are being made to get everyone home. Shortly after Diab devoured the yacht, cell phone signals returned, and the Mylan airport systems came back online. All those who suffered minor injuries at the festival are healing.

And something good has come from the horrific experience: perspective. Those who paid ten thousand dollars or more to attend the festival will never forget what they went through, and all are saying they're grateful just to be alive. "It makes me realize that what I used to worry about doesn't matter so much," said Lauren Gruber, from Scottsdale, AZ. And Preston King, 21, from New York City, said that he's made a decision: He's selling his Lamborghini and using the proceeds to start a charity that supports impoverished teens. "I got to experience what it was like to be hungry and desperate this weekend," King explained. "It was a huge wake-up call. Nobody should have to go through that, ever. We all need to be kinder to one another. Money isn't the only thing that makes the world go round."

(Additional reporting by Elena Sykes.)

25

I HAD NEVER worked so hard on something in my life.

It all happened so fast: the conversation with Rob, the guy at CNN who'd reached out, and then the commission that I write something as quickly as possible and ping it back to him so they could have the "exclusive" before anyone else, and then my frantic actual writing of the story—thankfully Lavender had a laptop I could borrow. Though, um, the absurdity wasn't lost on me: I was writing a story for CNN on Lavender's computer. I *definitely* had to be dreaming.

I was able to conduct the interviews with other concertgoers because so many of them had been brought onto Lavender's boat. Thanks to the restored Wi-Fi signal and the help of a guy named Freddie, who claimed to be a master hacker—and he *was*—I was able to break into Captain Marx's emails and see all of his messages and Myla East contracts. Paul was a fountain of knowledge, obviously, as he had most of his research memorized.

I wrote for six hours without stopping, barely noticing when the sun came up, barely acknowledging Elena when she tiptoed into the little suite I'd holed up in to deliver me a cup of coffee. My eyeballs felt like they were going to fall out. My brain ached. But finally, it felt right. I clicked into my email and attached the file to a message to Rob at CNN. After I sent it off, I resisted the urge to read the piece all over again and troll it for all of the myriad mistakes I'd no doubt missed. I refreshed the laptop screen over and over again, wondering when Rob would get to it, calculating what time it was in Atlanta. Maybe Rob was in a meeting. Maybe Rob was busy doing something else. Or maybe Rob *had* read the piece and thought it was total amateur work written by an eighteen-year-old girl who definitely had no place in journalism.

But then he wrote back: *It's perfect.*

The piece went up an hour after I sent it along. Once it appeared on CNN—the *lead* story, no less, the *breaking news*—I stared at it in shock. Millions of people were reading it right now. Millions of people were learning the truth and the terror. And that was all because of me.

"Well, that's it," Elena said after she read the piece through. "You're going to be famous now. You realize that, right? They're going to want you on TV for interviews. *Today. Good Morning America.* You'll go to Hollywood. They'll probably make a movie about you."

"What?" I smacked her playfully. "Well, if they're going to make a movie about me, then they're going to have to make a movie about *you*, too."

"And me," Paul added.

Elena shot him a sweet look and lightly touched his hand before pulling away. "And of course you."

At this point, the sun was high over the water. We were sitting on the deck of Lavender's yacht, eating from a tray of sandwiches Lavender's culinary team had prepared. Behind us, the Red Cross had set up a station, and volunteers were treating those who'd been wounded at the festival. A couple of people were hooked up to IVs. One guy had a nasty head wound. As I looked out onto the water, I saw a Red Cross speedboat heading for the island again, some large, canvas body bags in its hull. My spirits sank a little. They were collecting the corpses on land. Those innocent people. They thought they were running toward safety. What were their last moments like? How *scared* had they been?

The most horrible part was that because of the confusion and lack of cell service, a few of the bodies were still unidentified. We'd created a meeting station on the yacht where people who hadn't connected with friends could hang out in hopes of them showing up or post MISSING signs. But even so, some people were on different yachts—we were even afraid some were still out at sea after everyone took to the water. It would be sorted out eventually, but I couldn't imagine the agony parents back home must still be going through. To hear the grisly tales . . . to hear of some sort of *thing* at large . . . to understand that a wealthy, selfish man purposefully put your child in harm's way—it disgusted me to my core.

But I wasn't the only one. Nobody was on Marx's side. No one had come forward to stand up for him, to make excuses. Even the Twitter trolls who'd joked that they hoped all the privileged millennials who got to go to Solstice would drown in the sea slunk back into their hiding places, their tails between their legs. It was one thing to cyberbully out of jealousy, but another to kick a group of people when they were down. Every musician Marx had worked with came out and expressed their shock, apologies, and deep regret. Lavender's people were fielding phone calls from other musicians and music industry people begging to come to Solstice and help out or at least donate money. I heard rumors of a charity being set up to honor the people whose lives had been lost, including Eric. And like I said in the article, people were starting to think deeply about materialism, excess, and what life was really about. I couldn't believe I was saying this, but something good actually *had* come out of this experience.

I just wished we hadn't had to go through all the pain. And I certainly wished nobody had lost his or her life.

"I'm surprised you didn't add in your interview with the insurance company to the article," Elena said. "Especially what they said about how they would have come after Marx for fraud."

"I thought about it. I think the article said what it needed to say," I said. The conversation I'd had with the advisor who'd put together the documents for Marx's policy was a blur by now, though I remember the guy's shock when I'd told him Marx's grand plan. He'd told me that they would have figured it out eventually—no one reaps a claim of more than two billion dollars and gets away with it. But I guess it didn't really matter what would have happened, because it was over. Marx was in the belly of the very thing he was hoping would make him even richer than he already was. It was totally fitting.

Elena's phone beeped. She glanced at it, and then turned the phone over. I coughed awkwardly. "Steve again?"

She rolled her eyes.

Paul perked up. "If he's still giving you shit, I can talk to him."

"It's cool," Elena said quickly. She placed her hand over the phone. "He can't believe that we're really over. But it's not even worth getting into."

"Then don't," I said encouragingly. Elena gave me a determined nod. There was something different about her this morning. She seemed as exhausted as the rest of us, and her makeup had all worn off, and her hair was a mess, but she stood taller and talked a little louder, and just seemed . . . *happy*. I didn't think it was simply because Paul had come into her life. Elena would be leaving soon enough—and who knew what would happen with them after that. But it was like she finally believed what I'd told her about Steve not being good enough. It was like she finally understood how great she was . . . and she was owning it.

Then my phone pinged. I still wasn't used to my phone reacting after so much silence. My mother's name popped up on the screen. *Read your article*, her message said.

I sucked in my stomach. There was no punctuation. No emojis. I couldn't gauge her mood . . . or what she thought. Despite my parents' earlier relief that I was alive and okay, I knew that soon they'd come back to earth and probably ground me for the rest of the summer. There was no way I'd be seeing much of Hayden when I got back to Atlanta. All I'd be doing was going to the internship and working at the diner. I was *okay* with that—after what I'd been through, I felt lucky to be able to return to these opportunities when some people weren't coming back at all.

But at the same time, I'd worked so hard on the piece, and I could feel my mother's judgment seeping through the phone screen. I knew where she stood on me wanting to be a journalist. I knew she'd find it frivolous.

I was about to write back when I saw the little bubbles pop up that indicated my mother was still typing. A new text appeared on the screen. *Adri, I had no idea how talented you are.*

My jaw dropped. Another text came in.

Dad and I have been talking. Really talking. What's happened has given us some perspective. We realized we haven't listened to you. We haven't given you chances and freedom. I hope you understand why, but maybe it's not fair to you.

I just stared at my screen. Was this really happening?

And look, if you don't want to do the internship this summer, you don't have to. You should write for CNN. After this article, they'll probably want you. We know you'll get into a good school. We just want you home, safe and sound.

I must have been making strange noises, because Elena leaned over to see what I was doing. "Whoa!" she gasped after reading my mother's texts. "Has your mom's account been hacked?"

"I—I don't think so," I said shakily. "I think it's . . . *real.*"

I let the phone fall to my lap, letting what had just happened sink in. I was going to do it. I was going to write. I would get to fulfill my own destiny. I was going to get to take charge of my own life.

"I'm so happy for you, Adri," Elena said softly, taking my hand.

I leaned my head on her shoulder. "I'm happy for you, too."

And then we turned toward the bow of the ship—a cheer had risen up. Behind the Red Cross tent, Lavender stood on a small stage. Someone had set up a microphone and some speakers, and a DJ began to play the silky beat of a very familiar song. My jaw dropped for the second time in under a minute. Was it happening? Were we actually going to get the private concert we'd been promised?

Lavender looked out on the crowd that had assembled, her grin wide and magnificent. "My lovelies, if I can't come to Solstice, I'm going to bring the Solstice here."

People cheered again. Several raised their phones into the air to record the moment. I thought about the hashtags that would come out of this. The silver linings everyone would talk about. Lavender's performance wouldn't make up for what we'd endured, but it was sure as hell nice.

Lavender leaned forward. "I've written a new song this morning. You're going to be the very first to hear it. It's called . . . 'Diab.'"

Elena shoved me excitedly. An addictive island beat started up. Lavender's silky voice began to sing lyrics about Myla and its beauty . . . but also its curse. The song gave me chills. I could tell it would be an instant hit.

"Come on," Elena said, offering her hand. I stood, though on exhausted legs. Yet the music flowed through me, invigorating my body. Lavender swayed back and forth. On the horizon, planes took off from Myla Airport, transporting the rescued back home. Tomorrow, Elena and I would leave as well. Would we ever come back here? I wondered, too, where Diab was just this moment. Deep down? Digesting? I thought of how its eye had looked at me, and then it blinked with startling humanity as I thought-pleaded for it to eat Marx instead. It was like the thing had *listened*. Like the thing had a soul. What *was* Diab, really? Would we ever know? It was tragic that it was dangerous, but did we also have a responsibility to take care of it, as a creature of this planet? I glanced at Paul, who was gaping at Lavender, tapping his toe to the music. I'd have to ask him about that. Maybe I'd come down here next summer to take part in his research. From a safe distance, of course. And definitely without any glow sticks for miles.

I blinked hard, trying to be more in the moment. The music. The relief. That I was here, whole and okay, and that I'd get to go on. I moved with Elena to our favorite dance moves, the ones we'd practiced in her bedroom when we were younger. And we laughed together, and suddenly, finally, it felt like we were on the trip we were supposed to have had all along. If only for a moment.

"Happy Solstice," Elena said into my ear just before she executed a spin.

"Happy Solstice," I said back to her. And I meant it with all my heart.

Acknowledgments

Huge thanks to Erin Stein, Weslie Turner, Dawn Ryan, and Brian Luster at Macmillan for bringing me this project and letting me play around in this hyperbolic world. Also huge thanks to Janice Lynn Mather and all of our early readers for your careful reads for island details and character authenticity—you are lifesavers. And to my son, Henry, who may someday feel lured to attend a festival like this: If it seems too good to be true, it probably *is*.